FATAL ERROR

(Book 2 of the BackTracker series)

Eileen Schuh

FATAL ERROR

Book 2 of the BackTracker series

www.eileenschuh.com

FIRST EDITION paperback

Imajin Books - www.imajinbooks.com

October 20, 2012

ISBN: 978-1-926997-93-3

Cover designed by Sapphire Designs - designs.sapphiredreams.org

Other Novels by Eileen Schuh:
The Traz
The Traz: School Edition
Schrödinger's Cat

Praise for FATAL ERROR

"In *Fatal Error*, Eileen Schuh gives us a wise, haunting, deeply moving sequel to *The Traz*. The very best in today's motorcycle gang stories just got a little better. Her character of Katrina is the Scarlet O'Hara of the new generation. Unforgettable!" —Betty Dravis, best-selling co-author of award-winning *Six-Pack of Blood*

"In *Fatal Error*, author Schuh creates a compassionate tale of human behaviour and consequences. Writing with her trademark depth and intelligence, she draws us into the compelling world of teen-runaway Katrina Buckhold." —Donna Carrick, award-winning author of *The First Excellence*

"Eileen Schuh weaves a subtle plot where nothing is quite what it appears. Katrina's continuing journey is a painful one as she lays old ghosts to rest and tries to find her place in the adult world." —Joanna Lambert, author of *Between Today and Yesterday*

"*Fatal Error* held me as captivated as *The Traz*. A great sequel." —Jacinta Zechariah, book reviewer for World Literary Café

Dedicated to those who do their best to serve others and to those too young to understand.

Acknowledgements

Thank you to my husband, Alvin, who supports me while I write stories about other men.

Thank you to my children for being much better behaved than the youngsters in my stories.

Thank you to my grandchildren for inspiring me to occasionally visit the real world.

Thank you to all those who bought my first book and waited patiently for this one.

Thank you to Cheryl Tardif of Imajin Books for displaying incredible confidence in me and my craft.

Thank you to everyone who reads my books. You make my day.

CHAPTER 1

Northern Alberta Police Detachment, Edmonton, September 1996

Katrina shivered, curled her feet under her on the chair and wrapped the afghan tighter around her. She'd not felt warm since the cold wash of the rescue chopper had whipped about her on the ridge.

It had been a long flight. When they'd finally set down, someone had hustled her through the deepening cold of the September dusk and had sat her in this small corner office.

She shivered again. The intense chill reminded her of that frigid October night a long time ago. Ages ago, it seemed.

Or perhaps that night had never existed.

Perhaps what had happened in that dark Quonset was just a shifting, circling, recurrent nightmare. A wordless collage of violent images. A dream thing she'd always be able to stifle by concentrating on other matters.

Beyond the wild beating of her heart and the chattering of her teeth, she heard ringing phones, radio static and clacking boots. The familiar police station sounds reminded her of her father—and of Chad, the undercover officer who had promised to meet her here tomorrow and find her a safe home with a real bed.

A shadow appeared, pooling darkness at her feet.

Katrina looked up.

An imposing, heavyset, grey-haired man, absorbed in a file of papers in his hands, stepped into the room. Stiff, starched and formal, with sergeant stripes on his shoulders, he looked so much like the father she'd lost. He was a lot heavier, but had the same soft blue eyes and the same uniform.

"I understand you're—" His eyes met hers. A look of shock cut across his face. "How old are you?"

"Fourteen."

He scowled. "Katrina Buckhold?"

She hesitated, then nodded. Her birth name sounded weird. Since the age of twelve, she'd used the alias "Sarina" when hanging out in places she knew she shouldn't, like the back rooms of the King's Ace Bar and The Traz biker gang compound.

"You're fourteen?" The man's eyes darted between the file and her face.

"Do I look like I'm lying?"

The man scrunched his brows and was silent for a long moment.

"This changes things," he said finally. "Stay here. I'll be right back."

He headed toward the door, but stopped and turned. His eyes flickered over the room as if it were a struggle to look at her, as if he'd much rather be somewhere else. "I apologize. My name is Sergeant Kindle."

Katrina flashed him a quick grin. *He thinks I'm just a stupid kid.*

CHAPTER 2

"Debra!" Sergeant Gabe Kindle roared as he threw Katrina's file on Constable Debra Carter's desk.

Debra tucked a wayward strand of brunette hair behind her ear, hit the hold button on the phone and looked up. Although she was only in her early twenties, Kindle thought there was a hint of quiet wisdom in her hazel eyes. "Yes, sir?"

"Why is the kid in my office? I thought *you* were taking care of her."

"Sarge?" a constable called from across the room. "The Americans are on line one again for you. Saying it's urgent."

"Tell them one moment." Kindle gritted his teeth. To Debra, he said, "I have an international operation against the bikers coming down and I don't need screw-ups like this."

"You said you wanted the murder witness in your office as soon as they got here."

"I wanted the *murder witness,* not the girl."

"The girl *is* the murder witness."

"This is no time for jokes."

"Sarge, I'm not joking. Chad just called it in. Katrina Buckhold is the mystery witness Shrug was refusing to turn over."

"Are you serious?"

He picked up the file and searched through the pages, most of which were blank. He let out a huff and scanned the room for the officer who had fielded the American caller. "Constable Morgan! The Americans, what are they after now?"

"Their SWAT team is ready to go in after The Traz, but the paperwork isn't. They need that info you promised them for their search warrant."

"How is that urgent?"

"There's destruction of evidence happening inside the South Dakota clubhouse, while SWAT sits on the grass outside the gates waiting for their legal right to enter."

"Fine. Tell them I'll be right with them. Debra, where were we?"

"I was saying Chad called in the information on the wit—"

"Why didn't anyone tell me this until now?"

Debra's face reddened. "You were teleconferencing with border officials and said no interruptions. I put the message on your desk."

"I haven't had the privilege of sitting at my desk for forty-eight hours. Why didn't Chad tell me this yesterday, last week, last month?"

"He didn't find out until the rescue helicopter landed at the biker compound. The pilot had the girl aboard, but was waiting on the ridge for the murder witness. That's when Shrug told Chad that the girl was also the witness and ordered the chopper to leave before the tactical team moved in and bullets started flying."

"What do we know about this girl?"

"Remember that car accident in Calgary a year ago last summer? The one that claimed a police officer and his wife? The girl is their daughter."

"You're telling me I have the orphaned daughter of a cop sitting in my office and she's a witness to a brutal gang slaying?"

Debra shrugged. "That's what Chad said."

"And two undercover police officers didn't tell me until now?"

"Like I said, Chad didn't know—"

"It was Chad's job *to* know," he snapped. "That's why he was sent in there. To ensure that everything was above board with Shrug. It's unlikely he failed to notice a girl was running with a biker gang."

"Sarge, Chad told you there was a young girl who needed to be rescued. He had no idea she was the witness. You know full well what Shrug's like. If there's something that man doesn't want you to know, you won't know."

Kindle resisted the urge to shout. "I sent Chad in to make sure stuff like this wasn't happening. If those two have screwed up this operation with their foolishness, I'll not only have their careers, but also their necks."

"Sir?" Constable Morgan called out. "The Americans want to know if they should call back."

"I'll be there in two minutes."

Debra reached for the file. "I'll look after the girl, Sarge. I'll locate her guardians and find her an ultra-safe location for the night. We can deal with the witness thing tomorrow, after Chad gets here."

"Let Calgary know I want Shrug here too."

"Sir, if you want Shrug here, you'll have to ask the FBI to capture him. He's long gone. Took off moments after the tactical team swept into the biker compound. He's across the border by now."

"What the hell's he doing in the U.S.?"

"He's got a biker, Stack Jacobs, that he's set up for something big down there."

"And that's more important than what's happening up here?"

"Apparently."

"I'm guessing this Stack guy did something to really piss Shrug off?"

Debra flinched. "Killed a puppy. I'm sure there's more to the—"

"Has Shrug gone totally insane? First I discover his secret murder witness is a child and now he's gone AWOL? Maybe I *should* sic the FBI on him."

When Debra entered Kindle's office, Katrina Buckhold was swaddled in the grey chevrons of a crocheted blanket. Long amber curls shimmered across her small shoulders. With her feet tucked beneath her, she stared at the floor.

"Katrina?"

The girl gave an obstinate toss of her head, then looked up, her brow furrowed and her jaw taut. She had the bluest eyes Debra had ever seen.

"Yeah?"

Debra smiled, hoping to calm her. "I'm guessing you are at least fourteen."

"Do you always sound this idiotic, or has it just been a long fucking day for you?"

"Pardon?"

Katrina flung the blanket aside and unfurled her legs. "You said you guessed I was at least fourteen. What a load of crap. It doesn't take a genius to know you'd never have guessed I'm older than ten, if that file in your hand didn't tell you otherwise. I get along better with people when they're honest with me." She folded her hands in her lap and stared at her feet, which were now swinging about five centimetres above the floor.

"I apologize."

Debra stepped behind Kindle's desk, sat and studied the girl. Witnesses to gang murders tended to be half-bald burly men with tattoos and facial hair. She wasn't sure how to deal with one as vulnerable as Katrina.

"I'm Constable Debra Carter. Sergeant Kindle asked me to get things in order for you."

She tried to imagine how someone so young would feel about witnessing a murder. It hadn't been a simple murder, either. The bloody and violent crime scene had left even the most experienced of the homicide investigators shaken.

Katrina slouched until her toes touched the floor. Then she crossed her arms and yawned. "Just find me somewhere to sleep tonight. A sofa will do. After all, I slept on Shrug's couch for over a year."

Debra opened Katrina's file. There wasn't much in it other than the notes she'd scribbled while taking Chad's desperate call from the ridge.

"I'll find you somewhere to sleep and it won't be a sofa. But first I need to get in touch with your guardians."

"That's not likely to happen. Chad will look after me tomorrow. He has plans in place for me."

"Constable Chad Leslie?"

Katrina looked up at Debra through long, dark lashes. "Yeah, he promised me everything is set."

"I see. Well, in any event, Constable Leslie won't be around until tomorrow, so tonight I have to get in touch with your guardians. That information doesn't seem to be in your file."

"Good."

"You're going to give me that information."

"Not likely."

"Then I'll call Children's Services." Debra reached for the phone.

"Steven and Elizabeth Cooper."

"Do you know the Coopers' phone number?"

"I know the phone number of everyone who ever gave me one, plus many more."

"For now, Mr. Cooper's is all I need."

Katrina rattled off the number. "He's a lawyer, you know, so don't mess with me."

"I'm trying to help you."

"Anyone who uses the phrase 'Children's Services' in the same breath as my name, gets no damned stars from me."

"Did you have a bad experience with Children's Services?"

Katrina gave a sardonic giggle. "Know any kid who's had a good experience?"

"You were reluctant to give me Mr. Cooper's name and number. Did you have a bad experience with him too?"

"Can't say I did. However, I can say *he* had a bad experience with *me*."

"How so?"

"After Grandpa died, I had no living relatives, so my parents named the Coopers in their will as my guardians." Katrina's eyes misted over and she blinked several times before the ice returned to them. "Cooper's a lawyer and my legal guardian. I'm fourteen and ran with The Traz for a year. Think that was a good experience for him?"

"Well, let's find out." Debra picked up the phone. "This is a Calgary number?"

Katrina nodded.

"I remember your parents' accident, Katrina. I'm very sorry about what happened."

"My mother killed my dad. She couldn't have him for herself, so she took him from me. She was driving drunk."

"I didn't know that."

"It wasn't a secret. Sure, they blamed the other driver for coming across the centre line, but Mom's blood alcohol level was higher than the other guy's."

"I'm sorry it happened."

"Being sorry does shit all good."

"I suppose, but perhaps someday you'll find that sharing your sadness will make you feel better."

"Why would I want to feel better? My father's dead."

Hearing the coldness in the girl's voice made Debra's heart ache for her. "But *you're* not dead, Katrina. You have your whole life yet to live."

"That's what Chad said. You can't let Cooper take me to Calgary. I won't go back there with him."

Debra dialled the number. "Let's see what Mr. Cooper says."

CHAPTER 3

Debra Carter's residence, Edmonton

Katrina was asleep when a rap on the door called her to face the day.

"Mr. Cooper's here to talk with you," Debra called. "Are you awake?"

"Yeah."

She let the luxury of Debra's spare room soak into her soul. She'd been exceptionally relieved when Cooper had agreed to let the female officer bring her home. If she'd had to over-night it in some crowded and cold foster home...well, she wouldn't have still been there in the morning when they came to check on her.

Despite the money and power possessed by The Traz, she'd had nothing to call her own on the compound, other than her computer and clothes. No room of her own. Not even a bed. For a long time, she hadn't cared. She'd been as barren and empty inside as her life had been on the outside. It wasn't until Chad had come at her with soft promises that she'd started to miss what she'd had before her parents died.

She snuggled deeper under the pink satin duvet. She thought of Steven and Elizabeth Cooper and how cold and strict they'd been. She remembered Mr. Cooper obsessing about the money she'd inherited. She wondered if he'd won his battle against her parents' life insurance company.

Last year, before she'd run away with Shrug, Cooper had tried to collect the rest of her parents' life insurance. He'd spent way more time on the phone talking with the agent than he'd spent talking to her. The insurance company argued that because her mother had engaged in the criminal act of drunk driving, it didn't have to honour the policies' double-payout clauses in the event of accidental deaths. Since Katrina already had a million dollars from each of her parent's policies, she couldn't understand why Cooper thought she needed more. However, he refused to stop fighting for it.

Debra rapped again. "Katrina, you haven't gone back to sleep, have you? I must leave for work now and Sergeant Kindle's waiting for you down at the detachment."

Katrina sighed. "I'm coming."

She didn't want to deal with Cooper or Sergeant Kindle. It was only the thought of seeing Chad that finally got her feet on the floor.

Cooper was seated on a couch in Debra's living room. He stood when Katrina entered the room. "I hear you've been a pretty busy lady lately."

She knew he was trying to sound gentle, but it didn't work. He was staid and lawyer-ish, always had been.

"It hasn't been good."

With reluctance, she accepted his bony, cold handshake.

"They're not too happy with me, Katrina. They don't think I've been a very good guardian."

"You had a tough job." She didn't want to look in his eyes. She spotted a slit between the front room curtains and stared out at the street.

Cooper stepped between her and the window, then slipped his hands into his pant pockets. "I'm just warning you."

"Warning me?"

"They're talking of assigning you a new guardian."

"I...wow." She chewed at a broken thumb nail. Now that she was off the biker compound, perhaps she could get a much-needed manicure.

"Well, I'm glad I have your support."

As usual, he misunderstood her. Cooper pulled her to him for a hug. She stiffened and stepped away. His shoulders sagged as he let out a deep sigh.

He's pretending I've hurt his feelings, acting like he wants to be my friend. Not likely. Chad, where are you when I need you?

"There are issues I want to go over," he said. "Legal things. You must tell me what you've been doing this past year."

"I can't."

"Come." Cooper reached for her hand. "Sit with me on the sofa and we'll talk. Before we meet with the Sergeant, I need to know what went on."

She wriggled her hand free. "You don't want to know what went on."

"Yes, I do." His eyes were moist, as if he were actually feeling sad for her. "Please talk to me, Katrina. I promise I won't get angry."

Her eyes started to tear. *I can't tell him what happened. I can't tell anyone. Ever.* "I can't."

"Sit, please." Cooper patted the sofa. "Let's talk about other things."

Needing distance, she sat in the chair on the other side of the coffee table. For a moment, he stared sadly down at her. Then he sat down on the sofa.

"You go first," he offered.

"How's Elizabeth? Last time I talked to you she'd just been diagnosed with breast cancer."

"She's not doing well."

"Worry about her then, instead of me. Chad will look after me and keep me safe."

"Who's Chad?"

"Constable Chad Leslie. An undercover cop. He's the one who convinced me to leave the bikers."

"Well, I don't know what he promised, but I'm your legal guardian and no one plans anything for you without my say-so."

"I understand that."

An uncomfortable silence fell between then.

She struggled to think of something to say, afraid that if she didn't talk, Cooper would again start questioning her about the gang.

"What happened to my house in Calgary?" she asked.

"It was sold."

"And my stuff?"

"We kept what we felt might be important to you. The rest was donated to your mother's favourite charities."

She squeezed her eyes shut. "Okay." *It's all gone. The last remnants of my life with my parents, sold and dispersed.*

"Did you know there was a handgun stored in the basement, Katrina?"

"Yes."

If Shrug hadn't interrupted her thoughts that early September morning a year ago, she'd have gone home, gotten that pistol and shot herself. She clearly remembered the day Shrug had eyed her up at the restaurant and asked if she wanted a ride on his Harley. *A ride to hell and back.*

"Don't tell Elizabeth," Cooper whispered, flicking a look at the doorway, "but I kept the gun for you. If you don't want—"

"The gun was Grandpa's."

She envisioned her grandfather's face and could almost hear his voice. He'd taught her how to control her breathing and heartbeat—a must for hunters and sharpshooters. When her dad took her to the shooting range to fire off his service revolver, she'd hit the target every time because she knew how to hold steady.

"Ah, I see."

"Grandpa used to take me hunting. I loved that."

Thinking about her grandfather and dad was depressing her. She needed to focus on something less sad.

"It's okay about selling the house, Mr. Cooper. I didn't want you to sell it before, but everything's different now. Like I said, you don't have to worry about me."

"I'm your guardian. I have to worry about you."

There had to be something she could use to convince Family Court to transfer her guardianship and money to Chad. *Maybe I can convince Cooper that he doesn't want me. Or trick him into admitting he's been negligent.*

"I know you don't want to look after me, especially if Elizabeth is sick. I stress her out."

"Elizabeth and I both care a lot about you, Katrina. I admit we were a little lost being thrown into a parenting role when we'd never had children of our own, but we fully understood what you were going through. We ached for you."

He's lying. "You were going to send me to a foster home."

"Elizabeth and I did the best we knew how for you. When it wasn't working..." He shrugged. "We were scared for you, dear. We were looking for help to get you out of your grief, off the streets and back into school."

"It didn't work, did it?"

Cooper sighed. "No, it didn't."

"You seem to have had trouble looking after me, but I don't remember you ever having trouble looking after my trust account."

"Don't insinuate I'm in this for your money. Every penny of your trust is still there for you."

My turn to lie. "I didn't mean it to sound that way."

"Katrina!" Cooper slapped his gaunt knees. "Your dad and I were very close. He confided in me about the problems you were having even before the accident. I know all about how upset you were when your grandpa passed and about your mom drinking too much after his death. I know there were problems between your mom and dad, and that you were skipping school. However, when I agreed to be your guardian in the will, neither your parents nor I believed it would actually come to that, especially at such a difficult time for you. Elizabeth and I did our best."

"And then you gave up on me."

"No!"

"Yes. After I ran off, your life was more pleasant, wasn't it? And when Elizabeth got sick, not having to deal with me was a bonus."

Cooper jumped to his feet and paced the room. "I reported you missing immediately. Sent the police looking for you."

"Wow. That must have taken an entire five-minute phone call. I know you didn't really care that I was gone. You even used the quarter million dollars I wired you to keep me out of your life."

"Katrina! Don't make things up."

"I'm not making things up. There's plenty of paperwork to prove what I'm saying."

"The paperwork will show I bought the land you wanted with the money you wired me. The title is your name in trust."

"Yes, but where do you think I got that kind of money?"

His face blanched. "You said it came from your grandpa."

"Although Grandpa was wealthy from his investments, I wasn't *in* his will. Don't tell me you didn't check that out. I know you would have. Somehow though, it didn't matter to you, did it? It was much less trouble to just do as I asked. It kept me out of your life."

"You said your grandfather gave you that cash before he died. I had no reason to doubt you."

She snickered. "Mr. Cooper, I was with a biker gang. Do you really think that money came from IBM investments?"

"What are you saying?"

"Perhaps it was the proceeds from other investments which bought the land? Perhaps from cocaine? Guns? Theft? Bribes? If I were you, I wouldn't push this guardianship issue too hard. Wherever that money came from, I don't think the fact you accepted it from a kid running with bikers will look good."

Cooper's mouth gave a nervous twitch. "I see."

Katrina crossed her arms. "Like I said, Chad will look after things for me."

CHAPTER 4

Northern Alberta Police Detachment, Edmonton

At the detachment, Katrina and Cooper walked into a roomful of proficient looking people. The boardroom table stretched forever, its shiny white top reflecting the sterile glare of the overhead fluorescents. There were legal advisers, Crown prosecutors, investigators and even a stenographer. Katrina was dismayed to see Chad wasn't among them. She tucked her hands in her jacket pockets while Sergeant Kindle made the introductions.

"Considering the circumstances," he said, "and for her protection, I'll only name the child as 'Katrina.' If anyone has need for her full name, please speak to me after the meeting."

It was when he introduced Sabrina Whiteheart from Children's Services that Katrina's heart began to race. *Something's not right.*

Sabrina's lips were too red, her short blonde hair too stiff and the shoulder pads beneath her navy suit jacket too bulky, as if she were trying to look older than she was.

The adults murmured greetings, then followed Sergeant Kindle's lead and sat. Katrina remained standing.

"Sabrina," she said. "What are *you* doing here?"

The woman's eyes widened, but before she could reply, Sergeant Kindle spoke. "We have some very serious issues to deal with, Katrina. We must make sure your interests are well protected."

His quick, intrusive answer made no sense. "My guardian is here and he's a lawyer. I think he can protect my interests."

"That may be the case," Sabrina interrupted. "I'm just here to observe." She stared at the table in front of her.

Katrina glared at the woman. *She won't look at me because she's lying. She's here to take me away from the Coopers and lock me up in some foster home.*

She sank deep into a chair, wishing she could disappear. She wouldn't live with strangers. She'd run away again...somewhere, anywhere.

Chad, where are you?

"Katrina, you're a valuable member of our team," Sergeant Kindle said. "As you're a minor, we need to ensure you're both well protected and able to make fully-informed decisions. We wouldn't want, uh, questions raised in the future about...the way you were dealt with."

He's choosing his words much too carefully. He's hiding something.

"She's a member of what *team*?" Cooper asked. "What *future* are you talking about? Do you have plans we don't know about?"

Sergeant Kindle held up a hand. "It'll be a while before we get into that. We'd first like to talk in general about what happened during Katrina's year with The Traz."

"And for what will this information be used?"

"I'm sure Katrina wants to know how things went on the compound after she left. And we'd certainly like to hear her story..."

Sergeant Kindle's voice droned on until Katrina tuned it out. This wasn't at all what Chad had promised. He'd told her he'd find her a home where she could start a new life free from Shrug's control and safe from The Traz bikers.

Sergeant Kindle took a deep breath. "We need to know—"

"Where's Chad?" Katrina interrupted. "He was supposed to be here to look after me."

"Chad's not coming to look after you," Debra explained. "I think you can understand he's busy with other matters."

A dark, familiar feeling swept over her. On the biker compound, when she'd stared into Chad's dark eyes, she'd been so sure he was being honest. But now he was too busy to keep his promises? *Fuck him.*

"Excuse me, Sergeant Kindle," Cooper said. "What will the information she gives you be used for?"

"It will help us in our investigation. Debra, why is the girl asking for Constable Leslie?"

"She told me Chad made her promises about keeping her safe, finding her a home. I haven't talked to Chad about it, but it may have been before he knew..." Debra stopped, glanced at Katrina and then cast Sergeant Kindle a knowing look.

Before Chad knew what? What is it they're hiding from me?

"Katrina hasn't even had the opportunity to be checked out by a physician," Cooper said. "Considering the company she's kept for the last year, perhaps we have our priorities wrong here. She's not prepared for any of this and neither am I."

"I'm not prepared for what, Mr. Cooper?" Katrina asked.

"Am I to understand you're insisting she be seen by a doctor before we continue?" Sergeant Kindle cut in.

Cooper leaned forward, blocking Katrina's view of the sergeant. "In the interests of the child, yes."

He thinks if I'm out of the room, Sergeant Kindle will reveal his secret. What an idiot!

"I'll have the staff physician look at her immediately," Sergeant Kindle said.

Cooper gave a terse nod. "I'd appreciate that."

Shit!

The whole episode with the doctor had been an embarrassment to Katrina, from being checked out for sexually transmitted diseases to questions about physical abuse and drug use. *None of that stuff would've happened at the compound. Shrug took good care of me. Except for—*

What had happened in the compound was no one's business and she'd told the doctor that. She was out of the gang now and Shrug was no doubt behind bars with the other biker. *He doesn't matter anymore. Nothing matters.*

She flopped onto the waiting room sofa and waited for Cooper.

"Katrina?" Cooper waved at her. "There you are."

As he got closer, she saw lines of worry wrinkle his face. "What's wrong?"

"I'll tell you everything later. How did it go with the doctor?"

"Fine. I'm totally okay. She just gave me some vitamins."

"That's good."

Cooper stuffed his hands into his pockets and stared down at her. For some reason, the look in his eyes made her feel like crying. She shifted uncomfortably and lifted her chin. Shrug had taught her it was dangerous to be weak.

"What do we do now?" she asked.

"Let's find a quiet place to talk. It's warm out. How about we walk down by the river?"

Outside, Katrina drank in the astounding beauty of the Alberta September. Across the river, gold leaves glittered behind the red berry bushes lining the bank. Interspersed in the dazzle of fall colours were the spruce trees, stretching their deep green toward the rich, late-afternoon sun. The sky was a cloudless blue dome and the air was thick with the pungent scent of autumn. Fallen leaves, some mottled and others striped, crunched beneath their feet.

This was the time of year when she used to go hunting with Grandpa. Hunting ducks and geese involved autumn skies and sunrises and sunsets. And colourful reflections in ponds. She'd always remember the calls of the birds echoing off cool morning mists and the warmth of a retriever, shivering with excitement.

But those moments were gone.

When they were away from traffic and pedestrians, Cooper motioned her to stop. She took a spot on a park bench and watched the diamond sparkles racing downstream on top of the wavelets.

Cooper joined her on the bench. "Sergeant Kindle wants to question you about a murder."

She froze and the world became deathly quiet.

"Talk to me, Katrina. What happened?"

A flock of snow geese came into view, myriad white birds moving across the intense blue sky, their shimmering wings gilded with the glow of the low-lying sun.

"I don't have a clue what you're talking about, Mr. Cooper."

"Someday you'll have to talk about it."

Shrug had said those exact words to her just days ago.

"I can't talk about something that didn't happen," she said, just as she'd said to Shrug. "Aren't the geese flying a bit early this year?"

Cooper's cell phone rang. The geese honked. A jogger ran by. Cooper's phone jangled again.

Her heart raced and she could hardly breathe. "You should answer your phone. You have a business to run."

Cooper shrugged. "I have voice mail. They say your testimony could be vital to getting murder convictions."

She liked the way the shadows of the trees made parallel lines across the grass at her feet. *What would it be like to live on a planet with two suns?*

Cooper's phone impatiently beeped.

The shadows would be so different. It would change perspective, alter the seasons.

His phone beeped again.

"I know nothing about a murder," she said. "I can't help them at all."

Autumn leaves rustled in the lengthening silence between them.

Cooper rose. "The geese actually started flocking three weeks ago. They say that means we're in for a long, hard winter."

CHAPTER 5

Holiday Inn, Edmonton

The door to the adjoining hotel room was propped open and Katrina could hear Cooper's quiet snores. But she couldn't sleep, couldn't even close her eyes. She'd worked so hard to forget the terror in that Quonset and no one this side of the compound was to have known she'd been there.

She pulled the quilt over her head. In the dark, she heard her frantic breathing and felt her racing heartbeat. She inhaled deeply, then exhaled.

Did Shrug tell someone? Did Gator?

Terrifying images of faceless people doing nameless things emerged from the darkness.

"100, 99, 98, 97," she whispered.

Colours and sounds. None of it made sense.

"65, 64, 63, 63..."

Liquid red—dripping, flowing, gushing. The haunting echo of an endless scream.

"10, 9, 8, 7, 6, 5, 4, 3, 2, 1, 0."

Her watch beeped midnight, and she pulled the quilt from her head and breathed in the cool night air. The light filtering in under the door and between the drapes created ominous shadows in the room.

"3.14159 26535 89793 23846 26433." That was the start to the infinite value of pi. She knew more. "83279 50288 41971."

She'd never be able to learn it all because it was infinite. *Like my terror. Endless.*

"69399."

Like a scream in a metal shed that lasts forever.

"37510..."

When Katrina opened her eyes, the first rays of dawn were peeking through the hotel curtains. She tiptoed to the window and looked fourteen stories down to the lazy morning traffic. Edmonton seemed quieter than Calgary and was much flatter. There were no mountains to the west, just building after building until the city was swallowed by the horizon.

"Katrina?" Cooper said from the doorway. "It's early yet. Why are you up?"

"I can't sleep."

"Shall we go for breakfast?"

"I don't eat when I'm upset."

"Come anyways. Have a piece of toast or at least a glass of juice."

"Fine."

She grabbed a change of clothes and headed into the bathroom.

Then they went downstairs to the restaurant.

As they waited for their breakfast, she watched the shadows of the ceiling fan rhythmically sweeping across the café tabletop. She calculated the speed of the fan and looked up to confirm. When the blades swept away from her, they changed shape and almost disappeared before slowly morphing back to full size on their return. The fan was doing thirty revolutions per minute, just as she'd figured.

"They want us both back at the police station," Cooper said.

"I'm not going."

The waitress's shoes squeaked. Dishes clanked onto their table. Silverware tinkled.

Katrina picked up a glass of orange juice and swirled it. The juice rose and fell against the sides. *Tomorrow I'll learn the mathematical equations for wave action. If I combined that with the chemical formula for orange juice, I can write this breakfast on a piece of paper and toss it in—*

"They're sending an officer for us, Katrina."

"I can't go back there!" Her voice pierced the quiet.

The two other early-rising diners in the room turned to stare at her while in the kitchen, dishes clattered.

"Very well." Cooper forked some omelette into his mouth, chewed and swallowed.

She wanted to run, but where would she go? *Cooper sold my home, so I can't go there.*

"3.14159 26535 89793 23846 26433, " she whispered.

"I'll phone and let them know we can't come. It's okay, dear. Have some of your toast and finish your juice."

Katrina concentrated on slowing her breathing. Shrug had told her that emotional people were vulnerable because they couldn't think straight. They couldn't see straight either, he'd said. She blinked rapidly a few times. Now was not the time to become vulnerable or blind.

"Mr. Cooper, you're a lawyer. You must let them know that I won't talk, that I know nothing. That I have *nothing* to tell them."

"I'm not going to be your lawyer. You need someone who specializes in juvenile law to represent you. I'll stick to being your guardian."

"Then as my guardian, call Sergeant Kindle." She tapped Cooper's cell phone. "Now! Tell him I'm not coming. I have the right to remain silent."

Cooper flipped open his phone. "I'll get you a lawyer. You might be surprised at how limited your rights are."

"Limited?"

"Your rights will have to be balanced with your obligation not to obstruct a police investigation."

"I swear I know nothing about—"

Cooper patted her hand. "It will be okay, dear."

There has to be a way to get him to listen to me. Maybe if I blink lots, talk sweetly, look up at him through my lashes.

She curled her foot under her thigh, cupped her chin in her hands and tilted her head. "Can you imagine how dangerous it would be for someone to witness a gang murder? And then to tell people about it?"

Cooper dialled. "The danger would be one reason not to talk. Another reason would be to avoid incriminating oneself."

Incriminating myself? Shit! "I'm a suspect?"

He raised the phone to his ear. "You need a lawyer, Katrina."

CHAPTER 6

Northern Alberta Police Detachment, Edmonton

Katrina slouched as far as she could in her chair and peered at the faces rimming the boardroom table. Chad was there today, across the table, but he hadn't even looked at her yet.

When she'd first walked in with Cooper, she'd been terrified. However, that terror had gelled into a massive ball of fury when they'd made her sit in the steno chair, pumped up higher than the rest because, as they said, she was so short. It made her feel like a baby in a high chair.

She was also furious with Cooper. He should've refused Sergeant Kindle's request to bring her to the detachment. He'd said they had no choice, but she knew otherwise. Canada wasn't a police state. Citizens had rights and freedoms.

So where are mine?

She shaded her eyes with one hand to hide her anger. Then she concentrated on becoming calm. Shrug had once told her it was easy to take advantage of people who were angry. She didn't intend on letting anyone take advantage of her—ever again.

Cooper flanked her on one side and on the other was Steward McMal, her new attorney. Cooper had told her McMal was the most experienced lawyer in juvenile law in Canada. But the moment she had looked into McMal's eyes, she'd known the man was an idiot.

Her gaze drifted to Chad. When they'd been together in The Traz, he'd always had a chuckle on his lips and a glint in his eyes. Not today. His face and heart were as stiff as his uniform. It was as if he were pretending he didn't know her.

"There is some question about the juvenile status," Sergeant Kindle began. "Guardianship issues were addressed..."

Cooper joined in, using longer sentences with more legal words and fewer pauses. Katrina didn't even try to understand all they were saying. As their voices droned on endlessly, she tuned them out. Her lawyer, McMal, kept cocking his head as if he were listening intently. She doubted he was, though.

Chad's chest rose and fell rapidly. Every few minutes, he shifted forward and opened his mouth. Just when she'd think he was about to say something, he'd release a heavy sigh, settle back in his chair and bite his bottom lip.

"I promise you she's being questioned as a witness, not a suspect," Sergeant Kindle said.

"Sergeant Kindle, sir," McMal said. "How can you promise something like that when you have no idea what she's going to say?"

"She's young," Cooper said. "She's been through a lot."

Katrina tapped her fingers on the table and cleared her throat. *Hello? I'm right here!* Nobody looked at her.

"We have a fairly good idea of what she's going to say," Sergeant Kindle said.

She slammed her fist on the table and stood up. "I'm not going to say anything! I know nothing about a murder."

"Oh, you *are* going to talk," Chad said.

"I am not!"

"You know details about the murder."

"I don't know squat. Besides, it's my right not to talk. Although, apparently, my rights are of little importance to anyone here today."

McMal touched her elbow. "Your rights are very important, dear."

"Really?" She stared at his fingers pressing into her skin. They were cold and bony just like Cooper's.

She looked back at Chad. *What is it he wants from me?*

Everybody here was after her for something. Sergeant Kindle wanted her to talk. McMal wanted her to shut up. Cooper wanted her money.

If she stared long enough into Chad's liquid dark eyes, she knew she'd be able to read his thoughts. She'd done it in The Traz. When they'd first met in the cycle shop she'd known instantly he was an undercover cop.

She locked her eyes on Chad and the world stopped.

"Sit." His hardened gaze was a silent warning for her to obey.

She slithered back to her chair. *If I could just have a minute or two alone with him...*

There was a pause in the conversation and she jumped in. "Sergeant Kindle, I want to be alone with...I don't want either my guardian or lawyer present. I have that right."

"You need at least one of us here," Cooper argued.

"You must make them listen to me," she said to Sergeant Kindle. "You'll be violating my rights if you don't. I've asked for Mr. Cooper and McMal to leave."

"I'm not sure—"

"They're not representing me fairly. They haven't done a thing I've asked."

"But you need someone. I could—"

"I must object," McMal said. "The child's in no state of mind to make this kind of decision. I insist on having her evaluated to determine her capabilities before we continue."

Katrina sent her chair spinning and stalked to the far end of the room. Behind her, the adults kept talking.

"I think you're underestimating her," Chad said. "Believe me, she's quite capable."

She couldn't agree with him more.

She ran a finger down the white enamel-painted bricks. The corporate boardrooms she'd been in with her mother had sported much richer colours and softer lighting. This boardroom, with its white walls, tiled floors and sparse trim smelled—she sniffed—like a laboratory or a hospital room. She looked at the bank of fluorescent lights and sniffed again. The room smelled like…evidence. Like facts. Truth.

"If she's asking not to have her guardian and attorney in the room, I believe we have to respect that," Sergeant Kindle said behind her. "Juveniles do have certain rights when it comes to—"

"You must tread more carefully," McMal warned. "We have to be sure she understands."

"She understands!" Chad shouted. "Her father was a cop. She has an IQ of two hundred and fifty. Believe me, she understands."

"I would be more concerned about the matter if she was a suspect," Sergeant Kindle said in a tone so soft that Katrina had to quiet her breathing and train her ears on the conversation to hear him. "But we're simply questioning her as a witness."

"As I've said before," McMal said, "how can you promise anything when you don't know what she's going to say? She could incriminate herself without realizing it and your promises fly out the window and the next thing we know she has charges laid against her."

"I'd like some time alone with her to make sure she understands what she's getting into," Cooper said.

She heard chairs squeaking and voices murmuring. A door slammed and footsteps approached. She reluctantly turned. Cooper and McMal stopped a meter from her.

"Katrina," Cooper said. "Watch what you're doing. If you had any part in what went down, don't say anything, dear. Let us be here for you.

There are wicked ways they can ask questions to get you to say things you don't intend on saying."

"I'm not an idiot."

"It wouldn't hurt for us to be here," McMal said.

"If you had half a brain between you, you'd realize it isn't charges against me that you should be worrying about."

McMal scowled. "If you were to get a homicide charge slapped against you, I bet you'd change your mind about that quite quickly."

"Compared to actually *getting* murdered, a mere murder *charge* would seem awesome." She turned to the wall and rested her forehead on the cool bricks.

"Steward, she has a point," Cooper said. "Tattling on a biker gang would put her in a precarious position."

"So would a murder charge."

"There may be things she wants to say to the police that she doesn't feel comfortable saying in front of us."

"That's exactly what I'm afraid of."

"I believe we have to respect her decision on this one."

"She ran with a biker gang for a year. I don't think that's an indication she's a pro at making good decisions. At least have a psychiatrist talk to her before agreeing to this."

Katrina whirled about and took a step toward him. "You're an idiot to think I need a psychiatrist!"

"I've changed my mind. I withdraw my offer to represent her." McMal strode toward the exit.

Cooper's stiff shoes squeaked closer to her. "They're desperate for your testimony," he whispered. "There's a good chance to work a deal for you."

"If there was any chance in hell you'd work the deal I want, I'd let you. You have no idea what I want."

"You're not an expert at making deals. You need legal help."

"I'll take my chances."

"Don't. You'll regret it."

Katrina put her hands over her ears and pounded her forehead against the wall. "3.14159." She pounded her head again. "26535 89793."

Cooper's shoes squeaked away.

"23846 26433…"

She was nearing the one hundredth digit of pi when she heard Chad's voice behind her. "It's okay, Katrina. Cooper and McMal are gone now." He gently drew her hands from her ears and rested a familiar arm about her shoulders. "Come, Sarina."

She laid her head against him. She could smell his cologne—the same scent he'd used in The Traz. He hugged her tighter. Then he led her back to the table, pulled out a chair and she sank into it.

"Katrina," Sergeant Kindle said. "I'd like you to tell us what happened."

I can't tell him. I can't tell anyone. Ever.

She closed her eyes and willed her heart to thump slower.

Slower. Slower.

Just as Grandpa had taught her in the forest.

CHAPTER 7

After the murder, she'd curled up on Shrug's couch, shrank the world until only her breath and her heartbeat existed, and hadn't moved for three days. She could do it again. Grandma Buckhold had taught her how to meditate, taught her she mustn't try to enter a trance. She should just let it happen.

There was just four of them now in the boardroom—Katrina, Chad, Sergeant Kindle and Debra. As voices swirled about her, she watched her thoughts tangle and tumble. As she exhaled, she imagined her fear leaving her soul on each wind of breath. She filled her body with strength and peace. She drank in the universe, released and relaxed.

"Katrina?" Chad called. "Do you want to know how the tactical team made out?"

It doesn't matter. It didn't happen. None of it.

"She'd probably like to know who was arrested and what the charges are," Sergeant Kindle said. "Maybe she'd like to know who's still on the loose?"

The universe is a safe place to be. Big breaths…in and out.

"Do you want to know if the bikers are aware you betrayed them?" Chad said.

It hadn't happened. She hadn't been there. Reality existed only in the mind, and her mind was empty and quiet. If no one heard a tree fall, it made no sound. If no one spoke of evil, it did not exist.

If no one heard a scream…

"Katrina." Chad's voice was so low it came to her as a vibration—his soul talking to hers. "Tell me about the blood and missing fingers."

He can't know about that.

"Tell me what you saw."

I saw nothing, heard nothing. It did not happen.

"Lukas—"

She lunged across the table. "Don't say that name! Don't say that!"

Chad's dark eyes drilled into her, unblinking. She raked at his face, but he caught her hands. "I'm sorry, Katrina. I am so very sorry."

He knows I was there. He knows how to make me cry.

Katrina blinked as a stream of tears rushed down her cheeks. She yanked her hands away. Helpless and hopeless, she sank into a chair and cradled her head on the table

"Chad, what did you say to her?" Sergeant Kindle asked.

"She sounds pitiful, like a lost kitten," Debra said. "Katrina, can I get you something? Water? Milk? Something to eat?" She lifted a strand of hair from Katrina's face and tucked it behind her ear. "Hasn't she been through enough, Chad, without you making her cry?"

"I wasn't the one who took her to the Quonset."

No, it was Shrug who took me to the Quonset, left me in the Quonset. Left me.

"Enough!" Sergeant Kindle said. "There's a time and place for that discussion and it isn't here or now. Katrina, we're truly sorry to put you through this, but we need your cooperation. There's a tremendous amount at stake. Would you please talk to us?"

Someone had to make it go away. And it wasn't going to be Chad or Debra or anyone else, now that Sergeant Kindle had stepped in.

"I want my guardian," she sobbed into her arms.

"Katrina," Chad scolded. "You're playing games. Shut off the waterworks and turn on the mouth. Start fucking talking. Now!"

Sergeant Kindle cleared his throat. "Chad, language."

"I'm talking her language. Aren't I, Katrina?"

Chad's not here for me like he promised. He's here to make me talk.

"Your language is all lies," she said. "You've kept none of your promises to me."

"I take it you're looking to deal?"

"I'm looking to enforce a deal we already have."

Chad raised his eyebrows. "Tell you what. That's not going to happen, but there's nothing saying we can't strike a new bargain."

"We really aren't on opposite sides, Katrina," Sergeant Kindle said, attempting a smile. "We just want to talk to you."

"I don't talk to people who lie to me."

"I haven't lied to you."

"Chad lied to me."

"I lied to you?" Chad said. "No, Katrina. You're the liar around here."

"When did I ever lie to you?"

"Well, maybe not exactly lie." He dragged his chair closer to the table. "But you've been avoiding the truth for almost an hour. First with your 'trance.' Then your phoney alligator tears. Now your demands to see Cooper. Katrina, just get on with this. Quit trying to manipulate—"

She laughed. "Me, manipulate? I never promised you the truth, Chad. In fact, I never promised anything. But *you* promised me a home. Did you just forget to mention I'd first be stuck in a police station and interrogated about a murder that didn't happen—or whatever? Who's trying to manipulate whom?"

"Is this squabbling really necessary?" Sergeant Kindle said to Chad.

"None of this is necessary," Katrina said. "Can I please leave now?"

"No, you cannot. Sit!" Sergeant Kindle searched through the papers in the file in front of him. "Look, Katrina, I just want to share information on the gang. Can't we just do that? Is that so hard?"

She clamped her lips together.

"Perhaps if you addressed this issue of Chad's promises?" Debra suggested.

"Chad, can you address this issue of your promises?" Sergeant Kindle asked. "In a professional manner, please."

"Sure." Chad folded his hands and rested them on the table. "Katrina, I'm sorry I promised you things I can't deliver. And I really mean that. If things were the way I thought they were when I made those promises, you'd be out of here. Gone. Starting a new life. Sarina, look at me so you can see I'm telling the truth."

"Katrina," she corrected. "My name is *Katrina*."

"It was different in there. Different name, different situations. One had to say things and do things to survive." He lowered his voice. "I had to tell you things, promise things, for your sake, Katrina. To protect you. Look at me." His fist pounded on the table. "Look at me!"

He knows that if I look into his eyes, I'll start believing his lies all over again.

"I'm asking you trust me again," he said. "Make a new deal. One I can keep."

Her mouth twisted into a sneer. "I kept my end of our last deal. I did what you asked me to do on the computer. I disabled the perimeter sensors for your tactical team. I did whatever you asked. I owe you nothing. It's your turn now to do something for me."

Chad raised his hands in surrender. "I'm not arguing with you. You did everything I asked. I made promises to you in return. But I can't keep those promises. What I can do is give you a new deal."

"You mean you'll make me *new* promises that you won't keep?"

"Answer our questions and all promises will be kept."

She contemplated all the anxious faces waiting for her answer, waiting for her to cave to give them what they needed. But what about what *she* needed? They were pretending it was all so simple. What about the danger she'd be in if she answered their questions?

Isn't anyone going to warn me about the hours of questioning I'll face? Or admit to me that those promises won't be kept until I go through years of testifying?

She turned to Sergeant Kindle. "If I answer your questions, I can leave and start my new life in a safe home?"

"Eventually, yes."

She shook her head. "This is starting off real badly. Nobody's being honest with me."

"What do you mean?"

"You're asking me to do something very dangerous, while pretending you're not. You keep telling me you need me to talk. If you were being honest, you'd tell me you're going to need me to testify against the bikers in court."

"We don't know yet if we need you to testify. We have to find out first what you know."

She stood, legs apart, ready to fight. "Sir, that's two more lies. You know that you need me to testify and you know exactly what it is I know."

"We also must find out if you'd make a credible witness and we won't know that until you talk to us."

"Bullshit!"

A look of unease washed across Sergeant Kindle's face.

She crossed her arms in defiance. "I'm not saying anything."

Chad jumped to his feet. "Why not? Katrina, let's cut to the chase. I hate bureaucracy. How long did it take us to agree on our last deal, when you wanted out of the gang? Five minutes? Ten minutes? Today, we've been at it for hours and have gotten nowhere. I'll tell you what we want. Then you tell me what you want in exchange. It's what we did last time. That worked, didn't it?"

"It worked very well." She stormed up to him. "Except you didn't keep your end of the deal!"

"There will be no broken promises this time."

She slunk back to her chair. "Sure, Chad. Whatever."

"Here's what we want," he began. "Information about gang drug deals. Names, locations, dates, amounts. Are you with me so far, Katrina?"

"Whatever."

Chad pulled a notepad from his jacket pocket and set it on the table. "Tell us about the murder."

"No, I—"

He raised a hand. "The murder. And you will testify if we need you to." He tossed her the pen and pad. "Name your price."

"What are you doing?" Sergeant Kindle demanded.

"Working on a deal. She knows what we want. Now she has to tell us what *she* wants."

Katrina grabbed the pen and ground the nib into the paper beside the word 'murder'. "I'm not—"

Chad caught her hand. "This is a package deal. You don't get to edit it."

"In that case, there's no deal." She slid the pen and paper back to Chad.

He shoved it back at her. "Name your price."

"Not everything has a price."

"*Everything* has a price."

He was right about that. Shrug had taught her that everyone could be bought. *Chad just hasn't found my weakness, yet. But he will. I know he will. It's what good cops do—and good bikers.*

Chad blew out a frustrated sigh. "You know what I could say to you right now? I could say fine, you're free to go. Leave. You're of no use to us anymore. Just walk out that door. Go find your legal guardian lawyer friend—he's raging his way around here somewhere—and ask *him* to protect you for the rest of your life." He snickered as if the idea of Cooper caring for her was comical.

"Maybe I will," she said.

"Katrina, listen, that's *not* a safe option. You'll be an open target for the gang. You must talk. If you don't, we'll have no choice but to send you out on your own. You'll be deemed an uncooperative gang member. We won't be able to protect you."

"Those are my options? Talk or…?"

"Yep, that's pretty much it." He wiggled the pen in front of her. "What do you say? Go on. You've been holding out on us for hours. You must know what you want."

Once more, she stabbed at the word 'murder' on the paper, drilling the tip of the pen into the table. "I was holding out because I don't want this."

"Well, things are different than you first thought, aren't they?"

"I promised to never speak of it."

"You're not bound by any promises made back then. You did and said what you had to in order to survive."

"It was a promise I made to myself."

"You don't need that promise anymore," Debra cut in. "You can change your mind."

Katrina took a deep breath. "I'm scared of what will happen if I talk."

"You'll receive great protection," Sergeant Kindle said. "The best."

"I'm not scared of the gang. I'm scared of what will happen in my head. I'll crash."

"You can do it," Chad said. "I know how strong you are. You're not going to crash."

"Secrets are bad things," Debra said. "They can grow into monsters if you don't name them, put them to words."

What the hell difference does it make if I give my monsters names or not?

"You've never talked about it, have you?" Debra said.

Katrina shook her head.

"I could tell by the way you flinched every time Chad said 'murder.'"

"Words will make it worse."

"I don't think so, Katrina. If you can say the word 'murder,' you can say 'suspects, evidence, motive, opportunity.' These are tangible things to chase down and handle. If you just have a bunch of horrible feelings floating around, how do you do anything with them?"

"Words will *make* it real."

Chad's eyes zeroed in on hers. "It's not words that make it real. With or without your words, the murder was real. I can show you the crime scene photos. You can see how *real* it was." His jaw clenched and unclenched. "There was *real* blood all over the *real* place, Katrina. I bet there were *real* screams too, weren't there?"

Faces began to appear amidst the violent images that had been haunting her—Lukas, Shrug, Gator. For the first time she remembered the words that went with the images.

'Son of a bitch! I'll be right back.'

'Shoot him! Shoot him.'

'Look at me. Look at me. Look at me! Watch!'

Her hands and shoulders trembled. Her chest tightened until she could no longer breathe. *I'm going to die. I can't tell anyone what happened. Ever.*

"Chad, where are we going with this?" Sergeant Kindle asked.

"I don't know. Katrina? Where are we going with this?"

Sergeant Kindle grabbed Chad's arm. "Let's take a break. Debra, stay with the girl."

Once the door closed behind the two men, Katrina was able to breathe again.

"Are you all right?" Debra asked. When Katrina didn't answer, she added, "It's okay to cry."

Katrina had heard those words before, in Cooper's kitchen a life time ago, when two officers had come to the door with their news and sympathy. After they'd left, Cooper had said, "It's okay to cry."

She whipped around. "I didn't cry the night my dad died. I'm sure as hell not crying now."

CHAPTER 8

Chad returned to the boardroom, alone, and hung his jacket on the back of the chair. He rolled up his shirtsleeves and took a seat across from Katrina. Without his uniform framing his face and wrapping about his wrists, he looked much more like he did in the biker compound.

He smiled at her. "Katrina, do you want Debra to stay here with us?"

"No."

She heard the click of the door as Debra left. Katrina was alone with Chad, like she had been so often in the compound.

"Do you want Mr. Cooper here, or your lawyer?"

She shook her head.

"You asked why I thought you would want to testify against the bikers. You must have reasons of your own for wanting to do that?"

She studied his face, taking in the tired eyes and grizzled chin.

If there was anyone in the world who understood her, it was Chad. Perhaps he had reasons for breaking his promises. Police officers often had good reasons. She knew that.

Maybe he still cares about me.

There was no one else in the world she could trust right now, no one anywhere who could help her. And without help...

"I can understand why you don't want to tattle on The Traz," he said. "After all, those guys were your buddies for a year. Kind of like a family."

"A family?" She made a sound, half laugh, half grunt.

The Traz had been nothing like a family. Her family had been her dad and grandparents, who'd loved her, given her stuff, taught her things. And her mother, who'd mostly just been drunk. That had been her family.

"You ate with the bikers, played with them, rode with them," Chad said. "You did business with them and for them."

"That didn't make them *family*."

Perhaps Shrug was like family, though. He was about her father's age, but much larger in build. He'd often made her tea when things got tough. He'd dried her tears. When her nightmares had wakened her, he'd held her for hours in his powerful tattooed arms.

But he did other stuff that wasn't so great.

Then there'd been Zed. He'd been nice to her. At least he'd talked to her.

"Some of the guys were okay," she admitted.

Chad nodded. "And others were brutal. Remember Pepper? Throwing you against the wall?"

She remembered. Chad had been so worried that Pepper had broken her arm. He'd even given up his bed to her that night and slept on the couch.

"Remember when Stack wrung the puppy's neck right in front of you?" he asked.

Katrina's head jerked up. *There's no way he can know about that. Stack killed the dog months before Chad arrived at the compound.* "Who told you about the puppy?"

"It doesn't matter who told me. The point is it happened. Just like the murder happened, Katrina. And now is the time to talk."

"Are you saying I should talk to get even with Pepper for throwing me against the wall and with Stack for killing a dog?"

"Getting even might be one reason to cooperate. However, I'll bet you can think of better reasons."

"No, I can't think of one good reason to tell you anything. *However*, I can think of lots of reasons not to."

"Tell me those reasons."

"As if you don't know."

"I don't know what your reasons are. Tell me."

"For starters, I'd never be safe again in my entire life. They'll kill me first chance they get. Gangs kill traitors."

"With the police on your side, you'll be safe. We'd go to great lengths to hide your identity. You know that. You also know you have many reasons to help us. Tell me just one."

"No." She pushed her chair back from the table. "I'm going to find Cooper."

"Wait!" He grabbed her arm. "If your father were here, he'd insist you work with us, Katrina. He'd want you to help us."

"Don't talk about my dad. He has nothing to with this."

His fingers dug into her skin. "Your father was a good officer, a good man."

"I said don't talk about my dad."

"He was a good father. He taught you to be honest, didn't he?"

"I'm being honest."

Chad released his hold and leaned back. "Your father liked bikers?"

"No."

Katrina had been so close to her father, loved him so much. He'd called her 'beautiful' and often wrapped her in his arms. He'd told her she'd do great things because she was so smart and knew all about computers.

"It would've made him happy to know you helped the police take down the bikers," Chad said.

Half the reason she'd joined The Traz was to forget the cold feel of her dad's hand in the coffin. She grabbed the notepad and began to doodle. Her dad hated biker gangs. He would've been furious if he'd known she hooked up with The Traz.

"He would have been proud of what you did in the compound to help me," Chad continued. "If he was here, he'd tell you that."

Katrina threw the pen across the table, missing him by a centimetre. The pen clattered to the floor.

"He wouldn't have liked the fact that I was with the gang," she said.

"No, he wouldn't have. He would've been terrified for you. But he would've been happy you were able to safely get out."

"Dad can't be happy. He can only be dead."

"Although he's dead, you're alive, Katrina. You're still alive and you can help us."

"I've already helped enough. I'm not doing anymore."

Chad tore off her page of doodling and set a clean sheet of paper in front of her. He looked at the pen on the floor, then pulled another from his shirt pocket.

"You know what you have to do, Katrina. Write down some reasons you want to help."

"No."

"You can do this. I know you can. I remember how strong you were in The Traz. You stood up against men three times your size. Now you're safe in a police station. There's no need to be afraid."

"I'm not afraid."

"Then why won't you talk to me?"

"I *am* talking to you."

"Why are you afraid to talk to me about this stuff?"

"I'll talk to you about the drugs deals."

His stiff shoulders loosened. "Thank you. That would be good. You'll tell us about the murder too, right?"

"No."

"Why not?"

"I don't think I was there."

"I know you were there. Just like I know about the puppy."

She swallowed hard. "I don't think you know that."

"Katrina, the police know you were there. If you say you weren't, you're lying."

By the set of Chad's jaw and the look in his eyes, she knew he was telling the truth. Perhaps one of the bikers had made a deal with the Crown to tell what he knew in exchange for a lesser charge or a lighter sentence. Perhaps, but not likely. Bikers seldom talked to cops and never ratted out their brothers. But she wasn't a brother. She wasn't a Traz. Shrug had refused to even let her talk about belonging to the gang. Maybe the bikers were going to blame it all on her.

"It's…it's not something I'll talk about."

"It was terrifying, wasn't it?"

He waited, but she said nothing.

"With your testimony, we'll get convictions. When we found out there was an eyewitness to the biker murder, we considered ourselves lucky."

"It wasn't lucky that I saw it! I—" She clamped her mouth shut. *Oh God. I just confessed to seeing the murder.*

"It's not lucky for you, but it's good for the police."

Chad acted as though he hadn't noticed what she'd said. But she knew he'd heard her admission. Cops always noticed such things.

"Now what are we going to do for you, Katrina?"

All her defences came crashing down. She had to talk. She didn't have a choice. She'd be killed if she left police protection. Or worse— she'd get blamed for the murder.

I have to tell him everything. About Shrug and Gator and Lukas. And about that cold October night in the shed.

She was going to rat out a biker gang.

"Let's talk about witness protection," he said. "Do you know what that is?"

"No."

"You're lying."

Of course he knew she was lying. Her father was a cop and she was a genius.

"I have all day, all week, Katrina. How long do you want to stay here?"

"What the hell is it you want from me?"

"I want you to talk. In exchange for talking, we'll grant you witness protection. You'll get a new identity so those you testify against can't hurt you."

"What if I don't talk?"

He stared at her for a long moment. "If you're not going to talk, just get up and walk out. I'm tired of this, Katrina. But remember, if you don't talk, the murderers may walk out of here. They know you witnessed their crime. They'll know you helped me dismantle their drug business. Do you think they'll figure out who disabled the perimeter sensors before the tactical team swept in?"

Katrina jabbed the pad of paper. "With my new identity, I don't want to go back to school."

"What do you want to do?"

"I'd like to be twenty-one. Have a high school diploma with all my final marks in the high 90's. Because as soon as the trials are over, I'm going to university and take computer sciences."

Chad nodded. "Write it down."

"I don't want them to give me a different name. No one in the gang knew I was Katrina Buckhold, so they won't be able to track me down if I keep my real name."

"Note that down too."

She scribbled her name in bold letters. "I need to be 'Katrina' because my father named me. He loved me and wanted me, but my mother didn't. I heard her say that once."

"People don't always say what they mean, especially if they're drunk."

"She wasn't drunk. I was four, sitting right there at the table with her in Cambridge Bay. It was the middle of winter, cold out and dark. She said to my dad, "It was *you* who wanted her, not me.""

Katrina's hair fell over her face, hiding her sad smile from Chad. "I'll be living like an adult, so I'll need money. I must have access to my trust fund."

"Write it down."

Tears burned the corners of her eyes.

"Finished?" Chad asked.

She didn't want to be finished—because terrible things would happen next.

Blinking back her fear, she said, "You'll tell me how the sting went? Who got arrested and what the charges are?"

She wondered what they'd nail Shrug with. The last time she'd seen him, he'd been packing an UZI while the tactical team was sweeping in.

"Eventually, yes," he said. "You can write that down as part of the deal. I can tell you that no one on either side got hurt during the raid."

"The poisonous mushrooms I fed the guys before the cops got there worked?" She set down the pen and tucked her hair behind her ears.

With a half-smile on his lips, he pushed back his chair and reached for the notepad. "I don't know what you're talking about."

He was lying. He knew all about the Amanita muscaria mushrooms. She had shown them to him. *He told me to throw them out, but I didn't.*

"I know some of the bikers were escorted to the hospital immediately after the raid with mysterious ailments." He rose and moved toward the door.

"None died?" she asked, wondering why he was covering for her.

"No, they all recovered." He looked over his shoulder. "You're damned lucky they did."

CHAPTER 9

Cooper marched into the boardroom, waving the signed agreement. "Katrina, are you sure you want to do this?"

"No." She wasn't sure about anything.

"But they told me you'd agreed."

"I did agree, but that doesn't mean I wanted to. I had no choice."

"There are always choices. You should've let me stay in here with you. I could've worked out—"

"Don't you get it? I have no choices."

"There are always—" Cooper bit back his reply and sat down beside her. "I'm sorry for scolding you."

"The deal's fair, right?"

"It's nothing special. Other than the part about changing your age, it's more or less what they'd do for any witness."

"It's also what they won't do if I refuse to cooperate, isn't it? I either cooperate and receive police protection, or I don't and I'm dead. I'm not asking for your opinion. I just want you to make sure it's written so they can't change their minds down the road."

"Don't set your heart on this agreement. It hasn't yet been approved by the higher-ups in the police force. I doubt they'll let a child your age assume an adult identity and a multimillion dollar estate."

"Why not? It would be the best way to conceal my identity after I testify. Besides, by the time the investigation and trials are done, I'll be damned near twenty-one anyway."

"More likely sixteen or seventeen."

"Is it me you're worried about, or my trust money?"

Cooper ran a hand over his chin. "I'm concerned about you, of course. I'm also nervous about you having access to that kind of money, especially considering what you told me about the funds you acquired while you were with The Traz."

"I won't have a chance in hell of ever getting back into the drug business if I testify against The Traz, if that's what's worrying you."

"I suppose you have a point." He sighed.

"There's one thing I want you to check for me." She pointed to the agreement. "What happens if I can't?"

"Can't what?"

"What if I can't talk about it? I don't remember what happened that night. What if I'm no help to them?"

Cooper scanned the document. "There's nothing specific about that in here. Only that your demands won't be met until after your testimony. And, of course, you'll be protected until then."

"What if the bikers say *I* killed Lukas and I say *they* killed him, and the jury gets mixed up and they all go free and I ratted them out and—"

"Your police protection isn't dependent on a guilty verdict, Katrina. If you testify, no matter what the jury decides or the bikers say, you will be enrolled in the Federal Witness Protection Program."

"And if I don't talk, the cops won't protect me and the bikers might not be found guilty and they'll be let go and they'll come after me because they know I know and they'll be scared I might tell."

As she contemplated her fate, she twisted a lock of hair tight around her finger. The tip turned from pink to white to purple.

"I'm in danger from the gang whether or not I testify, so I might as well...*right?*" She released the strand of hair and tossed it over her shoulder. "I *need* the Witness Protection Program, right?"

Cooper lifted a shoulder. "I don't know. Maybe. There are things we could do on our own to hide you, especially with your kind of money. But I'm not an expert at such things."

"What if I can't talk about the murder?" Hot tears raced down her cheeks and she rested her face on the cold table. "I have to, don't I? I don't have a choice."

"No," he said, his voice old and tired. "You have no choice."

"But I don't want to talk. I don't want to remember."

"We all know it's going to be hard on you, Katrina. Sergeant Kindle suggested he could bring in a psychiatrist to help during questioning."

She sat up. "A what?"

"Although the doctor would be there to help you remember and to get you through the rough spots, he works specifically for the police. I'd rather it be me there for you. Or legal counsel of some sort. If you don't like Steward McMal, I can get another attorney, someone more in tune with you. There are many who wouldn't mind representing you."

Lawyers, psychiatrists, witness protection, Cooper. It wasn't supposed to be like this. *I was supposed to be free of the bikers, in a safe home. Chad promised.*

Cooper gave her shoulder an awkward pat. "You can refuse to have the psychiatrist there."

"Should I?"

"Did you have a part in the murder?"

"I don't know. I've never let myself remember that night. What if I killed someone?"

"It's okay, dear. You don't have it in you to have done something like that—unless you were being threatened in some way."

"How do the police know I was there?" she cried. "How would they know? I doubt any of the bikers told them there was a witness."

Cooper shrugged. "Fingerprints, perhaps. DNA."

She glanced at her fingers. They dripped with bright, warm blood.

Then the image vanished.

Sergeant Kindle and Chad entered the boardroom.

"Mr. Cooper, please wait in the hallway," Chad said, holding the door open.

With an impending sense of doom, Katrina watched her guardian leave the room. She'd just sat back down when a stranger walked in.

"This is Dr. Holeman, our forensic psychiatrist," Sergeant Kindle said.

Katrina stood up so quickly that her chair toppled over. "I can't do this."

She thought she'd be given some time to think about what she'd say. That it would take a day or two for the higher ups to approve the agreement. That the Crown Prosecutors Office would have to look at it— for days.

Shit! It's too soon. I'm not ready.

"Hello, Katrina." The psychiatrist held out his hand.

Her head jerked toward Chad. "Let's talk later. I need to rest. I'm so tired. It's been a long—"

"Please, have a seat, Miss Buckhold." Dr. Holeman had a comforting voice. "I hear you've had a very long day. We're going to start out slowly."

Katrina blinked. Nothing in the room was in focus.

"You're very frightened. Is there something I can do to make you feel safer?"

"No." She righted the chair and slumped into it, despondent. "There's nothing anyone can do."

The doctor sat down beside her. Everything about him was average—normal length brown hair, normal brown eyes, normal features. She guessed him to be a bit younger than her father.

"May I call you Katrina?" Dr. Holeman asked.

"Yeah, whatever."

She felt the spastic rise and fall of her chest. Her fingers dug into her palms, her jagged nails cutting into the skin. Her jaw tightened and her molars ground together.

"Close your eyes and get as comfortable as you can."

She couldn't believe she'd agreed to talk. She remembered nothing of that night in the metal shed. How could she talk about it? How could she testify?

"You're safe," Dr. Holeman said.

How can I ever be safe from The Traz?

"Take a deep breath and let me know when you're ready."

She looked wildly about. Across the table from her, ivory blinds blocked a bank of windows. Above her, rows of humming fluorescents descended from dappled ceiling tiles.

Her face burned. Sweat broke out in beads across her forehead. She unclenched her hands and wiped them on her jeans. Then she crossed her arms. If she laid her thumbs just the right way on her lace sleeves, she could feel her warm, smooth skin between the petals of the crocheted flowers.

"Katrina, close your eyes," Dr. Holeman suggested. "It'll help you relax."

"I don't want to relax."

"Why not?"

"If I relax, I might remember things I don't want to."

"I thought you agreed to talk about it."

"I didn't want to agree."

"Katrina," Chad snapped. "Stop it."

"Stop what?"

"Stop playing games. I have here in your own handwriting what you want from us in exchange for talking." His voice dropped to a rumble. "Telling the doctor you didn't want to agree is coming awfully close to lying."

She turned back to Dr. Holeman. His face seemed far away. He began to shrink, smaller…smaller. She looked down at her hands. They were disappearing bit by bit.

"I don't have to do this," she said, stumbling to her feet.

The room teetered. She needed to leave, to run. Darkness seeped in from the corner of her eyes. She could no longer see the door. She whirled around, desperate to find an escape. But there was none.

Voices that weren't making sense chattered in her head. The world pressed against her. Tighter. She was shrinking.

Then Chad's familiar scent, the smooth baritone of his voice, the anxious whispering of her name, pulled her back from the brink.

"Katrina?" Chad called.

Far away, like at the very edge of the universe, she heard her own galloping heartbeat and desperate panting.

"Katrina!" he called.

Gradually she became aware of Chad and the doctor beside her, with Sergeant Kindle just behind them.

"Are you okay?" Chad asked, brushing her hair away from her face. "You looked like you were about to faint."

She pushed away his fumbling hands, lurched toward the table and found her chair. Afraid she was going to burst into a thousand pieces, she sat and hugged her knees tightly.

"We're going to start out slowly," Dr. Holeman said. "If things get too difficult, let me know, okay? We're recording this conversation so the police can use the information you share with us in their investigation. Do you understand?"

She nodded as she gasped for air.

"You're hyperventilating and that will make you dizzy. Take deep, slow breaths. That's right. Do it again for me. Good. I want you to go back in your mind to the morning of October 26th last year. That day has come and gone and has no reality anymore. It can't hurt you because you're just remembering that day. Big breath in, Katrina. And out."

I like the doctor's voice. It's deep, rhythmic. Sounds like he's reading poetry.

"Was the morning of October 26th sunny?" Dr. Holeman asked.

"I don't know. I was too worried to notice." Her voice sounded so fragile beside the resonating bass of the doctor's.

"On the morning of October 26th, you were worried about something. Is that correct?"

"They're talking about taking me out tonight."

"Who's going to take you out tonight?"

"Gator, Shrug and…"

"Who else?"

Vague images appeared in her mind, washes of color and patterns, but nothing discernible.

"Pete and Todd."

"Take another deep breath for me, Katrina. That's a girl. It's not going to be a pleasant outing, is it?"

"Shrug says I'll do fine."

"You called him Shrug?"

"Yes, and he called me Sarina."

"Did you tell Shrug you were worried?"

"Yes."

"What did you tell him exactly?"

"I told Shrug I didn't want to go."

The images were condensing. Faces appeared. Lukas. He was screaming.

"No!" Her eyes flew open.

Dr. Holeman covered her hand with his. "The police need this information to solve a murder and arrest those responsible. You're going to help put these people in jail so they can never do it again."

Locking up the gang won't bring Lukas back to life.

No, locking up The Traz wouldn't make her life better. It would put her in more danger because they'd blame her for ratting them out.

"Let's keep going," the doctor said with a smile. "Close your eyes again and relax. Focus on your breathing. In...out."

In the gang...out of the gang...in a body bag.

"After you told Shrug you didn't want to go with him that night, what did he say?"

"He said I had to go with them. He said it would be all right, not to worry."

"Were things later that night all right?"

She was going to get Shrug in trouble. She didn't have to. The bikers were the only other ones there. Nobody would know if she lied. "No, I'm wrong. Shrug didn't say it would be all right."

Chad let out a growl that made her jump. "Katrina, quit lying. What did Shrug say to you?"

She glared at him. "I'm not ly—"

"Shrug's not worth lying for. None of those guys are. Your information will be useless to us if it's not one hundred percent the truth."

"It's hard to remember things. I'm not purposely lying. I—"

"That's another lie. Shrug told me you can remember hour-long conversations, word-for-word. I'm pretty sure you can remember *exactly* what happened."

"Hard to remember doesn't mean I can't remember." She pouted. "It means it *upsets* me to remember."

"Listen to me, Katrina. I'm going to tell you why the truth is so important. You have no idea what I already know, so it's very risky trying to get something past me. The defence is going to have access to your statements. They'll say if you lied about one thing, maybe you lied about it all. You can't just sprinkle a bit of truth here and there between the lies. It has to be true—all of it. Do you understand?"

"Yeah, I understand."

When he was with her in the gang, Chad had told her he felt they shared a soul. He could simply look in her eyes and discover what she was thinking. Perhaps that's how he knew when she was lying.

"From now on," he said, "I want you to imagine your father is in the room here with you. Draw on his presence for your strength. Because for you, that's what this is all about, isn't it? You were so close to your father. You respected him. He once told you that you were going to do great things with your life."

But I tarnished all that by running with The Traz.

Chad crouched beside her. "Today you have the chance to set things right. This is your chance to do something that will make a big difference to the world. That's what greatness is. That's what your father saw in you—someone strong, full of goodness, honest."

"My father is dead."

"But you're not. Let your father's love and wisdom live on through you." He nodded to Dr. Holeman.

"Okay," the doctor said. "Back to that day—October 26th. Were you excited about going out with the boys on the bikes?"

Her dad had taught her about right and wrong, lying and telling the truth, and crime and law enforcement. If she didn't tell the truth today, all the good years—the good things her father had done for her, her father's life—would mean nothing.

"Were you happy to tag along?"

"No, I didn't want to go."

"But you did. Why?"

"Shrug must've told you what was going to happen," Chad interrupted. "But you went anyways?"

With a sigh, she shut her eyes and returned to the memory of that day. "No, he only told me I had to go. And not to worry. It was going to be all right."

"Good, that's how I want you to answer," Chad said. "Because I *know* that's the truth."

"Thank you, Katrina, for being honest," Dr. Holeman said. "Shrug told you everything would be okay and you believed him. But you didn't know—"

"I knew someone was going to get killed that night."

"How did you know that?"

"A few days before, Shrug and I went to a meeting in the clubhouse. All the guys were talking about a new gang, The Blue Torpedoes. These kids thought they were tough. They were making crystal meth and selling it in the bikers' territory. Gator said The Traz had to put a stop to it, teach all the new little home-grown gangs a lesson. They had to make an example out of Lukas."

"Lukas was the murder victim?" Dr. Holeman asked.

Katrina nodded.

"What were the exact words the gang members used?"

"Todd said, 'We have to take them bastards out before they start really screwing us over.' Then Pete said, 'If we can get just one of them fuckers real good, we could scare the rest of them out of it.' Then Gator said, 'Make it a front-pager with lots of colour.'"

"What else do you remember them saying?"

"They talked about which Blue Torpedo to kill."

"Why did they decide on Lukas?"

There were many reasons The Traz had chosen Lukas. But one was so…disturbing.

She clenched her hands. "I suppose they had lots of reasons."

"Katrina, why did they pick Lukas?" Chad demanded.

"I don't know. What difference does it make?"

"You were there. You heard then talking about it."

"Not much was said." She turned to the doctor. "It was like Gator had already decided it was going to be Lukas."

"And he didn't say why?" Dr. Holeman asked.

"Said something about Lukas mouthing off to Stack and Pepper."

"Stack and Pepper wanted it to be Lukas?"

"I don't know. Gator wanted it to be Lukas and no one but Shrug argued much. Shrug was kind of not wanting it to go down at all. He said the Torpedoes were all punks, and if The Traz was smart enough it could find better ways to scare them. He said he really didn't want to do a front pager and have the cops all over the gang. He had some big cocaine deals in the wings and he didn't want to lose them. But no one listened to him. They just called Shrug a 'prissy ass.' They'd say, 'Is that woman of yours turning you into a prissy ass?'"

Dr. Holeman's forehead creased. "Woman?"

"Yeah, they called me that, but it wasn't like I really *was* Shrug's woman. It was just a nickname."

"Then what?"

"Then Gator said to Shrug, 'I got two clean fuckers trying to run my show, and I don't like that.' He meant Shrug and me. Shrug had been turning a lot of the guys against Gator, and Gator knew that. 'Ain't it about time that woman of yours got her hands dirty?' he asked. And Shrug said calmly, 'I have no problem with that.'"

Katrina paused for a moment. Her head wanted to explode. "I don't like talking about this. I think I've said enough."

Dr. Holeman glanced at Sergeant Kindle, who shook his head. Then the doctor pressed on. "They told you the time had come for you to get your hands dirty and prove you were loyal to the gang."

"Shrug always looked after me, so it was like if he agreed to get me involved, he was showing loyalty too. Gator's men would've killed Shrug if he didn't do what Gator wanted. Gator had been hinting to the gang that Shrug was a cop. It wouldn't have taken much to make them believe that. Then the gang would've turned on Shrug and killed him. You don't need evidence and stuff in the gang. You just do whatever you want. Even if they thought he *might* be a cop, they'd have killed him."

Just like they're going to kill me for ratting them out.

"So you felt you had to do this," Dr. Holeman asked.

"I *knew* I had to do it or Shrug would die. And then I would die."

"Katrina, after Shrug agreed you'd 'get your hands dirty,' what happened at that meeting?"

"I don't know. He sent me home."

"Did you see him afterward?"

Her eyes pooled with unshed tears. "About three hours later Shrug came home. He was very quiet. He kept looking at me. He'd start to say something, then he'd stop. He paced around the room. He wanted me to tell him I didn't mind getting my hands dirty."

"Did you tell him that?"

Tears streamed down her face. "No."

"Why not?"

"Because...I—" A sob stole her words.

She recalled that night. Until then, Shrug had been so good to her. Kind. He'd bought her things. Made her tea. Listened to her. She'd helped him make his cocaine deals.

"I was hoping he'd change his mind. I...didn't...want...to...go."

Her weeping took her back to Shrug's kitchen, to a time when things had been different. When *she* had been different. When Lukas had still been alive.

"I understand how scared and unhappy you must have felt," Dr. Holeman said, his voice full of compassion. "But Katrina...look at me. You're here at the police station with us. You're safe. You're not in the compound with Shrug. You don't have to feel sad and scared anymore."

"I was angry at Shrug for getting me into this, even though I knew he had no choice. We were both dead if we didn't do it."

Dr. Holeman touched her arm. "What happened the night of the murder?"

"I heard a bunch of bikes leave. About an hour and a half later we took off."

"Who was with you?"

"Gator, Pete and Todd."

"Was Shrug there?"

"Yes, I rode with him."

"Where did you ride to?"

"The Quonset. It's like a big metal warehouse with a dirt floor, out in the middle of nowhere. It took us a long time to get there."

"Did you see anyone on your way there?"

She closed her eyes, struggling to remember if they'd passed anyone. "No. We went down side roads and trails. Sometimes I thought we were going in circles. When we got near the building, I saw lookout bikers on the hilltop."

"What time was this?"

"It was starting to get dark. It was the end of October so it must've been around five or six o'clock."

"Go on, Katrina. You're doing great."

She remembered how dark it was when they'd arrived at the Quonset. And how fricken cold. She'd had icicles on her cheeks.

"Do you recall going into the warehouse?"

"It's black in there," she said, slipping back to that day. "There are no windows and the door closes behind us. I can smell the leather of the bikers' jackets. I hear Lukas groaning. And Pete breathing beside me. I remember thinking he was like my Grandpa's black lab when the rifle came out, whining in anticipation."

"Excuse me," Chad cut in. "Pete was whining?"

"No, Grandpa's dog whined."

"What kind of noise did Pete make?"

"None."

"How did you know he was excited then?"

"I—" *Shit! I just said it was too dark to see anything—and it was.* "I could smell he was excited."

"You could 'smell' he was excited?"

"It was too dark to see anything, so how the hell else could I have known?"

"Go on."

"It was so dark. I felt sick and dizzy. I didn't know up from down. I couldn't believe we were there to murder someone and it wasn't bothering Pete. Or anyone else. Gator turned on a flashlight and I saw Lukas in the middle of the floor. We all started to walk toward him. Lukas didn't move."

"Was he standing?" the doctor asked.

"No, he was crumpled on the ground, in the dirt."

"Did he try to run away?"

Her eyes drifted shut again. "No."

"Why not?"

"I don't know, Dr. Holeman."

"When you get closer and Gator shines the light on him, what do you remember noticing?"

"I remember he was pretty beat up. I remember him looking up at us. I thought he'd be begging for mercy, but instead he looked angry."

"Tell me about Lukas's wounds."

"There was blood trickling down his forehead."

"What else, Katrina?"

"He kept groaning in pain, yet his expression was furious."

"I want you to remember what was so painful. What was making him groan?"

Lukas is staring at me. He thinks I'm betraying him.

"Katrina!" Chad's voice sliced through the air.

She blinked. "Yes?"

"You were disoriented because it was so dark in the warehouse," he said. "You said you were upset because no one else seemed to care they were about to murder someone. In fact, Pete seemed happy. Lukas is crumpled on the floor, groaning. Why? You don't have to relive that night. Just tell us about it. Remember it."

Exhausted to her very core, she let out a ragged sigh. Then she took a fortifying breath. "Lukas's legs are broken."

That's what Chad wants.

He didn't want to know about the hurt in Lukas's blue eyes or that she'd never get the chance to tell Lukas why she was there. She'd never get to say, 'I'm sorry.'

"He can't run away and he can't fight back," she said.

"What happened next?"

"They walk around him and poke him a bit, kind of taunting him. They get really angry when he spits at them. I think it would've been better if he'd…cried instead. He was mad and that made them do worse things."

"And then?"

Lukas will scream. And there will be blood.

"I want to go home."

Dr. Holeman nodded. "I know you do. But a long time ago you saw these guys kill Lukas. Right now you're in a police station and Lukas is *dead.* He's not groaning or bleeding. And you remember how he died. What happened next, Katrina?"

"I can't say it."

The doctor eased closer and laid a reassuring hand on her shoulder. "We need to know what happened. Then you can go home."

"I need to go home *now.*"

"You're almost home. Tell us what happened next."

It was obvious they weren't going to let her leave until she'd told them everything. A few more sentences would buy her the freedom she desired. She could finish this—she *had* to finish it, once and for all.

"Gator put a lantern in my hand and flicked it on. He moved my hand so Lukas was in the light. Gator had this funny smile on his face. He said to me, 'Watch carefully, because if you don't, who knows what might happen.' Then he winked."

Memories flooded her mind. "They all started making a big show of pulling out their weapons. Pete had this long knife. He moved it in the light so it glinted into Lukas's face. Then he turned his head and flicked the knife so the light bounced off the blade into my eyes."

Pete smiled at me, an evil smile.

"Pete ran the blade across Lukas, touching it to his throat, his heart, his crotch. Gator kept his eyes on me. He was making sure I kept watching." She forced her eyes to stay open, to only describe the images, not feel them. "Todd had his arms crossed as he circled Lukas and Pete. He whispered something, but I couldn't make out the words. Lukas tried to keep his eyes on Todd, but Pete kept running the blade down Lukas's body."

"Did Todd have a weapon?"

"He had a handgun under his jacket."

"Did Gator have a weapon?"

"I didn't see one."

"What about Shrug?"

"I couldn't see Shrug. He was behind me. I wanted to look at him, but I couldn't take my eyes off Lukas because Gator kept telling me to watch." Her voice trembled. "I didn't want to watch. It would've been better if I'd not seen anything. I don't think I did, really."

The memories began whirling, an ever-changing kaleidoscope of violent, wordless images. She couldn't fight them off.

"I was there, but it didn't seem real. After a while it became like a dream. I was just pretending to watch so Gator wouldn't..." She struggled to find the facts, but they weren't there. Only pure, raw emotion existed. And terror.

I've got to suck it up. I have no choice.

Slowly the visions began to arrange themselves in sequence.

"Pete ran the blade across Lukas's palm, then he glanced at Gator. Gator nodded and then quick, like that, he sliced off Lukas's little finger." She rested her head on the back of her chair.

"Keep going."

"Blood started going everywhere. Shrug said, 'Son of bitch!' and then whispers to me, 'I'll be right back.'"

"He left you there?"

"Yeah."

"That bastard!" she heard Chad shout.

Her eyes shot open. Chad was on his feet, his notebook on the floor and his lips a rigid line.

"Tone it down," Sergeant Kindle said.

Katrina watched their altercation with interest. Sergeant Kindle seemed to be sending Chad a message, while Chad searched his boss's face as if expecting—demanding—something.

Sergeant Kindle gave the doctor a grim smile. "Could we take a short break? Five, ten minutes?"

"Sure," Dr. Holeman agreed.

Sergeant Kindle turned back to Chad. "I'll get Debra to take Katrina outside for a walk. The child needs some fresh air."

Katrina cringed at the word 'child.' Yet for the first time in her life, a part of her yearned for the simplicity of childhood.

CHAPTER 10

Fifteen minutes later, Katrina followed Debra back into the boardroom.

Sergeant Kindle and Chad were already seated at the table with the doctor.

"Is the weather nice out there?" Dr. Holeman asked.

"It's a little cool," Katrina replied. "But probably about right for September in Alberta."

It had been a tense stroll. When Debra wasn't looking at her feet, she was glancing back at the detachment. Katrina knew that's where she'd rather have been.

Katrina sat down across from Chad. Although the fire was gone from his eyes, the muscles around his mouth were still taut.

She wondered if everyone had thought Shrug was the murderer and that's why they were upset when she'd said Shrug left. But she'd seen Chad's eyes. He'd been angry, not disappointed or surprised. Maybe it upset him to think of her all alone with Gator and his men…in an ice-cold shed…with blood on her hands.

"Do you feel refreshed?" Dr. Holeman asked. "Ready to go at it again?"

"Yes, I'm ready."

"We're going to talk about the weapons. Pete had the knife and Todd's revolver was sticking out from under his shirt, right? You said you didn't see Gator with a weapon and you didn't know if Shrug had a weapon."

"I didn't say that. I know Shrug had a gun. He always carried one."

The doctor flipped through his notes. Everyone stared at him, waiting for him to say something. "You said Shrug was behind you."

"He *was* behind me."

"So you didn't see his gun."

They were trying to confuse her. It wouldn't work. "I didn't see it, but I know he had it."

"Do you know what kind of gun Shrug owns?"

Shrug's revolver had been the worst part of the night. Maybe she should've let them think he didn't have one. That way, she wouldn't have to talk about it. But how would she explain all else that happened? She could play ignorant. It would be hard for them to prove she was lying. "I don't know much about guns."

"Did you ever hold or touch Shrug's gun?"

Her eyes flared and she stared at Chad. *Are my fingerprints on that gun? Is that how they know I was there?*

Something in Chad's eyes told her they didn't know anything for sure.

"I never touched his gun."

"Did you ever hold Todd's—?"

"These are bikers! They don't go leaving their guns around for people to touch!" *No, they just pass the gun to you and say, "Shoot him! Shoot him..."*

"Katrina!" the doctor called.

She was surprised to find she was standing, drenched with sweat, her hands clenched at her sides. She ran her palms down her pant legs to dry them, hoping she'd kept Gator's words in her head, and not said them out loud. She sank back into her chair.

"Did *you* have a weapon in the warehouse, Katrina?"

"No." She held her breath and listened to her heart thumping.

"Has she answered your questions about the weapons?" the doctor asked Sergeant Kindle.

Sergeant Kindle thumbed his notes. "For now."

Katrina couldn't see his face, couldn't tell what he was thinking. Did he suspect she was lying? Did he have proof she was?

Across the table Chad scowled at her.

Yup. He knows I'm lying.

"Okay, Katrina," Holeman said. "The officers tell me they're surprised to hear Shrug left. Wasn't he supposed to be proving his loyalty that night?"

She'd never thought about why Shrug had left. What she did remember was being sure he wasn't coming back. When she'd needed him the most, he'd left her.

Why?

Chad raised his brows and tapped his pen on the table. He looked exactly like her dad used to look when he was waiting expectantly for her to give him an answer he already knew. He'd take a call from the teacher, hang up and turn to her. 'Were you in school today?' he'd ask, even though he'd just been told that she hadn't been anywhere near a classroom.

"Wasn't Shrug supposed to prove his loyalty that night?" Dr. Holeman repeated.

Chad's eyes drilled into her, daring her to give any answer other than the right one. She glared back. *He's wrong. I don't know why Shrug left.*

"Katrina, what's going on between you and Chad?" the doctor asked.

"He knows stuff that I don't." She could see it in his eyes and his clamped lips, in the tension across his shoulders and in the restless movements of his hands. He knew much more than just the reason Shrug left her there.

"Of course he knows things you don't. He's an investigating officer."

Chad was about to say something, but Sergeant Kindle cleared his throat and Chad remained quiet.

"Chad knows something he thinks I should be told," she said.

"Perhaps," the doctor said. "But he might have good reasons not to tell you."

"Maybe he knows why Shrug left. I don't."

Dr. Holeman looked at Chad. "Do you know why Shrug left?"

"I have a pretty good idea."

"Katrina says she doesn't know why he left. Is that good enough for you on this issue?"

"No, I'm not convinced he left." Chad shook his head. "I think you're covering for him, Katrina. I think he was there all along."

She let out a huff. "Are you calling me a liar? It was dark in there. I had to keep my eyes on Lukas. All I know is Shrug said he was leaving and then I no longer heard him breathing behind me. No longer caught the scent of his leather jacket."

"Okay, okay." Chad settled back in his chair and stretched his legs.

"During the break," Dr. Holeman said, "Chad told me he wanted to know how you felt when Shrug left."

Katrina kept her eyes on Chad. "Shrug had been touching my back, whispering things like, 'Hold on. You're doing good. It's almost over. It will be clean. It will be quick.' Things like that."

"Then when things got messy, he left?" Cynicism dripped from each word. "Was he being a 'prissy ass'?"

Before anyone could stop her, she made a beeline for Chad, stopping just inches from him. "I'm in this warehouse, watching this guy with broken legs getting his fingers cut off, one by one." Her face was close enough to his that she could feel the warmth of his breath. "Do you know how loud a man can scream? Do you know what screams sound like in an empty metal warehouse? Do you know how much one person can bleed? Do you know how far blood can spurt?"

She curled her fingers into fists and yelled, "Do you know how long one scream can last before another begins?" She lowered her voice to a whisper. "Do you know how long it takes a man to die?"

He didn't answer.

She gazed into his eyes. "At this point, I don't really give a shit where Shrug is or what Shrug's doing."

"I understand," he said. "Katrina, believe me, I understand."

Dr. Holeman patted Katrina's chair. "Sit down."

Sitting was the last thing she wanted. *I want my dad. I want Lukas...Shrug. I want Chad to hold me, like he did in the compound.* She sat down anyway.

"While Lukas was...being tortured," Dr. Holeman said, "did you see Shrug anywhere?"

"No."

"Does that answer your question, Chad?" the doctor asked.

"Yes. That answers my question."

Katrina knew if Chad wasn't in uniform, if they weren't in this room with his boss staring at him, he would've reached out and hugged her. To him, she wasn't just a witness in a murder investigation.

"Katrina?"

She reluctantly shifted her gaze to Dr. Holeman.

"I want you to keep looking at me. Let's go back to Lukas. Someone cut off his fingers, you said. Who?"

"Pete."

"What were Gator and Todd doing while Pete was...busy?"

"Todd was circling and taunting Lukas. Gator was off to the side, crouching and staring at me as if waiting for me to...do something." She shrugged. "I don't know what he was waiting for. I didn't like him staring at me. Why was he looking at me and not at what Pete and Todd were doing? I wasn't doing anything except holding the light."

"What was Shrug doing?"

"Shrug wasn't back yet."

"What else happens to Lukas?"

"He just, like, bleeds to—" She bit back the word 'death.'

"And?"

"He finally quits screaming and slumps to the floor. Pete..." *Where are the words I need, the facts?* "Pete lifted Lukas's head by his hair." *I'd once run my fingers through those same dark curls.*

"What did he do next?"

I don't have the words for you, but here's your fucking fact.

She made a slashing motion across her neck.

"Pete slit Lukas's throat?"

Katrina nodded.

It was hauntingly quiet in the boardroom. Quiet like the shed had been when the screaming had finally stopped.

Shrug had told her that's when Lukas died. That none of what happened after that was important.

What if he was wrong? What if Lukas had still been alive?

The screaming had ended, but the horror hadn't. So much more had happened. So unspeakably much more.

"Can I go now?" she asked in a timid voice. "I'm finished. That was the murder. Where's Cooper?"

"What did everyone do after Lukas died?" Chad asked.

"We went home, back to the compound." She looked at Sergeant Kindle. "Can I go home, please? Now."

He shook his head. "A few more questions, Katrina."

"What did Gator do afterward?" Chad asked.

"Stop asking me questions!"

"What did Gator do next?"

She wanted to scream. "He motioned me to bring the light closer to the bod—closer to Lukas."

"And then?"

"And that's all." She took a step toward the door. "I need to go."

"Let's get this over with," Dr. Holeman said quietly. "You're almost done here. No use having to come back again in the morning. We need to know it all."

"I-I can't."

"Yes, you can. Shrug came back. Tell us about that."

With her back against the door, she folded her arms across her chest. "Gator pointed to where he wanted me to stand with the light. He...jostled me, adjusted the light and stuff. The guys all bent over and inspected the body. They joked about it, laughed at how much blood there was."

Katrina hated what had happened. Hated what she'd done.

Her voice dropped to a nearly inaudible whisper. "They put their hands in Lukas's blood, then looked at their fingers."

"Pete, Todd and Gator did this?"

"Yes, they all did, like they're playing Follow the Leader, or something."

"And then?"

She closed her eyes, trying to remember everything the cops would have found in that shed. There was the Traz jacket Todd had tossed over the body to advertise the kill. The pistol, which might have her prints on it. The lantern, which definitely *did* have her prints. And they would've found things she hadn't yet talked about—gunshot wounds.

"What happened after that, Katrina?"

"Todd took off his jacket and threw it over the body. It landed so everyone could see the Traz patch on the back."

It hadn't happened exactly like that, but it was close enough.

"Todd walked off a ways and Gator started staring at me again. Then he went after Todd and I saw Todd take his gun out and give it to Gator. That's when I noticed Shrug was back." She massaged her head.

Wait! Everything's getting messed up! One little lie and nothing's fitting together like it should.

"Go on," the doctor encouraged.

"Gator motioned me to move away from Lukas." That hadn't happened at all, but the lies kept coming, faster and easier. "He put the pistol to Lukas's head and shoots." There, that lie covered the bullet wound. Now for her fingerprints and the gun left at the scene.

"Then he said to me, 'Your turn,' and he holds out the gun and signals me to come to him. Shrug whispers to me, 'Go take the gun, but tell him dead is dead. Then throw the gun behind the body and walk back to me.' So that's what I did."

"And then?"

"Gator, Pete and Todd left. It was so cold I was shivering. Shrug wrapped his arms around me."

That part was true. Shrug had picked her up and held her. She remembered nothing after that. Nothing until she woke up in Shrug's cabin three days later.

She looked across the table at Chad. His eyes were as moist as hers. Nobody asked her to say more, but she wanted to. She wanted someone to know, someone to care.

"He gave me his coat and tried to warm me." Her tears erupted in a torrent and Chad passed her a tissue. "He kept saying he was sorry, that it was supposed to be clean. Afterward, we left. It was over."

She was drained, worn out. She wanted to go home and sleep forever.

"When Shrug left the first time," Sergeant Kindle said, "did Gator seem to notice he was leaving, or that he was gone?"

It was dangerous to be talking when she was so tired. What if she forgot what lies she'd told and mixed up her stories?

"He must have. Gator was staring at me the whole time and Shrug was right behind me." She yawned.

"Think back, Katrina," Dr. Holeman said. "When Pete sliced off Lukas's first finger and Lukas started screaming—"

"No, Lukas didn't scream at first. He just looked at his hand, staring at where his finger used to be, watching the blood." That part was true.

"Okay, so Pete has just sliced off the first finger and it's very quiet.

What do you remember Gator doing?" Dr. Holeman persisted.

"Gator nodded to Pete. I knew something was about to happen."

"What did Gator do right after Pete sliced off the first finger?"

"I don't know. I was watching Lukas, wondering why he wasn't screaming. When I did look at Pete, he had his hands on his hips and was staring past me at Shrug."

"What was Shrug doing?"

"I was too scared of Gator to turn around and look. But that's when Shrug said, 'Son of a bitch!' and left."

"Did he say that loud enough for Gator to hear?"

"Yeah, Gator heard."

"Is there anything else about that night the police should know?" Dr. Holeman asked.

She shook her head. "That's it."

The doctor glanced around the room. "Are there any more questions?"

"I suggest we take another break," Sergeant Kindle said. "I'd like to review her testimony with the others, give Katrina a chance to think if she missed anything."

Terrified, Katrina paced the room where she'd been instructed to wait. Her legs were wobbly and her hands shook.

Did I just talk myself into trouble?

There had been times when Sergeant Kindle and Chad had simultaneously shifted in their chairs and refused to meet her gaze. And there was something about the way they looked at each other.

They knew she was lying.

What if they don't give me police protection? What if my lies help the bikers go free? What if Gator chases me down and cuts off my fingers? What if—

"Katrina?" Cooper said. "Come, sit for a while. I want to talk."

She reluctantly obeyed.

"Steward McMal's on his way down here," he said.

"Why?" Her eyes narrowed. "Has something happened that I need a lawyer?"

Cooper smiled. "I'd like to think everyone always needs a lawyer."

"Yes, I'm sure you do."

"They want your fingerprints. They say if they can match yours to unidentified ones at the scene, they can rule out anyone else's involvement. Steward's coming down to advise us on that."

"I told them why my prints might be on the gun."

"What else did you tell them?"

"I can't remember." That was close to the truth.

CHAPTER 11

A week later, Katrina was back in the boardroom. She hoped it would be a quick visit, that the questioning was over. But she was pretty sure she was here because the police had found out she'd lied.

She stood up and circled the table, wondering if Sergeant Kindle would be mad at her for lying. *Will Chad be disappointed?*

If her dad were here, would he understand she'd *had* to lie?

She'd once read an MSN online psychology forum that said the mind automatically made up things to fill in what it couldn't perceive or comprehend. That's sort of what she'd done—made up things to fill in those parts of the story that were too awful for words.

She paced in ever-widening circles, planning her strategy. She'd tell Chad that trying to talk about what happened was like trying to tell someone about a bizarre dream that made no sense. It was like trying to explain the colour red to a blind person. Or like trying to write Beethoven's Fifth in English.

"Katrina?"

She whipped around. Chad strode toward her, a determined look on his face. Afraid he'd run her over, she took a step back. His eyes were on her, dark slits beneath furrowed brows. He was not slowing down. She backed up until she hit the table. When his toes were mere centimeters from hers, he finally stopped.

He looked down at the report in his hand. "Question," he read. "Did Shrug ever give you his gun to hold? Answer: no."

He flipped to the next page. "Question: Do you know what kind of gun he had? Answer: I don't know much about guns." He dropped both hands to his side and scowled at her. "I happen to know you're very well versed in all manners of firearms."

He threw the report on the table, widened his stance and clasped his hands behind his back. "What's wrong with these answers, Katrina?"

She shoved her fists into his chest. "Back the hell off!"

He didn't move.

"What's wrong with these answers, Katrina?"

"I lied."

"Ah, you lied." He gave a quick nod. "I love it when people are honest about lying."

"I had to lie."

Chad blew out a frustrated breath. "'I lied.' That's *it?* No apology? No excuses? No desire to set things right? A kid is tortured and bled to death, murder convictions on the line, and you simply *'lie'?* No big deal, Katrina. Been lying all your life, why should this be different?"

"It's not like that."

"Remember when I told you that you might want to tell us about a lot of blood and missing fingers? Remember that?"

She had to get away from those accusing eyes of his. "I want—"

"You didn't like it, but it got you talking. Shall I whisper something else to you?"

"No, don't." She tried to squeeze by him, but he grabbed her arm.

"Ah, so you know what it is I'm about to whisper?"

"Chad, don't make me. Don't make me remember."

"Let's see..." He retrieved the report. "How about this? Somebody wrote here, 'Ask Katrina why you found only one body there, instead of four, or maybe even five.' What does that mean, Katrina? Aside from fears about your own life, I don't remember you mentioning anything about anyone else's life being in danger that night."

Her stomach cramped and bile rose in her throat. She swallowed hard.

"Let's all sit down, please," Dr. Holeman called from the doorway.

Chad backed away, but didn't take his eyes off her.

Nausea overwhelmed her and a wave of dizziness swept over her. She teetered for a moment, then sank into the nearest chair.

"Katrina," the doctor said, taking the chair beside her. "We have to go back and make it right. You have to tell the truth this time."

"No," Chad said. "We're not going back. We're going forward. You had a gun in your hand that night, Katrina."

"A gun?"

"I know you did. Truth time."

She pondered this for a moment. *Can the truth really set me free, like Dad always said?*

"Whose gun was it?" Chad asked.

"Shrug's."

"Not Todd's like you said before, but Shrug's?

"Yes."

"How did you get Shrug's gun?"

"He gave it to me."

"When did he give it to you?"

"Before he left me there. He put it here." She motioned to the small of her back. "Tucked it into my jeans under my jacket. No one saw him do it."

"There was blood on that gun."

"Blood? On the gun?"

"That night, before you pulled that gun out of your jeans, did you get blood on your hands?"

"Yes," she whispered. "Gator put blood on my hands. We were squatting by the body. Gator stared at me. I thought he was going to kill me. He touched my hands, rubbed them. Then Gator snapped his fingers and Todd passed him a gun. I thought Gator was going to kill me, but instead he held out the pistol. 'Shoot him,' he said. 'Shoot him.'"

"Who does he want you to shoot?" Dr. Holeman asked.

She closed her eyes. "Lukas."

She remembered reaching for Shrug's pistol beneath her jacket. Remembered touching the ice cold metal.

Then I—

A brilliant flash and the crackle of static scorched her brain.

Everything turned black.

From far away, Doctor Holeman shouted, "We're losing her!"

Then Katrina heard nothing.

CHAPTER 12

Holiday Inn, Edmonton

Katrina had been in the hotel for almost two weeks and had yet to see the sun peak in. Although the window blinds were open, her bedroom was always in the shadow of the adjoining tower. The perpetual gray suited her mood. Made it easy to sleep—all day.

Made it easier to forget.

"Katrina," Cooper said, smoothing the blanket before sitting on the bed.

He reached out to pat her hand, but she shoved in beneath the pillow. She turned away, longing to be alone.

"I don't know you that well," he said. "However, I knew your father very well. And I know you weren't raised this way, full of lies and deceit."

She felt the pressure lift from the bed as he stood.

"I understand why you lied, Katrina. You've been through way too much this past year. Too much for a grown man, let alone a girl your age. Grieving your grandpa, your parents, witnessing a murder."

"I didn't lie about the murder."

"You've lied about so many things nobody knows what to believe anymore. You even lied to me about your doctor's exam. It was more than just vitamins she gave you."

She clenched her teeth. "How do you know? That's private information."

"When you passed out during the interview, I accessed your medical file."

"So who the hell else knows what's in there?"

"Katrina..." Cooper rested a hand on her arm. "You can't go this alone, dear. You've had a hellish year and you need help and support to work through it. If you don't want to talk to me, let me get someone else here to help you."

"I can look after myself fine."

"You may be intellectually advanced, but you still have the emotional needs of a young teen. You need guidance, support and love."

She pushed his hand away. "I don't need anything."

"Then why did you pass out in the interview room?"

"If you read my medical file, you'd know why. I have low iron. That has nothing to do with your stupid kinds of needs."

"Katrina—"

"Iron is close to vitamins, so I don't think you should be calling me a liar."

"There were other—"

"I don't believe you, so shut up about it!"

She wormed her way under the covers and drew the blanket over her head. It wasn't fair she couldn't have *any* secrets. It was nobody else's business. It was *her* body. It had nothing to do with the murder, or drugs, or anything else.

"I want you to talk to a psychiatrist or some kind of counsellor."

"No."

"It will help you deal with things."

"I'm dealing."

"You're not dealing with anything. You're lying in bed."

"Don't worry about me. I'm doing fine."

"Some of what you told the police doesn't gibe with the evidence." He sighed. "And an iron deficiency doesn't account for the hand marks on your—"

"Go away!"

"Someone in that biker gang struck you. Since you wouldn't talk about it even to the doctor, I believe there was likely other abuse."

"No!"

"I—"

"Don't talk about it! Ever!" She burst into sobs.

Cooper's footsteps moved toward the door.

"Sergeant Kindle wants to finish questioning you," he said. "When you're feeling up to it."

"I'll never feel 'up to it,'" she said beneath the blanket.

In his office, Kindle studied the undercover officer sitting on the other side of the desk. What was the connection between Chad and the girl? He seemed far more invested in young Katrina than was professional.

"I can't believe it's boiling down to this," Chad said, pushing a full coffee mug toward Kindle. "The defence will be all over the girl's inconsistencies about what happened after the murder, no matter how irrelevant."

"Perhaps."

"If we hadn't asked about what happened after the murder, we wouldn't be having this problem," Chad said. "Except, of course, we had to ask so we could explain the partial print on the gun left at the scene— Shrug's gun."

"No." Kindle tapped a crime scene photo with the end of a pen. "We had to ask to explain the bullet wound in the vic's head."

It irked him that, because someone hadn't done their job properly, he'd not known that the gun left at the scene was Shrug's— until Katrina had told them. If he'd been prepared, the questioning might have gone a lot smoother.

"Did Shrug shoot Lukas? Is she covering for him? Did he set her up?"

"Listen to yourself! You're not making any more sense than the girl is."

"You don't think Shrug is the shooter?"

"I *know* he's not the shooter. The girl is. But we've already got one-and-a-half wrong versions of things from her."

"Did the print results come back from the lab?"

"Yeah."

"It's hers?"

"Not an exact match, but it's too small to be a man's. There were no other kids in that shed to put a print, in the vic's blood, on that gun—not as far as we know. Everything points to Katrina, touching the gun and firing it."

All the girl seemed to do was lie.

"It won't look good if we keep questioning her until she comes up with the answers we want," he added. "It also won't look good if we have Shrug on the witness stand saying one thing and her saying another."

"The autopsy confirmed Lukas was dead long before he was shot," Chad said. "Considering what she's already told us about Lukas's torture, why would she stumble over admitting she shot a dead man?"

"Dr. Holeman says it's because it concerns her direct involvement. The other stuff she just watched. This, she *did*. Putting a bullet through a human being's head, whether that person is dead or alive, isn't likely to be anyone's highlight of the day."

Chad scratched his chin. "Perhaps if we promise we won't lay charges against her, she'll feel freer to talk. I'm sure we can get the Crown to agree to grant her immunity. That might get her guardian on our side too. Maybe with Cooper's encouragement she can get through this."

"I've thought of that, but it's not something I want to do unless we absolutely have to." Kindle took a sip of coffee. It was a bitter. "If the Crown can tell the jurors she's testifying on her own accord, with no deals or promises, she'll be much more credible to them."

"Speaking of credible, if Shrug—"

"No, stop right there. I don't want anyone speaking of Shrug until his testimony is on the books and the convictions are in."

"Are you afraid we might say something that will mar *his* credibility on the witness stand?"

"Shrug's an officer of the law. He's credible. His history with the girl may have been unethical, immoral and perhaps illegal, but it had nothing to do with the integrity of the sting against the bikers. It should have no effect on the guilt or innocence in the murder case."

Chad downed his coffee and moved the nearest file to make room on Kindle's desk for his empty mug. Kindle scowled, but Chad seemed not to notice.

"I'm thinking his history with the girl has a lot to do with the murder case," Chad said. "I'm damned sure he left the girl alone in that Quonset because he didn't want to witness the murder. He would've been forced to drop his undercover operation to assist with the homicide investigation if he'd stayed in that shed. There's just no way he wanted to give up everything he'd worked three years—"

"For Christ's sake, Chad, it's not at all like Shrug to do something like that. He left to get help." At least he hoped to God that was the reason.

"It's not like Shrug? I didn't know the man until three months ago. Is it like Shrug to involve a minor in a police sting?"

"If you're thinking I'm covering for him, you're wrong. The matter of him and the girl will be fully investigated. If there were things happening that shouldn't have been, he'll face the music—after the trials."

"Sarge, this is the reality. It's October 26th and Shrug's in the middle of nowhere, surrounded by bikers who don't like him. Where the hell do you surmise he would be going to find help?"

"Enough! Save your concerns until after the trials. Concentrate on the matters at hand. Dr. Holeman wants to talk to the girl. *Alone.* In a more comfortable setting. Record the conversation for us. How does that sit with you?"

"I'd like to be there when he does it."

"Holeman said you antagonize her."

"Antagonize her?"

"You've talked about her and Shrug, but I want to know what the hell kind of relationship *you* had with her in The Traz."

"She adored me."

"She doesn't seem to adore you now."

"She's angry because I didn't keep my promises."

"While she was adoring you, what were you doing?"

Chad chuckled. "Fighting off her advances."

"That's funny?"

"Look, I just happened to be there. Her crush on me wasn't something I had a hard time handling."

"She's only fourteen, Chad."

"Yes, she's only fourteen. But—"

Kindle scowled and Chad clamped his lips closed.

"You complain about Shrug using her," Kindle said. "What's all this about you using her to help with computer work and perimeter sensors?"

"That's different. With me, she knew which side of the law I was on and I never asked her to do anything illegal."

"Maybe not illegal, but dangerous."

Chad shrugged. "Disabling the sensors wasn't dangerous. Who better to disable them than the kid who was always out wandering around in the bushes and fields? Shrug or I doing it would only have raised suspicion. *That's* what would have been dangerous."

"Ah, I see. It was far better to endanger the girl than yourselves."

"No, it wasn't like that." Chad straightened and looked him in the eye. "Sarge, the atmosphere in the compound was explosive. Shrug or I doing anything suspicious would have put a whole lot of people in danger. Not just Shrug and I—the girl, too. The entire tactical team. There were no easy choices in there." He looked at his feet, squeaked his shoe over the worn tiles and sighed. "No easy choices."

Chad got up and walked to the door. As he wrapped his fingers around the knob, he turned back. "Don't you dare compare what I did with Katrina to what Shrug did. Perhaps you'd like to ask Shrug about the licking he gave her?"

Kindle blinked in surprise. "Shrug spanked her?"

"Oh, I'm sure he'll give you all kinds of solid reasons for doing it, but in my books there's no reason for a man in this profession to do that, especially to a girl her age. None! It was an outright assault and I'd be willing to testify to that. Reconcile *that* with your misguided opinion of him." Chad stepped into the hall, then looked back at Kindle. "And don't *ever* compare me to him again."

Kindle ignored him and focussed on the crime photos. Was it possible that one young girl could bring down his top two men?

CHAPTER 13

Dr. Holeman's Office, Edmonton, October 1996

Katrina pressed her cheek into the smooth black leather of Dr. Holeman's recliner. *I wish I could sink right into this chair and disappear.*

"I'm recording our conversation," the doctor said. "What you say will be shared with the investigators of this murder case. Do you understand?"

She nodded.

"What you say must be the truth. It will later become part of your sworn statement. Do you understand that?"

"Yes."

"What happened after Gator told you to shoot Lukas?" the doctor asked.

"It was the worst part of the night."

"You've told me about the brutal murder of Lukas. Is it worse than that?"

"It's what happened inside me. I…"

"Yes?"

"I suddenly became calm. Unbelievably calm."

"This was after Gator said, 'Shoot him,' that you became calm?"

"Yes. I was no longer afraid. I-I wasn't anything inside. I stopped shaking and my mind took over. I knew exactly where every person in that shed was standing. I looked Gator straight in the eye and reached behind me for Shrug's revolver. I was deathly calm. I knew what I had to do."

"You pulled out the gun?"

"I totally confused Gator. He just kept looking at me, his hand out, passing me Todd's pistol. 'This is the last thing I ever do for you!' I said."

"What did you do next?"

"I shot Lukas in the head."

There! I said it. Now you know.

"Shrug—*someone* said Lukas was dead *before* I shot him, but...I thought dead people's eyes are closed. My dad's were. I grabbed Lukas by his long hair, pulling his head off the floor. His eyes were open, looking at me. I put the muzzle to his temple. I thought I had killed him."

"How did that make you feel?"

"I was calm. Unafraid—as if I was ready to surrender to fate."

"You know now that you did not kill Lukas, that he was dead before you shot him?" She nodded. "What happened after you shot Lukas?"

She floundered for words. "When—before the echo faded, Gator was in my sights."

She'd been so close to killing Gator. She'd have killed them all. Todd was right behind Gator. Once Gator fell, a quick shot and she'd have had him in the heart. Pete would've been rushing toward her with his knife. She'd have breathed deeply and evenly, and kept her heart beating slowly, steadily. She would have killed them all and it wouldn't have bothered her one little bit.

"You pulled the trigger?" Dr. Holeman asked.

"One last stare into Gator's cold eyes and I began to curl my trigger finger. But Shrug reached from behind and swatted my hand. He rushed past me and grabbed Todd's gun from Gator. He said, 'I saved your life, you son of a bitch.'"

"You were calm during all this?"

"Totally. I was strong. I was going to shoot them all. No one could have stopped me. They were basking in their success, their guard down, stoked on their own power, convinced I was their next victim. They'd never known me to fight back. I'd been terrified of Gator since my first day in the compound. He knew that. Expected that. The Traz thought women were trash and had never been afraid of one."

"What would you have done after you shot them?"

"Turned off the lantern," she whispered. "Sat in the dark." *Alone. Cold. Calm.* "And shot myself."

"You'd have committed suicide?"

"My friend was dead. What would there be to live for after I killed those who did it? With nothing to live for, there was nothing to fear. Being fearless made me feel powerful and calm."

"Shrug knocked your hand. Did you drop the gun?

"No. But it was no longer aimed at Gator."

"What happened after Shrug took Todd's gun from Gator?"

"Shrug wanted me to give him back his gun."

"Did you?"

"No."

' "After Shrug asked for his gun and you refused, what happened?"

"Shrug began raising Todd's pistol at me and I aimed back at him. Too much time had passed, though, and I was scared and shaky. The others were no longer distracted. Todd ran toward Gator, while Pete ran toward me. I knew my plan to shoot them all wouldn't work anymore. They'd kill me before I had a chance to kill them."

"What did you do?"

"Pete was behind me. I thought he'd have his knife out, but when I faced him, he didn't. I aimed the gun at him and he just put up his hands in surrender."

"You didn't shoot him?"

"I no longer felt powerful. Shrug was behind me with a gun pointed at my back and neither of us had Gator and Todd covered. I kept my aim on Pete and backed up far enough so I could see Shrug and Gator. Shrug said to the boys, 'Leave. All of you. Now!' And they did."

"Then what?"

"Shrug walked over and took the gun from me. Then we stood for a long while just looking at each other."

"What did Shrug do with the gun after he took it from you?"

"Nothing, at first. He went to slip it under his jacket, but I said, 'No! Leave it here.' So he tossed it behind Lukas into the shadows."

"And?"

"And we left."

"Why did you want the gun left there?"

"To claim the scene. It was ours, Shrug's and mine. We'd won. Gator may have murdered Lukas that night, but he lost The Traz."

Chad watched Kindle and Debra as they listened to the recording of Katrina's interview with Dr. Holeman. He saw their faces pale when they heard the girl admit she wanted to kill the gang members and then herself.

Debra shivered. "It was after the murder, wasn't it, Sarge, that Shrug reported to you he had control of the gang? Is that how it went down? Katrina's the one who got him the power?"

"Perhaps," Kindle said.

Chad massaged his temples. "This changes things. Our witness is no longer just a poor little kid unwittingly caught up in murder. She was armed the entire time and almost took them all out, if what she's saying is true."

"Shrug will be here tomorrow. If I can trust my gut, his story's going to pretty well match hers."

"Yeah," Chad murmured.

"There's not a soul in the world that can argue she wasn't acting in self-defence."

"Do you really believe she can shut down her emotions like that?" Debra asked. "A terrified child one moment and planning a mass murder the next? Steady enough to aim a pistol?"

"She had to, in order to survive" Kindle said.

"She does it all the time—shuts down emotionally," Chad said. "Switches from one mood to another at the drop of a hat. You've both seen her do that here. I wonder if this strange emotional control of hers began that night of the murder or was it something already familiar to her."

"Shrug will know," Debra said.

"Perhaps he knew way back when he recruited her. Maybe uncanny control of emotions was the skill he was after."

"Don't go there, Chad," Kindle warned.

"You're not going to ask him about it? Not going to find out before the trials how the hell it was that the girl ended up riding into the compound on his bike?"

"Don't tell me how to do my job. I know Shrug a lot better than you ever will."

Chad studied Kindle. "Does anyone know anything about that miserable titan, or do some of us just think we do?"

"I know him."

"He fooled a biker gang for four years. Are you saying Shrug can't fool you?"

"Oh, Shrug could fool me. However, I know that man's heart well enough to be sure he won't." He pulled the tape from the machine and passed it to Debra. "Get this transcribed."

Chad didn't buy it. If Shrug wanted to deceive Kindle, he'd do it.

"I think sometimes he does fool you," Debra said. "That child's voice on the surveillance tape Shrug handed in? I think we can now safely assume it was Katrina's voice. Didn't Shrug have you convinced it wasn't a kid wearing the wire?"

Kindle shook his head. "No."

"I thought you said he told you the wire wasn't hidden on a child."

"What he said, Debra, was, 'Does that make sweet sense to you? Have your sound experts listen to it again.'"

"Ah," Chad said. *Shrug manipulated you.* "He left it to you to decide what to do with the truth."

"I decided to send you in to keep an eye on things and...you did a piss poor job of it." Kindle shoved back his chair.

"I kept her safe. Got her out." *Saved her life.*

"Only after involving her even further in the operation. You were with The Traz for less than three months and look how it screwed your perceptions—to the point where involving the girl seemed okay to you." Kindle stood up. "Shrug was under for four years, Chad. Don't you be judging him—or me!"

He tossed his pen on his desk and strode to the exit. "You want my job?" He flung open the door. "You can have it!" He stalked out.

The door slammed shut, and Chad watched Kindle's pen teeter on the edge of the desk and then drop to the floor.

"He's under a lot of pressure," Debra said. "I know the brass is breathing fire down his neck over Shrug."

"And justifiably so."

"He's dealing with his bosses on top of everything else."

Chad was amazed at how calm she remained, despite Kindle's recent tirade. There was a soft glow in her eyes, as if she were telling him life was fine. Everything would work out okay.

Will it? He hoped so.

"Sarge has invested a lot in this operation," Debra said. "He had a big budget and put many of his men in danger. He doesn't want to see it all get wiped out."

"That won't happen. What Shrug did with the girl—or what I did, for that matter—doesn't affect the integrity of the sting. Child endangerment charges might kill Shrug's career, but it's a legality the bikers can't claim was unfair to them."

Debra rested a hand on his arm. "Think about it, Chad. If the defence finds out Shrug, as a Crown witness, is under investigation by the force, they'll squash him on the stand, relevant or not. Do you really think these bikers deserve that break?"

"They deserve nothing." He was very conscious of the warmth of her hand. "I'm stressed. Want to go out for a coffee with me?"

Debra reached down and retrieved Kindle's pen. "It's not a good idea."

"Why not?" He saw her swallow hard and was afraid of what her answer might be.

"I saw how you were looking at me, Chad. We shouldn't be getting involved personally when we're working on this investigation together."

"Why not?"

"I'm stressed too. Both of us need to be able to go home at the end of the day and get away from it all. That won't happen if we start mingling our personal and professional lives."

"A raincheck on the coffee? Cashable after all this is over?"

"Maybe."

"Only a maybe? Is there's someone else in your life?"

"I don't know," she said as she moved toward the door.

He watched her leave, then kicked at the chair leg in frustration. *You don't know? What the hell does that mean?*

CHAPTER 14

Northern Alberta Police Detachment, Edmonton

When Kindle walked into his office, Shrug was there, clean-shaven and in uniform, lounging in the chair across from Kindle's desk. He reeked of cigarette smoke.

"It's about bloody time you got back here, Shrug."

"You miss me?"

"Not in a fond way."

Shrug slid a pack of Nicorettes back and forth between his fingers. "I figured you'd have your hands full with the girl. Didn't need me around tickin' you off as well."

"I needed you around."

"Well, now you have me."

Kindle's lips tightened and his eyes narrowed. Shrug was overestimating his welcome.

Shrug quit grinning. "I take it that's not makin' you real happy after all."

"Every time I run into a roadblock in this case, your name is on it."

"That roadblock you're talkin' about, would that be my gun?"

"Why did you leave it there?"

"The woman wanted me to."

"The '*woman*'?" Kindle bellowed.

"Sarina."

"She's not a woman. She's a child. And from now on, you're going to refer to her that way."

"Sure, sorry."

"Are you telling me you left your gun at the scene because a child told you to?"

"I thought it was a good idea. Thought it would help you guys. You wouldn't have to waste time wonderin' whose gun put the bullet through the vic's head."

"We didn't match the gun to you until Katrina started talking."

"I can't help it if there's questionable intelligence around here. I know there's a record—"

"Why the hell was the girl there?"

"God damn it, it was bad." Shrug stood and wandered over to the window. "It wasn't supposed to go down that way. If I'd known what was gonna happen, I wouldn't have gone there myself."

"I know all about Gator foiling your plan to prevent the murder. I don't need to hear that excuse again. But you, of all people, should know that where drugs and money are involved, nobody's safety is guaranteed, especially a child's."

"It was bad. Fuck!" Shrug punched the wall. "I suppose I'm not supposed to be swearin' like that anymore?"

"Start practising so you'll look respectable on the witness stand."

"I've gotta quit smokin' *and* cussin'?"

"With all the trouble you're in around here, I'd say you better start now."

"It's just that the night in that shed was so goddamn bad, Sarge. They must've been torqued up on somethin' to be able to do that. It was evil, man. Pure evil." Shrug began to pace.

"You left the girl in there with them."

"Christ, I had to try to do somethin'. It wasn't gonna stop with Lukas, you know. I thought with my winnin' personality I could convince some of Gator's boys out back to help me stop it."

"Didn't work?"

"Nope. They didn't know what was goin' on in the shed. They didn't want to flip sides and end up bein' on the losin' one. All I know is no one expected both Gator and me to walk out of there that night. Shit, I was sure beginnin' to think it wouldn't be me."

"Why did you give the girl your gun?"

Shrug turned and glared at Kindle. "I can't believe you just asked me that."

"Answer."

"I had to leave her alone with those thugs. What the hell was I supposed to do, give her a whistle?"

"Could we maybe say something like you gave it to her to protect herself while you went to get help? The prosecutor and jury might like that a whole lot better."

"When the jury hears what the jury's gonna hear, they ain't gonna care why I gave the woman a gun."

"It's not just the jury you should be worrying about. Down the road, you're going to look into the eyes of a disciplinary review panel."

"Whatever."

"They're going to come down hard on you. It's going to be rough, Shrug."

"They might not be a fount of wisdom, but it doesn't take much to understand why a man gives his woman a gun when he has to leave her in a place like that."

"The *girl*. Calling her your *woman* conjures up bad images."

"It wasn't like that." Shrug stopped pacing. "She didn't say it was like that, did she?"

Kindle shook his head. "She didn't say and we didn't ask. But she does say people called her your woman."

"Is Sarina okay?"

"No, *Katrina's* not okay. She's kind of like you, Shrug. Real shook up. Not liking to remember."

"She would've killed us all. And I wouldn't have blamed her one bit."

"Why did you stop her?"

"She's what, sixteen?"

"Thirteen at that time, Shrug. Thirteen."

"What seemed like an excellent idea that night would've lost its appeal pretty fast. She wasn't thinkin' straight. She was suicidal. If she'd offed us, you would've found her body with ours."

"The hardest part for her to talk about was what happened after Lukas died. Tell me what went down."

"I took her home. Let her sleep for three days."

"Before you took her home."

Shrug returned to his chair, sighed and closed his eyes. "I walked back in there and she had my pistol levelled at Gator's heart. Steady as can be. Cool. She—shit!" He hunched forward.

Kindle held his breath, waiting. Finally he said, "If there's something we need to know that we don't, you've got to tell us. We can't have any surprises. If anything happens to get these guys off..." He let Shrug fill in the blanks.

"I suppose her aimin' the pistol kinda destroys the image of a vulnerable, credible witness?"

"I'm sure the defence will jump on the fact Katrina was armed and perhaps more involved in the murder than she's saying."

"You can present her to the jury as a hurtin' orphan in too deep. Lookin' for love in all the wrong places. That ain't the reality, though. That woman's got the devil in her soul. What all did she tell you about Lukas?"

"I don't get to tell you what she said. Why don't you tell me about

Lukas?"

"Uh…well, she tell you the reason he was chosen?"

"You probably know the reason better than she does."

"You did good to get her to talk, Sarge. She'd never say a word to me about it. Denied it happened."

"We got her through it."

"She know about me yet?"

Kindle shook his head.

Shrug smiled. "She ask about me?"

"Stay away from her, Shrug. Far away."

CHAPTER 15

Northern Alberta Police Detachment, Edmonton, November 1996

"Chad?" Debra called from the hall outside his open office door.

He looked up. She was clasping her hands under her chin as if praying, and her face was furrowed with worry. It rattled him to see her so tense. She was usually composed.

"Come in. Have a seat."

She hesitated for a long moment, her eyes darting from his face to the desk to the window. She walked in and took the chair nearest his desk.

"What's the matter, Debra?"

"Sergeant Kindle sent me to get you. He can't fend off our legal department any longer. They're insisting Katrina be told Shrug's an officer."

"Oh." Chad felt his own tension rise.

Debra fiddled with her fingers in her lap, then peeked up at him from under long black lashes. "How do you think she'll react?"

"I don't know how the girl will react. However, I'll bet her guardian reacts with a lawsuit."

"A lawsuit, I can handle. It's Katrina I'm worried about."

"Why?"

"She's believed all along that Shrug is a biker. She's going to feel betrayed that none of us, including Shrug, told her the truth."

Debra's worries started to gnaw at Chad. "Maybe she'll be relieved he's not a gang member."

"She might eventually feel relieved," Debra said. "However, right now I'm guessing she won't know what to feel—other than deceived."

"She's been through a lot, but she's strong. I think she'll be okay. But once the Coopers get a hold of this info, I'm not sure Shrug will be."

"Kindle's going to try to convince them to overlook the matter, at least until after the trials."

Chad let out a huff. "I wish him luck."

"I think Sarge has a good shot at keeping this out of the courts. And the media. For now, at least. Cooper wouldn't want the girl to go through all this questioning and the upcoming trials only to see Gator and his boys walk free because Shrug screwed up."

"Are you saying you think if people find out about Shrug's relationship with the girl, the gang will get away with murder?"

Debra lifted a shoulder. "It's hard to predict how a jury will view such things, but there's no doubt if the defence finds out Shrug is under investigation for things he did while undercover with The Traz, they'll be asking the jury to question his credibility as a witness. It will colour Katrina's testimony too."

"Maybe."

Debra stood and rubbed her hands together. "We have to go. Kindle wants you to be the one to tell Katrina. He's going to be there, but he wants you to deal with the girl so he can deal with the guardian."

With a sigh, he said, "Lead the way."

Chad took a seat across Katrina and Cooper. He wondered whose idiotic idea it was to break the news to them in the huge instruction hall. He'd have chosen a much smaller room with carpeting to soften the echoes and perhaps a warm fireplace crackling in the corner.

"I've got something for you, Katrina." He shuffled the sheaf of papers in his hand. "This is the list of the bikers we arrested, along with the charges I promised to show you. I've pencilled in their aliases so you'll know who we're talking about. Before I give it to you, there's something we need to discuss."

Katrina held out her hand. "There's always something more you need from me before I get anything."

Within seconds, she was tossing Cooper the first page and running her eyes down the second. Chad watched her face, but there was little he could tell from her expression.

When she flipped to the last page, he spoke. "Shrug's not on there because he's an undercover cop."

Katrina stopped moving. Her fingers froze to the page.

Is she even breathing?

"Katrina?" He swore her face was turning blue.

She slowly turned to Cooper, who was pulling out his cell phone, his wide eyes glued on Sergeant Kindle's face. Katrina glanced at Kindle and then turned to Chad. He first saw confusion in her eyes and then saw the light dawn. Her lungs finally drew in a desperate breath and an involuntary gasp shook her.

"Shrug is what?" she whispered.

"He's one of our undercover officers," Chad repeated.

Katrina spun to face Cooper. He was engrossed in conversation with Sergeant Kindle and also, she surmised from the phone at his ear, with McMal.

She turned back to Chad, wondering how he could betray her like this.

So this is how he knew what Shrug said to me. How he knew about the puppy and the gun. How he knew exactly when I was lying. This is the secret Sergeant Kindle and his guys had been fretting about that first day in the boardroom and what all the 'protecting my rights as a juvenile' shit was about and why Sergeant Kindle called in Children's Services. None of it had been for my benefit. They'd been protecting their own asses.

She flicked her eyes back to Sergeant Kindle, who was now sitting on the edge of the table, intently talking to Cooper in as low a voice as he could.

It can't be true.

She peered into Debra's eyes. And then she knew.

It is true. Every word. It's why everyone was so upset about Shrug leaving me alone in the shed. Because he's a cop! A fricken cop! And he left me there!

She walked to the far end of the room, dizzy, disoriented and nauseous.

Chad touched her shoulder. "Do you want to know more?"

"It's not true. You're just saying Shrug's a cop because you think I'm lying about stuff. You're trying to trick me!"

"Katrina, Shrug is really Constable Donald Hayes. It's true."

"No! A cop wouldn't do the stuff Shrug did."

"He had to do that stuff."

"If he's a cop, he's a very bad one. He was the gang leader."

"He was undercover with the bikers for a long time before you joined. He needed to become the leader to get his job done."

"He needed me so he could become the leader." Her voice cracked.

"I'm sorry."

"You're always sorry." She poked his chest. "Don't you get tired of being sorry all the time?"

"Katrina, calm down. Let's talk about it."

"He used me. He fucking used me." She ground her teeth in frustration.

"He'll have to answer to that."

"When?"

"Perhaps after the trials are over."

"You knew? You all knew?"

"We all knew about Shrug, of course. None of us knew anything about you until...well, until I met you in that cycle shop."

"Great. And then *you* used me."

Chad sat on the corner of the table and patted the space beside him. "Sit."

She obeyed and stared into space. Everything she thought she knew about Shrug—everything he'd done and said—was a lie. She'd based her life on his lies. All her feelings, all the reasons she'd had for doing things, the decisions she'd made—none of it was real. The entire last year of her life no longer made any sense.

She crossed her ankles and swung her legs. Faster...

"I can imagine how you must feel," he said.

"You have no idea how I feel."

"You were alone and needed someone. Now you find out the one adult you did turn to is not what he seemed."

"I thought he was a biker." She looked up at the ceiling. The concentric lines of the brown watermarks snaking across the white reminded her of Shrug's tattoos. "I guess he was actually better than what he seemed."

Chad chuckled. "That's one way to look at it. You might have been a lot worse off if he had been a real biker."

"Nope. A real biker wouldn't have picked me up in the first place. That should've been my clue. I now know why I wasn't scared of him. I think I sensed something in him."

She stilled her legs as a terrible thought entered her mind. *What if Shrug doesn't honour his promise to keep our secret? What if he's already told?*

"Chad, what do you know about me? What has Shrug told you?"

"He didn't talk to anyone about you."

Her thoughts raced. If Shrug *was* a cop, he'd likely learned about her from Rusty and Syd, the undercover cops she'd known from the King's Ace bar. What if they found out it was her who had witnessed the biker murder? What if everyone in the whole world found out the real reason Lukas died?

She grabbed Chad's arm. "I need to talk to Shrug."

"That's not going to happen."

I'll kill him if he's broken his promise! And he has to do something to shut up Syd and Rusty.

"Now, Chad. I need to see him now!"

"I know you and Shrug were close in the gang, but you have to let that all go. It wasn't what it seemed. Leave Shrug behind and get on with the life you've planned."

"He made me promises."

"You'll have to let go of his promises too."

"No!" She closed her eyes and cradled her face in her hands. "No..."

"What did he promise?

She'd recant her story, refuse to testify, be denied witness protection and end up being killed by The Traz. *Whatever!*

There was no way in hell she'd ever tell a soul *why* Lukas was killed.

CHAPTER 16

Chad couldn't get over the disarray of Kindle's office. The desk was piled with papers, and files were strewn about the floor. At least three half-filled coffee mugs sat on various surfaces. An old pizza box lay on a cabinet, one dried slice inside.

"Watch out for Shrug," Chad warned as he took a seat next to Debra in Kindle's office.

Kindle grabbed a file from the floor and spread it open on his desk. "What do you mean?"

"Shrug wanted to know if, considering he'd risked his life for this operation, I seriously thought he wouldn't risk his career."

"What the hell is that supposed to mean?"

Chad shrugged. "You're the expert on deciphering what Shrug means."

"Chad!" Debra elbowed him.

"From now on," Kindle said, looking at each of them, "no one involved in this investigation goes anywhere near Shrug. Understand?"

"Sarge," Debra said. "Shrug's been out of the loop for four years. He's quite alone. He doesn't have a support system."

Chad cast Debra a sideways glance. *What the hell kind of support have you been giving Shrug?*

"Shrug's getting all the support he needs." Kindle's jaw tightened. "From professionals. You're either involved in the investigation or involved with Shrug. Choose now."

"I'm not *involved* with him." Debra flicked a look at Chad. Then she stared at the floor, her cheeks red.

Chad's eyes narrowed. *She has something going with Shrug. How could I have not known? Why didn't she tell me instead of letting me think—*

"Katrina insists on talking to Shrug," Debra said.

"Why?" Kindle asked.

Chad sighed. "Something about promises he made."

"Promises?"

"Yeah. She wouldn't tell me what they were, but she seemed quite upset."

"She's not to talk to Shrug." Kindle's voice left no room to argue. "Come on, Chad. Keep this clean. I really don't need those two conspiring about what lies they're going to come up with on the witness stand."

"You think that's what it's all about? Lies?"

"I intend to find out. In the meantime, go and convince the girl that Shrug is not bound by any promises made to her while with The Traz."

"She knows that. In fact, that seems to be what's distressing her."

"Okay, then find out if she wants to change any of her story now that she knows."

"You're kidding, right? We're going to go after the third version of things?"

"If the third version is closer to the truth than the first two, yes."

Chad couldn't believe what he was hearing. Hadn't they wasted enough time on lies?

"Sarge," Debra cut in, "when Shrug said he'd risk his career, I don't think he meant he'd perjurer himself. You know he wouldn't do that. You said it yourself. You know his heart. Considering he used to be a—"

"Debra! Stay away from Shrug. Now, both of you..." Kindle motioned to the door. "Out. I have work to do."

As if on cue, his phone rang.

He waved vigorously to Chad and Debra. "And close the door behind you."

CHAPTER 17

Alberta Provincial Courthouse, Edmonton, December 1997

The past year and a half had been hell, and Katrina was terrified Gator's lawyer would ask if she somehow knew Lukas. Maybe suggest that the reason he'd been killed was to give her a chance to prove she was a Traz and not a Blue Torpedo. Shrug hadn't said anything, but Gator might've. The bikers all knew. They knew everything. Had they told their lawyers? Would they make her tell the world?

She could hardly see over the witness box as she was sworn in as 'Sarina' from behind the Plexiglas.

One of the defense attorneys was bound to point out she was a sharpshooter who'd been armed with a pistol and done nothing to stop a murder. Someone would suggest she may even have been part of it.

I'll be called a liar. A killer.

The defense lawyers would do whatever they could to convince the jury what she said wasn't true because, well, she was pretty sure if Gator, Pete and Todd didn't walk out of the court free men, a team of lawyers might end up dead.

She had already testified at several of The Traz drug trials and was accustomed to the fortified courthouse. But there was no doubt in her mind that this trial would be different.

Most of what she'd known and testified about at the drugs and weapons trials were the deals Shrug had worked, so her testimony hadn't been all that important. In fact, even though she was on the Crown's witness list, she sometimes wasn't called to the stand.

This time, though, she was the sole eyewitness, the crime was murder and Shrug had not been in the Quonset when that had happened.

After she was sworn in, just as at the drug trials, the defence objected to having her true identity concealed.

"It's impossible for us to research *Sarina's* background and determine her credibility," the defence lawyers argued.

The judge studied his notes. "The court-ordered independent witness report the defence has been given contains all information the prosecutors have about…Sarina." He glanced at Katrina. "Other than her legal name and a few other identifying matters. The defence's objection have been noted. The trial will proceed."

She was happy that the judge agreed to conceal her identity in the court room and have her only known as 'Sarina.' The media, the defence, the jury—nobody but the Coopers and a handful of investigating officers would ever know it was 'Katrina Buckhold' who had once rode with The Traz and testified against the idiots in court. For sure, witness protection would let her keep the name her father had given her.

Although she had talked about that night many times to the investigators and Dr. Holeman, it was different with Todd, Pete and Gator in the room. Gator glowered at her with the same animal look he'd used the night of the murder as he'd chanted, "Watch. Watch. Watch."

She was glad that on the night when the gang had voted to kill Lukas, Shrug had warned her to keep her mouth shut. That meant she wouldn't have to testify about what she'd said, only about what she'd heard and nobody had actually said Lukas was chosen because of her.

"Tell us," the prosecutor began, "about that afternoon in the clubhouse on the biker compound."

"Gator called a meeting," she said in a soft voice.

The courtroom became quiet as everyone strained to hear her speak.

"Shrug said I had to go…"

The questions from the prosecutor came one after another. She knew to answer the Crown's questions to match her statements to the police. Later, she'd answer the defense's questions as briefly as possible.

"Who was there?"

She told them.

"What happened that night?"

She stared straight ahead, avoiding Gator's glare. "Gator wanted to take a vote."

"A vote for what?"

"He asked who wanted to 'whack the kid.'"

"The kid?"

"Lukas."

"Did he say *why* he wanted to 'whack the kid'?"

"He said Lukas was shucking meth to Traz customers."

"What happened next?"

Katrina told him. She spoke of the darkness. It had been so cold. The clang of the metal doors behind her.

Lukas's moans.

She was about to tell the court about his broken legs and how she'd been holding the lantern, but suddenly she started sobbing. Surprised by her tears, she covered her face.

The questions stopped. Someone handed her a tissue and told her to take a sip of water.

After a minute, the prosecutor cleared his throat. "What happened next, Sarina? What did you do? What did you see?"

Questions and more questions until she'd told them everything up to the point that Pete had wiped the blade under Lukas's chin and the last of his life blood had poured out.

She wiped at her swollen eyes. Then she glanced at those she'd betrayed.

There was no remorse on Gator's, Pete's or Todd's face. They obviously didn't feel sorry for her—or Lukas. No shame, no guilt. They looked like they were pondering what she'd said, trying to find fault with it.

Soon their lawyers would be asking her questions. Would they ask about Lukas? Would they ask about the bullet through his brain? Would they ask about his accusing, haunting familiar blue eyes? Would they ask if she'd ever kissed—*seen*—him in the alley behind the King's Ace Bar?

She wouldn't answer that. Not now. Not ever.

She'd been warned that the defence would ask about Shrug's gun. It was the one thing they had—the gun left at the scene, with partial prints that were a likely match to Katrina's. The fact it was a police officer's gun meant she and Shrug were going to get grilled about it.

"What was the worst part of that night for you?" Gator's attorney asked.

She knew what he wanted her to say. She'd told Dr. Holeman the worst part was when she'd felt Shrug's heavy, cold pistol in her hand. The defense lawyer wanted her to say it, here in front of the judge, the jury and everyone. He wanted her to admit to being armed, to firing the pistol, to threatening his biker clients.

Katrina glanced at Gator. His eyes were fixed on her, unwavering, taunting her. Todd and Pete were looking ahead, as if utterly bored.

As if they know tomorrow they'll be out of here and back on their bikes.

"The worst part," she said, "was finding out there are people in this world like them. People who can torture and kill and not care. People..." Gator wasn't looking at her, so she caught his lawyer's eyes instead. "The worst part was not Lukas's screams. It wasn't all the blood everywhere. It wasn't his dismembered fingers. The worst part was when I looked into Gator's face and saw none of it bothered him."

Tears smudged her vision. Her mouth trembled at the memory of poor Lukas and she began to sob. Soon her cries were streaming through the microphone into the hush of the courtroom.

"Lukas didn't deserve that," she cried.

She wept for him, for her dad, for the girl she had once been—before The Traz had destroyed her. It seemed like she sat there forever, weeping and trying to wipe clean the stain of murder on her hands—in her soul.

"Are you finished with the witness?" the judge asked.

Katrina held her breath. *Please, please be done.*

"No further questions, Your Honour," the prosecutor replied.

"The witness may step down."

Exhaling slowly, Katrina buried her face in the rough jacket of the court security officer as he guided her past the jury.

Tomorrow will be different. Better. Tomorrow I'll start my new life.

CHAPTER 18

"We did it!" Chad grinned in the doorway to Kindle's office. He was in the mood to celebrate. "It took damned near two years since the charges were laid, but we got over two hundred guilty verdicts. No one walks free."

"Yeah, we did it." Kindle set down his pen and motioned Chad inside.

"You don't sound too happy about it."

"One battle ends and another begins. Time now for Shrug to answer for himself."

"Oh." Chad sank into a chair and stretched out his legs. "Rumour is, you're going to be sticking up for him."

"I will."

"Just because Shrug was willing to risk his career for this operation, doesn't mean you're obligated to risk yours."

"If it weren't for Shrug, you wouldn't have your guilty verdicts. Hell, you wouldn't even have had charges laid. The Traz would still be ruling the streets. The entire world owes that man."

"What does the world owe Katrina?"

"That girl has many ways to collect what's owed her. I'm Shrug's only hope."

"Even if Katrina sues, sir, dollars won't set things right for hcr."

Kindle flipped him an envelope. "She's not going to sue."

Chad's eyes narrowed in suspicion. "What's this?" He pulled out a cheque. "She's paying you one hundred thousand dollars?" It didn't make sense. "She gets control of her trust fund and the first thing she does is write you a cheque?"

"It's not my cheque. Read the letter."

Chad withdrew a piece of paper from the envelope. "She wants to fund a seminar to teach police officers ethics, especially where it concerns minors. She has a bent sense of humour." He chuckled, tucked the letter and cheque back into the envelope and tossed it onto the desk.

"I didn't find it funny," Kindle said.

"No? Does her money insult you?"

Kindle shoved the letter into an interoffice envelope.

"I'm guessing the buck doesn't stop here," Chad said. "Unless it's Shrug's. Sarge, how do you intend to defend an officer who recruited a minor into a dangerous police operation?"

"If I were you, I'd shut up. There's going to come a time when it will be *you* needing my support."

Chad gritted his teeth, then stood. "I guess I'll go get Debra and hit her up for a coffee. She gave me a rain check for when the trials were over."

Debra wasn't at her workstation. The sweater that was usually hanging on her chair wasn't there. No files or pens cluttering the desktop. Her monitor was in hibernation mode.

"Where's Debra?" Chad asked the receptionist.

"She booked the afternoon off."

"Did she say where she was going?"

"No, but she left with Shrug."

"Shrug?"

Chad's celebratory mood vanished.

It's Shrug, not me, she's interested in. She's been waiting for the trials to be over because of him. So she can date him.

The next morning Chad stood in the doorway of Debra's office and studied her. She had her usual look of calmness as she flipped through the files on her desk. The sun streaming in behind her caught the edges of her rich brunette curls and painted a halo around her. It wasn't only today that she looked angelic. She was always beautiful and soft.

He tilted his head. She hadn't struck him as someone who'd be taken in by an abrasive tattooed giant on the brink of losing his career for endangering a child.

He ruffled the folder in his hand. Debra looked up.

"Came by yesterday to collect on your rain check for a coffee date," he said, "but you weren't around."

"Oh, I'm sorry I missed you. I was with Shrug."

"Is something wrong? You don't look very happy."

"Nothing makes me happy lately."

"I wanted to celebrate the trial victories, but I can't find anyone around here besides myself that's happy about the convictions."

"I'm glad we got the convictions, but..."

"But what?"

"Shrug."

"Are you and Shrug...you know, a couple or something?"

"Tell you what," she said, standing. "Take me out for that coffee and I'll tell you all about it." She grabbed the sweater from the chair and strode to the door. "You coming?"

He wasn't sure he wanted to know about Debra and Shrug, but she was already out the door and into the hall before he could protest. He caught up, held the exit door for her and they crossed the street to the restaurant.

She said nothing the entire way. When they took their seats, she stared out the window, lost in thoughts he didn't want to interrupt.

Debra and Shrug...

The thought made him depressed. And pissed.

When the waitress brought their food, it didn't seem appetizing. He pushed it aside. And still, Debra said nothing.

Finally, he could stand the silence no longer.

"I don't understand all this concern for Shrug. It embarrasses me for my profession to think an officer of the law could even think of doing what he did."

"Chad!"

"I'd really like it if someone besides me had concern for Katrina instead."

Debra nodded. "I can't argue with that, but let me tell you something. The world sacrificed a gentle giant for that biker bust."

He laughed. "Are you calling Shrug a gentle giant?"

"He once was. He isn't gentle anymore."

"Shrug used to be gentle?"

Her serious eyes held his. "Before Shrug went undercover, he had a heart of gold. And a booming voice that never delivered one word of anger or deceit. He was devoted to children."

"And now?"

"He had to bury his goodness to take on the devil." She bit her bottom lip. "With more time, do you think he'll get that back?"

"It sounds to me like you think he has a good excuse for doing what he did. I can't think of one valid excuse for taking a kid into a biker gang."

"Perhaps you're right." She picked up her cup and stared into it. "Maybe I have to mourn the man he once was and accept what he is now."

"If that's hard for you, just remember what he put the girl through.

She's going to be scarred for life by what she witnessed and what she did. She will be forever in danger—all because of Shrug."

"Were you close to Katrina in The Traz?"

Chad glanced out the window, watching the traffic rush past. "She had these deep blue eyes. They seemed to invite you into her soul. But then, her quick mind stepped forth to keep you out."

"Sort of what Shrug said."

"She reminds me so much of Heather."

"Heather?"

"I had a twin sister. We could tell what the other was thinking simply by staring into each other's eyes. Heather said we shared a soul. She died when we were ten."

"I'm sorry."

"Kids are so…resilient. Or maybe just self-centred. I went on without her. Got busy with my own life, although I often wonder if I shouldn't miss her more. When I spotted Katrina in that cycle shop and she looked across the room at me," he shrugged, "I'm not sure to this day what it was I saw. Something."

"You're going to miss her now the trials are over and she's off with her new identity."

"I suppose I will." He glanced back at Debra. "We all will."

She smiled. "Even Sergeant Kindle. He really seemed to relish taking on a fatherly role with her."

"That's what I thought, until I found out he's going to be supporting Shrug during his disciplinary hearing."

"I don't think that decision has anything to do with how he feels about Katrina. Kindle blames himself for what happened with Shrug. He says he knew better than to leave a man undercover for four years. He also says he knew things were off-kilter, but did nothing." She caught Chad staring at her and fumbled with a napkin.

His pulse quickened and he lowered his eyes, hoping she hadn't sensed his passion or seen his cheeks redden.

I might still have a chance with her. I've got to come up with something to say or she'll think I'm daft.

He cleared his throat. "Katrina lied on the stand."

"How do you know?"

He shrugged. "I just do."

"Are you sure? Nothing she said seemed to contradict the evidence, or Shrug's testimony."

"Maybe Shrug lied too. I can't tell when that bastard's lying."

"What did she lie about?"

"Aside from the fiasco when she lied about the worst part of the evening?"

"That wasn't lying," Debra said, setting down the napkin. "That was answering a stupid question the best way she knew how. I can see how each day something different would seem the worst, depending on what one was remembering. When she was there in front of those bikers testifying, I can certainly see why she'd decide being with them was the worst part."

"Yeah, I know. But that wasn't the part of her testimony I was thinking about. She lied when they asked her why Lukas was chosen as the victim."

Debra frowned. "I don't think so. She said Lukas had been into trafficking meth and had insulted the bikers. We've confirmed all that. Shrug confirmed that. I don't think there was any lying happening."

"Maybe not lying. Maybe something was just left out. I mean, maybe there was another reason why—"

"We know there were other reasons. The truth of the matter was Shrug was vying with Gator for leadership of the gang, and this was the showdown. I'm not sure we can expect a young girl to realize what was going on behind the scenes."

Chad shook his head. "No, it's not that. Something *else*. Something personal for her." *Something only Katrina knows, but I'm going to find out.*

CHAPTER 19

"What would you rather be doin', Sarge?" Shrug drawled. He knew what he'd rather be doing, and it wasn't facing the disciplinary review panel next month.

"Probably just about anything in the world," Kindle replied. "In fact, filling out my income tax sounds better."

There was no doubt in Shrug's mind that Kindle was good at paperwork and management. For Shrug, the thought of sitting behind a desk all day wasn't very appealing. It might be his only choice, though. Even if they did let him keep his badge, he doubted they'd ever let him back on the street.

"I'm serious. If we were to walk away from here," Shrug waved his arm, "what would you do instead of...*this*?"

"What's your point?"

"We're not gonna make it through this internal investigation. So I'm wonderin', do we quit now or wait until after the verdict's in?"

"We'll get through it. If mistakes were made, we pay for them and move on."

Shrug wasn't sure they *would* get through it. Besides, it wasn't fair to take another man down with him, especially one like the Sarge. And there was no doubt in his mind, he was going down. How far down was yet to be seen.

Shrug scowled. If Kindle had all the facts, he wouldn't be dashing off memos on his behalf all the time and showing up at meetings. Or speaking to lawyers. But without Sarge's support, he was sunk.

I owe him. Lots. I gotta tell him everything, so he can back out now and save himself the embarrassment. Hell, save his career.

"It's only gonna get worse," he said.

Kindle pushed the Traz file toward Shrug. "In case you think I'm an idiot, Shrug, I do know there's something you're not telling me. I know we're not just dealing with how you got a minor involved. There are other issues, aren't there? Secrets?"

Shrug hunched forward in his chair and stared at the floor tiles. He owed Kindle his career at the very least and likely his life as well. The man had been a good friend. For many years. An excellent boss.

"You know what I say about my officers keeping secrets from me?" Kindle asked.

"Yeah. Your number one rule—if you can't tell your boss what you've done, you know you've gone over the line."

"You're supposed to think of that rule *before* you do something. Not two or three years later."

"There are other reasons for secrets. Not just because you've gone over the line."

"Although, in your case, you were probably over the line, right?"

"Yeah, probably."

"That's not helpful information." Kindle sighed. "Come on, Shrug. Come clean with me."

"There's nothin' I can say that's gonna make this any better. Why are you wastin' your time fightin' for me?"

"I don't mind giving my officers shit, but when someone else does it doesn't sit well with me. Besides, I have to support you guys. Nobody upstairs knows what it's like out there. Not a clue."

Shrug scratched his bristly chin. "I didn't intend for it to turn out this way."

"I know you didn't. We just have to prove that."

"Optimistically, what's the best thing you can see comin' out of this?"

"We admit error. We accept responsibility. We ensure it doesn't happen again. Take whatever retribution is dealt out. It doesn't mean you have to lose your career over it."

"That's how *you* think. Why would anyone else think that way?"

Kindle tossed him a manila folder. It was labeled: *Constable Donald Hayes*.

"This is my personnel file," Shrug said.

"Exactly. You're a well-trained officer, excellent record both personally and professionally, doing a very hard job in extremely trying circumstances for far too long time. You were isolated from the influences of your culture and submerged in one so different we cannot even imagine. You were trying to survive. Mistakes were made."

Shrug slid the file back to Kindle. "That may sound all right to you, but when you throw in recruitin' a thirteen-year-old girl into a biker gang, it don't balance no more."

It's been a hell of a long time since anything in my life balanced.

"I tried to balance risk versus reward, Sarge. Good versus evil. My job versus my sanity. But there weren't no balance with The Traz, and nothing balanced with the girl, either. If you knew her, it wasn't like she was thirteen."

"She was very much her age. Remember, we all knew her."

"I ain't gonna argue with you."

"It's not like you couldn't tell just by looking at her that she was a juvenile. She never lied to you about her age. Whatever maturity you saw in her that the rest of us missed is irrelevant."

"She manipulates—"

"I don't care if she manipulates. She was thirteen years old, a fact that cannot be offset by anything she supposedly did or didn't do."

"I just want you to understand where I'm comin' from."

"Shrug," Kindle said quietly. "It wasn't the girl's fault. Don't blame her for any part of this. We're the adults here. We made mistakes. There are reasons we made mistakes, but Katrina's personality isn't one of those reasons. Don't try telling me it was. And definitely don't try telling the disciplinary review panel it was."

"I didn't mean I was blamin' her."

"Have you been keeping your counselling appointments with Dr. Holeman?"

Shrug squinted. "Yeah, why?"

"Tell him."

"Tell him what?"

"Tell him where you were coming from. Tell him the girl was manipulative. That's what Holeman's there for. He has the luxury of listening without judging. Tell him all that shit. I warn you, though, don't tell it to me because I got nowhere to put it but on my boss's desk, and you don't want Peters sniffing your dirty shorts."

"I don't want shit like that floatin' around in my file somewhere."

"It's a hundred times better to have that shit floating in a file than floating in your brain. Get it out there, Shrug. It's the only way you'll come to grips with it."

"What's that supposed to mean?"

"Ask Dr. Holeman. You and I grew up together. I know you better than you probably do. As your friend, I want to be there for you. As your boss, I have to be tough. Work it out."

Shrug cocked his head to one side. "You can't be my buddy?"

"I don't have the skills to put it back together for you. I'm sorry. As your boss, I made mistakes. Dire ones with terrible results. And for that, I'm very sorry."

"Wasn't your fault."

"A lot of it was very much my fault, and if I don't admit that and take responsibility for it and make some changes, more men under my command will lose their lives—or their souls. Guilt is the downside of accepting blame. Being able to do something about what went wrong is the upside." Kindle glanced at the closed door and lowered his voice. "Tell me what you're hiding."

Shrug let out a grunt. "There's always two realities. Man's world and God's world. Sometimes they conflict, you know. What's right in God's eyes looks wrong to men."

"Wrong or illegal?"

Shrug didn't answer.

"If you've done something illegal and you're covering it up by claiming a moral obligation, I'm not buying it."

"No, I guess you wouldn't buy it. A man needs a deep, deep, spiritual understandin' to comprehend somethin' like that."

"Don't insult me. You're not superior to me in any way. Not in the moral department and definitely not in the police department."

"I know that, Sarge. I was tryin' to point out you're one of the deepest men I know."

Kindle's smile was full of umbrage. "You'd better rethink things if you're insinuating that because I'm so deep, if I knew your secret, I'd agree with your decision to keep it secret."

"Is that what I'm sayin'? I'll be damned." What had sounded like a great justification in his head, sounded pathetic with Kindle's voice wrapped around it.

"Let's test your theory. Tell me your secret and we'll see how I react."

Shrug pulled the pack of Nicorettes from his pocket and popped a couple in his mouth. His strategy was unravelling. If he kept mute—as he knew he must—neither he nor Kindle would be able to defend his actions.

"Nice try, Sarge. If we're gonna fight this internal review thing, let's get us some good lawyers. It's my experience they can twist anything around to make it look good."

"If that's the way you want to go with this, fine." Kindle pointed to the door. "Go get us a lawyer."

Shrug clambered to his feet, unnerved by Kindle's abrupt dismissal. "Am I really that fucked up?"

"Yes."

"Maybe lawyers aren't a good idea?"

"Didn't say that."

"Gettin' a lawyer ain't what you'd do?"

Kindle shrugged. "When you're fucked up, a lawyer is sometimes the only way to go."

CHAPTER 20

Shrug had been on Kindle's mind a lot since their meeting last week. He was worried that he hadn't given the man proper advice when he'd told him to hire a lawyer. Sometimes calling on legal help made even the innocent look guilty, especially in the eyes of law enforcement officials.

"You busy?" Shrug stood in the doorway to Kindle's office.

"Always. What do you need? Come in."

Shrug leaned against the doorjamb. "I've hired the lawyers. They're wantin' to meet with us."

"They? More than one?"

"One each, sort of. To play against each other."

"You make it sound like a theatrical production."

Shrug grinned. "It is. I oughta have got us some attorneys whose names frequently appear in headlines. You know, the ones representin' people like the Hells Angels or disgraced politicians."

Kindle's stomach lurched. "Who'd you get?"

"Nah, didn't get no one famous. Figured since we have to impress a panel of our peers and not a judge or jury, we need someone to fit the role of an *honest* lawyer, one who could act with deep respect for the rules that govern police behaviour."

"Act? A role?"

"And I get to direct."

"Ah, yes. You do realize the lawyers can't speak to the panel. It'll be you and I doing the talking."

"Yeah, we both talk good, so I'm not worried about that. These guys, Kraden and Henwood, will be there though, noddin' and nudgin', takin' notes and lookin' legal."

"I see."

"Their speakin' parts gonna take place in private. They're gonna tell us what to wear and how to hold our lips. What we wanna say and what we don't, *and* what to do if we get cornered."

"We're not on the stage in high school gymnasium, Shrug."

Shrug's smile widened. "But we'll do just as good as we did back then. You and I, we'll be stars again. We're gonna shine." The smile faded. "We have to, Sarge. Our careers are on the line."

"Seems to me our play-acting got us in big trouble back then."

"It got us women."

"We don't need women," Kindle said. "We need our careers. I think we ought to stick with honesty. That's what *I* learned from our acting fiasco."

He had enough of lies and deception. Lies always had a way of getting found out. It was time to step up, take responsibility. He'd put Shrug in the gang. He'd take the heat for that. And Shrug? Well, he'd have to come clean or lie like an Academy Award winner. Either way, that was Shrug's choice.

Shrug moved away from the door. "You still fightin' with me for the leadin' role?"

"I gave up years ago. Conceded to your superior acting skills."

"I think you're sayin' that to get my guard down. I figure my four years undercover with The Traz ought to merit some kind of award."

Kindle stared at him for a long moment, trying to find his old friend beneath the tough, rugged exterior. He wasn't sure any part of the farm boy he once knew was still there. "I'll have one engraved."

Shrug opened the door, then looked over his shoulder. "You free to meet these guys this afternoon?"

"Yeah."

"Fourteen hundred hours. Don't be late."

When the door closed, Kindle let out a ragged sigh. "Probably already too late, my friend."

"We'll fight this on two fronts," Lyle Kraden explained.

Kraden was a clean-cut forceful man. Mid-forties. Expensive suit. He sat behind one for the most impressive desks Shrug had ever seen. It was huge, rich and gleaming. Shrug wondered why legal offices were more intimidating than police stations. *I oughta bring that up with the brass.*

"On the first front, we want to build up the character of the officer— present an image of integrity, honesty, sacrifice," Kraden continued. "That shouldn't be hard to do with the excellent reports and evaluations on file. We have to play up the success of the sting, the number of charges laid, the convictions, the disruption to the gangs and the drug trade. Try to create a sense that maybe it was worth it, or at least could've been perceived as worth it from the undercover's point of view."

Kindle looked as apprehensive as Shrug felt, slouched in the huge, cushiony chair. Although comfortable and luxurious beyond reason, the chairs also made Kindle and him appear vulnerable and small compared to the lawyers in their straight-backed chairs behind the massive hardwood desks. Perhaps the austere interrogation rooms down at the detachment ought to be redesigned.

"The second front," the second lawyer jumped in, "is going to involve the girl."

Jasper Henwood was an antithesis to Kraden. The first time Shrug had been to his office, he'd been in jeans and a plaid lumberjack shirt. Today he was a bit more proper, but not much. He spoke gruffly. Shrug had even heard him slip in a cuss word now and then.

"We have to pierce her angelic image," Henwood said. "We have to find something on her."

"No!" Shrug said. "We will not do that."

"I have good evidence Katrina survived her ordeal with her virginity intact," Kindle said.

"Oh, come off it!" Shrug shouted. "So now I've kidnapped a virgin. Tell me again how that will help my case?"

"Well, if you kidnapped a virgin, at least you returned her a virgin."

Shrug glared at him.

"There were no signs of injury, drug abuse, or other forms of sex, either," Kindle added. "I was with Cooper when he accessed her medical file that day she fainted during questioning."

"That has to be unusual for a young girl running with a biker gang," Henwood said. "Shrug must have protected her very—"

"Yeah," Shrug interrupted, "except for one minor, unfortunate evenin' of torture and murder."

"This is more on your front," Henwood said, looking at Kraden. "Propping up the image of the officer. Slip it in unnoticed near the end, to avoid conflicting with my work of discrediting the girl."

"I said, don't sully the girl," Shrug snapped. "Don't go there!"

Henwood's brow arched. "Are you suggesting we'll find something?"

"I hired you and I'll fire you. If I ever hear you've been askin' around for dirt on Sarina, you're gone. Instantly. Do you understand?"

There was an awkward silence.

"You do realize," Kraden said after a moment, "that we're fighting for your careers here?"

"As I've said before," Shrug turned to Kindle, "I risked my life for this operation. Unfortunately, I risked the girl's life too and feel compelled now to risk my career for her." He lowered his eyes and his voice. "Sarge, I'm compelled to risk your career too. Sorry."

"I don't want to go into this with you hiding secrets from me," Kindle said. "Do you know something about her history I should know? I'm not saying we'll bring it up, but if it's out there I want to know about it and be prepared if it lands before us."

"I know lots about her, but you haven't in the past been prone to listenin' about it."

"If you have anything to say about her other than she's evil and the devil has her soul, I'm prone to listening to it now."

"Nope, that about covers it."

Kindle pulled Shrug aside. "What aren't you telling me? What is the secret? Did you talk to Katrina before we went to trial? Is that it? You conspired with her to keep a promise?"

"I was ordered to stay away from her."

"Did you talk to Katrina before we went to trial?"

"Yeah, talked to her once."

Kindle exhaled. "You were so right, Shrug. It does only get worse, doesn't it?"

"Yeah, but you can't say I didn't warn you."

"Do I even want to know what you two said to each other?"

"Nothin' bad." *Not in God's eyes.*

Kindle wagged a finger in Shrug's face. "I thought I was defending your actions when you were undercover. If you haven't found it within yourself to clean up since getting out of The Traz, I'm wasting my time. I'm not willing to risk my career for that. And if you messed with that trial…"

"Don't worry about it, Sarge. Justice was served." *Despite how messed up that trial was.*

CHAPTER 21

Northern Alberta Police Detachment, Edmonton, September 1998

Kindle paced around his office, waiting for Corporal Sydney Koots to arrive. Syd had barraged Kindle with emails and phone messages, identified himself only as an officer from the Southern Alberta Detachment with background info on Katrina that might help Shrug's defence.

Long before the trials began, Kindle was aware of rumours about Katrina being something other than the naive, orphaned, unfortunate, credible witness the Crown had painted her. He'd ignored the scuttlebutt because, although neither he nor anyone else believed the girl had been the epitome of virtuosity before joining The Traz, everyone knew that no matter what her past, she hadn't deserved to be subjected to the horrors in that shed. After all, it hadn't been *her* on trial.

He had reasons for believing Shrug ought to be forgiven for involving Katrina in The Traz, but none of those reasons related to the kind of person she was—or had been. He assumed the prosecutors had some idea of her past in case the defence brought it up to challenge her credibility. However, when the bikers' high-priced lawyers made no reference to anything nasty, it had been easy to let the subject slide.

It wasn't until this Syd fellow had hinted that what he knew might also affect the bikers' appeals that Kindle agreed to meet the man. He had the feeling he was about to uncover Shrug's secret—one he was pretty sure was not going to make him happy.

There was a rap on the half-open door.

A young man in a suit stood in the doorway. He was in his mid-twenties, sported a straw-coloured crew cut and had green eyes that moved nervously around the room. He held a briefcase in one hand, while the other was on the doorknob.

Kindle nodded and waved him in. "Syd?"

"Sydney Koots, sir."

Syd closed the door behind him and sat down. He laid the briefcase on his lap and began snapping its handle against the brass lock.

Kindle raised his eyebrows. "What is it you have for me?"

From the front pocket of the briefcase, Syd pulled out a five-by-seven photo and placed it on the desk. "Do you recognize anyone?"

Kindle looked at the shot, obviously a bar scene with several shady-looking characters doing what characters do in a bar. "Am I supposed to?"

"Let me show you."

Syd pulled a bulky laptop from the case and set it on Kindle's desk. Then he walked around, stood beside him and began typing. In moments, the same photo appeared on the screen.

"I believe you know this girl."

Syd zoomed in on a woman on a barstool. She was quite tiny, had long red hair and too much makeup. She was looking at something in her hand. Syd zoomed in until a familiar face filled the screen. The little mole under her left eye left no doubt who it was.

Katrina Buckhold.

"Another picture," Syd said, clicking the keys rapidly. "Same night. Who is it?"

"It's Katrina."

"We knew her as Sarina." Syd clicked back to the original photo.

"Where did these pictures come from?" Kindle asked, suspicious.

"Undercover shots in the King's Ace, once the seediest, most dangerous bar in Calgary. These photos are extremely high resolution. You can't zoom in like this on regular digital shots. They'd be too distorted to mean anything. These you can. High tech, you know."

"The girl was in the seediest bar in the city. So what?"

"I'm not finished." Syd clicked and double clicked. "She's looking down, right? At something in her hand. Want to see what she's looking at?"

Though Kindle didn't have the chemical analysis, given the girl was in the seediest, most dangerous bar in the city, it was undoubtedly a hit of something illegal.

He shivered as a cold uneasiness crept over him.

"There's more," Syd said. "That fellow behind her, his back is to us. But look…" He zoomed in on another shot. Filling the computer screen, the telltale Traz letters were blazoned orange on a black leather jacket. "The King's Ace wasn't the gang's favourite bar, but there were a couple of the Traz bikers who seemed to have something going on there. Maybe just watching. Lots of competing evil at that place."

"She knew The Traz? Before Shrug…?"

"I think she watched them more than they watched her. She wasn't what those boys were after. This fellow," Syd panned out and pointed at the screen, "the one beside her? You can't see his face from this angle. Check out the red collar. Now look at this photo—same shirt, same night, different angle. Recognize him?"

Kindle didn't at first, but then the face filled the screen. What had started as a chill became ice.

"She knew Lukas before?"

"Yeah," Syd said. "They were an item for a while, Sarina and him. For quite a while actually, until she got mad at him and they broke up."

"They had a fight?" Kindle asked.

"Yeah, some puppy-love stuff. Hell, she's only twelve here."

"Twelve? No, thirteen. She was thirteen when her parents passed."

"Oh, she was no orphan when this was going on. Look. The photos are time and date stamped. This was taken in March, three months before the car accident that killed her parents. See here? 2:45 on a Thursday morning."

"I don't know what to say." Kindle pushed back his chair and strode to the window. "I didn't know any of this. It's quite a shock."

"She was no saint," Syd pointed out. "No stranger to the underbelly of nightlife when Shrug picked her up. In fact—"

"Shrug knew her then, did he?"

"Yeah, well, he knew about her. We were the ones who knew her."

Kindle glared at the man. "We?"

"Me and Rusty James, my undercover partner. We were working the drug angle. Sarina was there mostly for the excitement. A cop's daughter, you know. Said her mother was hitting the bottle again. I guess Mom had stayed sober for years and then…well, Sarina couldn't deal with it. It was the wrong age for the mother to go missing in a bottle."

"You knew her quite well?"

"She was smart as a whip, that girl. Insatiably curious. With her innocent appearance, she could get the guys to tell her almost anything. Was great for us."

Kindle frowned. "It was great for you?"

"Yeah. All we had to do was promise not to tell her dad what she was up to and she'd get us any info we wanted. Easy stuff, man. No paperwork, no money."

"Excuse me," Kindle interrupted. "She was 'great' for you? 'Easy stuff'? Did it not strike you she was the twelve-year-old daughter of one of your own? In the seediest, most dangerous bar in the city?" He clenched his fists. "Did it not strike you maybe you should get her the hell out of there? I can't believe I'm hearing this."

"Sir, we're not social workers. Getting kids off the street isn't our job. We were sent out there to track the drugs, not to save souls."

"But that's the whole point!" Kindle shouted. "Why do you think you're tracking the drugs? Why are you getting the bad guys? So you can save souls! Is it just a game to you? Do you have no sense of what the real mission is?"

Syd cringed. "Sir, I know what you're saying, but...well...I wouldn't know how to get her out. I didn't know—"

"You don't know how to do that?"

"No, sir. Not really. We see it all the time. Kids younger than her. I had a ten-year-old boy sell me crack once. Hell, if we were out to try to save them all, we'd sure be busy. Busy with the delinquents instead of the dealers."

"So we leave the kids out there, buy their crack from them, bribe them for information, wish them luck—and *voila!* Ten years later we've made ourselves another Gator?"

"I see." Syd closed the laptop. "Look, sir, if this information isn't going to help, let's just forget it."

"I'm never going to forget this." *What else can I say? The guy doesn't get it.*

There was an awkward silence.

Syd swallowed hard, his Adam's apple moving with each gulp.

"How did Shrug get hooked up with her?" Kindle finally asked.

"I chatted to him about her once. He was looking for someone clean—not addicted, no police record. But, well, someone experienced, if you will. I mentioned Sarina. How she could get us information real easy. Then, after her parents got killed, she dried up on us. We found her down there once, drunk out of her mind. I got a cab to take her home and told Shrug if he wanted her, he'd better get to her because she was fading fast."

"Why was this not brought forward before the trial? And where were these photos during our investigation?"

"They were tied up in *our* investigation. Not these three in particular, but they were with the package. We were making a case to shut down the King's Ace and clean up that area."

"You knew what was happening up here in Northern Alberta. The trial was anything but a secret. No one thought we might want those pics up here?"

"I was told...I thought..." Syd shrugged. "I don't know."

"I see. You thought we did not want those pics up here. Who made that decision?"

"My boss was aware of the photos." Syd pointed to his laptop. "Should...I take it?"

"Yeah, go ahead. I wouldn't know how to work it anyway. If I need it, I have your name. Leave me the photo."

The man hastily packed up his computer and headed for the door.

"Syd," Kindle called after him. "I don't want those photos to disappear. You keep them safe."

After Syd was gone, he collapsed into his chair and stared at the photo. It meant so little without the computer manipulation, and so much with it. It wasn't the fact Katrina had a night life that bothered him, but rather that Shrug had known and hadn't told him. But worse than that, when the one and only eyewitness in a murder trial was a friend of the victim, it was something that should have been known.

His credible witness was now one with a deeply troubled past and a turbulent relationship with the victim. Adding those two things to the fact she had firearms expertise and was armed the night of the murder, it would have been a much different trial.

There was something else. Something Shrug had said in Kindle's office his first day back after the police raid. Something Kindle had intended on following up on, but hadn't.

What had we been talking about?

He replayed the conversation in his mind. Shrug had asked about Katrina, how she was doing, and Kindle had warned him to stay away from her. But before that...

What was it?

Kindle tilted the photo to reduce the glare. Katrina must have had a wig on, along with the makeup. It made her look somewhat older from a distance.

Did Syd say Lukas had been her boyfriend? Who has a boyfriend at the age of twelve?

And what was it that Shrug had said? They'd been talking about Katrina and Shrug had asked if she'd told Kindle about the motive for the murder. And there was something about Lukas...

"She tell you the reason he was chosen?" Shrug had asked.

Syd said Katrina and Lukas were an item.

"Until she got mad at him," Syd had said, "and they broke up."

Kindle cradled his head in his hands. "Oh God, no. Tell me it wasn't Katrina who chose Lukas."

CHAPTER 22

Dr. Holeman's Office, Edmonton

The evening sun streamed low through the bottom half of the wall of windows behind Dr. Holeman, making it difficult for Katrina to see his face.

"You're staying here late because you know I have something I'm trying to say, aren't you?" she asked. Her appointment had been scheduled to end a good half-hour ago.

"I sense you're struggling with something."

"I don't know if talking will make it better or worse." With her luck it would be the latter.

"It's sometimes nice just to share, even if there's nothing anyone can do to fix the matter. You've told me many terrible things and I believe talking about them has helped you."

"I was hoping not talking about…this thing…would make it go away, but it hasn't."

"Things sometimes sit for a long time in our hearts and minds before we're ready to talk about them. I believe that time is now, Katrina."

"I don't know how to say it."

"Do you want me to ask you questions and you can just answer and not have to think of what to say or how to say it?"

"You won't know what to ask," she whispered.

"I'll guess. Let me know when I'm getting close. Does it have something to do with your mother?"

"No."

"Something to do with the murder trial?"

Katrina nodded.

"Ah, let's see. Something to do with Lukas?"

Shocked to hear Lukas's name so soon, she bolted upright. "How did you know? What made you guess that?"

"What haven't you told me about Lukas?"

"How did you know?"

"Tell me, what colour was Lukas's hair?"

"It was dark brown. He wore it short, with a curl." She gestured to her forehead.

"What colour were his eyes?"

"Blue. They were very pretty when he wasn't stoked up on meth. He used too many drugs. Did you know that?"

"No, I didn't. What else?"

"Even though he was almost five years older than I was, we got along because his mother drank too much. Like mine. We talked about that a lot. He was a genius too and didn't find me freaky like the kids at school did. I tried to keep him from using drugs because he was so gentle when he was clean. But he was hurting inside. He told me drugs made him hurt less, but I could tell they didn't. When he was using, his blue eyes got cloudy. Sometimes, even mean."

"Lukas was your friend?"

The words ripped through her.

She hadn't heard that said since the night Shrug had made her tea in his kitchen—the night after the murder, when he'd promised she could keep it a secret forever.

"You and Lukas were very close at one time?"

Lukas had wrapped his arms around her and hoisted her off her feet. They'd kissed…beneath a summer moon, behind the King's Ace.

"He was your boyfriend?"

"Don't say that!"

Gator had said that and then named Lukas his victim.

Panic narrowed her vision and made her face hot. "I have to get out of here. I can't breathe." She leapt from the chair. "I have to go outside. There's no air in here!"

"Katrina, take deep slow breaths or you're going to faint again."

"I can't! I can't!" *Lukas's eyes. His open, blue eyes…*

The moon had sparked off his eyes that night. And in that dark shed, his hair had been covered in blood.

Katrina felt a hand on her shoulder.

"Please," Dr. Holeman said. "Please, sit." He led her back to the chair.

"Gator knew Lukas was my friend," she sobbed. "He chose him to kill because he was my friend. He wanted to make me watch my friend…"

"I know. I know."

"Shrug was saying to Gator, 'No! Not Lukas.' And I think Gator said something about why would Shrug care. He shouldn't care about his woman's 'other man.' Gator said it would be good for me to kill Lukas and prove I was Traz and not Blue Torpedo."

"That was cruel. Exceptionally evil."

"It's my fault! If I hadn't—if Gator hadn't found out Lukas was my friend because I mentioned it once..." She sniffed and wiped her eyes. "I didn't know. I wasn't thinking. I had no idea he'd use it against me. I should've known not to say that. Shrug had told me 'knowledge is power.' You're not supposed to say shit. You don't tell things. I knew better. It's my fault."

"Katrina, it's not your fault. The brutality of the murder belongs to Gator and his boys."

"No. God, no! If I hadn't told Gator that Lukas was my friend, Lukas would be alive."

"It wasn't you who killed him—"

"Lukas didn't know that. He didn't know I wasn't in on the kill." She curled up into a tight ball, wishing she could disappear. "Dr. Holeman, Lukas died thinking I'd betrayed him. I saw it in his eyes, his blue eyes that used to smile at me."

CHAPTER 23

Northern Alberta Police Detachment, Edmonton

Kindle arrived, breathless, at his boss's office. He'd taken the stairs rather than the elevator so he could have a few more minutes of thinking time. He wished he'd never met Corporal Sydney Koots.

"Come in," Staff Sergeant Peters invited.

Kindle sat down and gulped in a lungful of air.

"You have something of concern?"

"It's come to my attention sir, that Katrina Buckhold was a friend of the murder victim. She was also acquainted with some of The Traz bikers *before* Shrug engaged her in the sting. There is photographic evidence from the King's Ace. Police photos—"

"Why are you telling me this?" Peters interrupted.

"Sir, it's something that has to be told. It ought to have been told to me years ago. I don't want to be guilty of participating in a cover-up."

"The trials are over."

"But the appeals aren't. This information was never brought up at the—"

"If The Traz knew Katrina from the King's Ace, they likely knew about her and Lukas."

"It's not clear what The Traz bikers knew."

"None of what you've told me is privileged information only the cops had. Therefore, the fact we didn't bring it up at trial is irrelevant."

"But—"

"Does this have something to do with the internal investigation into Shrug's behaviour?"

"I'm sure it will affect that, but it's not my main concern. It's the murder trial. This information was withheld from the defence, purposely, by the police. Perhaps The Traz knew her from the King's Ace, but we're not sure. Then there's the question of the photos being withheld. The Crown prosecutor presented Katrina as an innocent, reliable witness. The pictures raise doubt about that."

"The defence could've brought it up. They didn't. I wouldn't worry about it."

"I'm not sure the bikers knew of the connection between the girl and the victim. And the defence could claim the Crown's refusal to reveal Sarina's true identity to the court kept them from finding out on their own."

"Well, I can't see how any of that information about the girl would've affected the outcome. Whether the victim was a stranger or a friend of the girl—murder is murder. I say what's over is over. Let's move on. The bikers have lost two appeals already. They likely won't be allowed to launch another one."

"Several people are in possession of this information. Some are starting to talk."

"What kind of people?"

"Our people."

"Who are they talking to?"

"Each other. Myself. Maybe their wives and girlfriends—I don't know."

"I still say, leave well enough alone."

"It's up to you, sir." Kindle stood. "I'd like you to think about it a bit more."

"I will." Peters gave a nod. "You'll be the first to know if I change my mind."

Shrug was in his office when Kindle got back. The undercover officer was hunched over, staring at his feet as usual.

"Katrina called me," he said once Kindle was seated.

"I know. I patched the call through to you."

Everything about Shrug was annoying Kindle today. His brooding, his size, his secret. His arrogance and complete disrespect.

He picked up a message from his daughter, swivelled his back to Shrug and returned her call. He ended the conversation, hung up and looked over his shoulder. Shrug was still silently staring at his loafers.

Chad rapped on the open door, a folder in his hand.

"Come on in," Kindle said.

Chad stared quizzically at Shrug. "This is…the background on the Craigon case you asked for." He handed Kindle the file and looked from Shrug's face to his loafers. "What the hell are you looking at, Shrug?"

"Fuck off," Shrug said, moving only his lips.

"You've been sitting in the Sarge's office for an hour staring at your feet and you have the nerve to say that to *me*? You're the one who should fuck off."

Shrug began to move and Kindle scrambled from behind the desk. "Chad, out!" He pointed at the door.

Chad locked his eyes on Shrug's. "Me?"

Shrug stood and puffed out his massive chest. "His way of sayin', 'Fuck off, Chad.'"

"Shrug, keep your mouth shut." Kindle stepped between the two men. "Chad, leave. That's an order."

Once Chad was out of sight, Kindle turned back to Shrug. He caught a sparkle of amusement in the man's eyes. "There's no humour here. As Chad pointed out, if you're not going to talk, leave. I have work to do. If you have something to say to me, you're going to have to say it out loud because I don't read minds."

Without looking back, Shrug walked out of the office and shut the door.

Kindle sighed. *Last thing I need is to referee those two.*

He sat down at his desk and picked up a pen.

The door opened. It was Shrug. He stood in the doorway for a moment, vacillating under Kindle's stare, then stepped inside and closed the door.

"Katrina called me this mornin'."

"We've been there already," Kindle said.

"You didn't ask me what she said."

"I've come to realize it's useless to ask you questions. You only tell me what you want to anyway. So if you've got something to say, out with it."

Shrug sat down. "You know why she called?"

"I didn't talk to her." Kindle flipped open the file Chad had brought.

"She said she'd told Dr. Holeman about Lukas and if there was someone I should tell it would be good for me if I did." Shrug took a deep breath. "Sarina had a night life for a long time before I hooked up with her. She was gettin' into pretty bad shape before I got her out."

"You make it sound like you were saving her."

"Maybe I was. I dunno. Seemed like a good thing to do at the time."

"How can taking a young girl into a biker gang even begin to look like a good thing?"

"She knew Lukas, eh? They were friends."

Moving to the window, Shrug jammed both hands in his pockets and stared out over the parking lot. Silent minutes slid by.

"I'll help you out here," Kindle finally offered. "But you have to sit and face me. You owe me that much."

Shrug strolled back to his chair.

"I'll take a guess," Kindle said. "The real reason Lukas was picked to be the victim? He was Katrina's friend."

Shrug nodded.

"So tell me again. Who did the picking?"

"Gator."

"You sure it wasn't Katrina?"

Shrug's eyes widened in surprise. "Why would you think that?"

"Katrina getting revenge on a boyfriend who had pissed her off?"

"Where the hell did that come from?"

"Since I don't read minds and nobody tells me this shit, I guess I kind of make it up."

"Jesus Murphy! I can't believe anyone would even think that of the girl."

"A defence team would've. A jury might've."

"No!" Shrug studied Kindle's face. "No? Ah, shit." He let out a tired sigh.

"You should've told me."

"There were reasons I didn't."

"Shrug, how did Gator know Lukas was Katrina's friend? Did Gator know her from the King's Ace?"

"You know about the King's Ace?"

"I've seen pictures. Ones of Katrina with meth, in the King's Ace. With The Traz in the King's Ace. With Lukas in the King's Ace." His jaw clenched. "Yeah, I know about the King's Ace. Did Gator?"

Shrug leaned forward. "You've seen pictures?"

"How did Gator know Lukas and Katrina were friends?" Kindle asked. "Did he know about the King's Ace?"

"No."

"No, what?"

Shrug straightened. "No, Gator didn't know about the King's Ace. That day when Pepper and Stack had their chat with Lukas over him sellin' meth to our coke customers, we were talkin' about it back at the compound and Katrina let it slip she knew Lukas. Gator jumped on it right away, filed it away in his evil little mind for future use. He was like that. Didn't seem at the time a dangerous thing for Katrina to say, just a few words. Gator looked in her eyes and saw what else she wasn't sayin'—that she loved the boy. Turned it into somethin' when it suited him."

"You're sure there's no way anyone in The Traz knew anything about Katrina, Lukas and the King's Ace before then?"

"A couple of the bikers knew the bar. I don't think they knew much about the girl or Lukas, though. They weren't there lookin' for kids."

"What were they there for?"

"Business."

"That's not helpful. Tell me."

"They were watchin' the big boys in the back. Tryin' to intimidate them with their presence—makin' sure no one even thought of movin' into their territory."

"Katrina—was she watching the big boys in the back too?"

Shrug frowned. "What do you mean?"

"Was she watching them?"

"Yeah, maybe. What's your point?"

"Any chance The Traz and Katrina got to know each other in the back room?"

"Want me to say *yes*?"

"What the hell kind of answer's that?"

"I've told you, Sarge, The Traz didn't know. You don't seem to like that answer. You keep askin'. I'm offerin' to give you an answer you like."

"I was hoping there was some other way the defence could've got this information."

"Gator knew Katrina was Lukas's friend. If he didn't tell his biker buddies or his lawyer, it ain't my fault."

"It ain't—it *isn't*—just the *friend* part. She was a drug dealer. A frequenter of seedy places after midnight. She knew the victim, a rival drug dealer, whom she'd just happened to split up with weeks before the murder. All information the police knew, had evidence of and didn't share with the defence."

"The Traz knew most of that," Shrug said. "Gator could've testified about it."

"There's no way the defence would ever let Gator testify and leave him open to be cross examined by our prosecutors."

"That's not our problem."

"They could, however, have had you or Syd testify about it."

"You're thinkin' they'll appeal? Again?"

"They don't know about it yet. The information is sitting up top right now. I'm afraid too many people know to keep it secret any longer. Upstairs might try to keep a lid on it. Don't know yet. So you're sure Gator chose Lukas as his victim because he was Katrina's friend?"

"Yeah. He just figured that fact would make his little plan all the more delicious. When it came to power plays he was tuned in like a calibrated seismometer. He could spot the weakest link before you knew you had one."

"Katrina was your weakest link?"

"He thought so. How hard could it be to terrorize a woman? Easy, man. And probably more effective than tryin' to terrorize me."

"Why didn't you get her out of there when you saw what was coming? Why, Shrug?"

"Dunno. Thought I could control it all, stop it. Not until I saw Katrina on the stand at the murder trial did it sink in. 'Til I saw her cryin' and heard her sayin' what it was she'd seen. How many convictions did we net? Two hundred and fifty-six?"

"Something like that."

"When she broke down on the stand, at that moment I just knew it hadn't been worth one conviction." He paused. "That one night just erased anything good that ever came afterwards."

"If you didn't recruit Katrina, you wouldn't have gotten control of the gang. You wouldn't have broken up the drug and weapons cartel on both sides of the border. It wasn't worth it?"

"Lukas wouldn't get murdered and Sarina wouldn't face a life of hell."

"But a thousand other kids become victims of drug abuse and violence because the gang's still operating."

"I know you don't believe what you're sayin'."

"Glad to hear that, Shrug. But the important thing is, do *you* believe what I'm saying?"

"Of course not. A good shepherd doesn't sacrifice even one lost sheep for the benefit of the flock. That's in the Bible."

Kindle turned his eyes to the window. There was a storm blowing in. On the prairies, one could always see storms coming. "I know the story. Anything in the Bible about why you didn't tell me Katrina knew Lukas?"

"Nope."

"If you don't explain yourself, you'll be making it into legal journals as the late victim of a boss's wrath."

"For her, Sarge," Shrug replied. "She couldn't accept she'd caused Lukas's death. I tried to get her talk about it, but she wouldn't. She'd just quit breathin' and stare off into space and sit motionless. I'm glad Holeman got her to talk."

"Dr. Holeman did pretty good for us, but how can you be sure he couldn't have got her to talk about being friends with Lukas *before* the trials?"

"Because after the trial I went to Holeman. Told him what Katrina wouldn't. That was months ago. Yesterday she talked about it to him for the first time."

"You told Holeman and you wouldn't tell me?"

"Tellin' *you* wouldn't have helped. She'd have lied about it. She'd have lost her integrity as a witness. She'd have shut down, like she did with me every time I came near the subject. You know, Sarge..." Shrug squinted. "You'd have lost her for your investigations, lost her as a witness for all the trials."

Kindle shook his head slowly, trying to process all of the new information.

"What do we do now?" Shrug asked. "What the hell do we do now?"

Kindle realized with dismay that all his well-laid plans to deal with the errors of the past were crumbling to dust. "I haven't got a clue."

CHAPTER 24

Kraden, Henwood & Associates Law Office, Edmonton, January 1999

Shrug shifted uncomfortably under the accusing eyes that were on him. Kindle and the lawyers were talking as if he weren't even there. He surmised that when a man messed up as badly as he had, respect would be hard to get.

"Kraden," Kindle said. "Are you willing to defend Shrug against obstructing justice and concealing evidence *in addition* to his involvement with the girl? I'm not sure I am."

"On the positive side, it does somewhat explain how Shrug was thinking at the time," Lyle Kraden said. "And it wasn't bad thoughts. His latter actions prove he was very protective of the girl. Driven by concern for both her sanity and reputation. We can work it from that angle."

Kraden tapped out a rhythm with his pen and turned to Shrug. "Focussing for now on the issues with the girl, we have here an excellent officer making a bad decision. Why? He and his good intentions are immersed in a culture of violence. His perception of reality becomes skewed. This girl is frequenting violent pubs in the wee hours of weekday mornings. She's drinking, she's sinking. She's perhaps suicidal. It somehow doesn't seem like so bad an idea to get her out of there."

"Good luck at making any of that sound good," Kindle mumbled. "But I'm with Shrug. We're not using the King's Ace information if upstairs decides to keep her history under wraps. We won't risk losing the convictions just to save our necks."

"Do we have to drag the girl into it?" Shrug asked, wincing. "I mean, it's just not nice to be talkin' about her like this."

"We can't *not* drag the girl into it," Henwood said. "She's the whole point here. We're not going to be mean about it. We're going to explain the alcoholic mother, the death of her parents, her quest for excitement. We won't portray her as evil."

"Has she or her guardians ever filed any kind of formal complaint against the police?" Kraden asked.

"No," Kindle said.

"An *informal* complaint? A verbal complaint?"

"No."

"Lawsuit?"

"No, but she did mail us a one hundred thousand dollar cheque to be used to train undercover agents on the finer aspects of ethical police behaviour, especially where it concerns minors."

"She did?" Shrug chuckled. The girl had spirit. That's for sure.

"It was a slap in the face. An insult."

"What the hell is that she-devil up to now?"

"Shrug, watch what—"

"Sarge, she's after somethin'. She's after somethin'."

"Yes, she's trying to make us feel guilty."

Shrug shook his head. Kindle didn't get it. "Oh, it's more than that. There's somethin' in it for her, no doubt. That woman sold her soul to Lucifer long before I got tangled with her."

"Girl," Kindle correctly. He cast sad eyes at Kraden and Henwood. "Shrug's still...it's not like him to see a child as evil."

"Can we get a psychiatric evaluation on him?" Henwood asked.

Shrug grinned. "Whatever you think will work."

"There is no humour in this," Kindle said. "You've got to get yourself together."

Shrug ground his teeth. "You sayin' I'm so crazy I think the woman's crazy? Is that it?"

"Girl. Child. Not woman." Kindle let out a groan. "She is someone's *daughter*. A beloved only child."

"Spoiled rotten beyond reason," Shrug muttered. *And more clever than Einstein and Newton combined.* "She's a master manipulator, devoid of a conscience. Believe me, Sarge. I know that girl."

"She really donated a hundred thousand dollars?" Kraden asked.

Kindle nodded.

"That's good." Kraden began taking notes. "Excellent."

"It is?" Shrug and Kindle asked simultaneously.

"Yes, let's run with it. The victim's voice. Can't you see? We're going to direct the panel away from accuse and punish. We're going to ease them into a scenario of 'Let's do something so this never happens again. Let's find out why good officers make bad decisions and have a plan to prevent it.'"

Henwood nodded. "Those Calgary undercovers with the photos—

how does it happen these pictures, relevant to an extremely high-profile murder case, exist and no one says anything? Why did that happen?"

"Because they're idiots?" Kindle suggested.

"Okay...so how does it happen we have idiots under—no, not that. How does it happen we're sending ill-prepared agents undercover? Who screens these guys and how? Who monitors them?"

"And you, Sergeant Kindle," Kraden jumped in. "You're angry Syd didn't do anything to get the girl off the street. He told you he had no training for that. Shrug probably didn't either. If that's what we want our officers to do, shouldn't we give them the knowledge and skills to do it?"

"I'd like to argue all that's needed is common sense," Kindle said. "I can't see it requiring a special skill and you can't teach common sense,"

"Perhaps we can screen better for it," Henwood said.

"The victim has spoken," Kraden said. "Loud and clear. Let's listen. Let's get the panel to listen. Did she go for a lawsuit? No. She went to solve the problem, prevent it from happening again. The force has to be big enough to do the same."

"But there are programmes in place!" Kindle protested. "It's not like we've been neglecting our guys out there."

"Your programmes obviously aren't working. Shouldn't someone be trying to find out why not? The system should be revamped, to make use of all the information out there, on the way the human mind works, what makes us tick. And what about personality profiling? Crime is changing, the nature of criminals is changing. We have to change too. We have to make it work."

"I don't like it," Shrug said. "We're gonna blame the system for my bad decision?" That wouldn't gain him any brownie points.

"Why not?" Kraden asked. "If the setup had been different, you wouldn't have made that decision. If the Calgary officers had gotten the girl off the street instead of using her, the decision wouldn't even have been there for you to make."

"It doesn't feel right. I don't think it'll look good if I don't bear responsibility. That has to be in there somewhere."

"Yeah, they'll probably be looking for that," Henwood conceded. "Nothing would tick them off more than arrogance and denial." He paused, glancing at Kraden. "We'll work on it."

"Remember," Shrug said, "the Calgary stuff is out if upstairs puts the lid on. You won't have that to work with."

"We can work without it," Kraden said.

The two lawyers tucked their notes into their briefcases and escorted Shrug and Kindle to the door. After a round of handshakes, Shrug followed Kindle out of the law office and down the hall.

When the elevator door closed behind them, Kindle faced Shrug. Something had been niggling at him throughout the meeting. "Syd left me with the impression someone told him we didn't want those pictures brought to light. It wasn't you, was it? Were you talking to Syd and James during the investigation?"

"Syd and James?"

"Did you tell them we didn't want the photos up here?"

"For Christ's sake, Sarge. Don't even be thinkin' that!"

"I prefer a yes or no answer."

"If they don't keep a lid on it upstairs, I imagine—"

"It'll get worse?" Kindle let out a sharp-edged laugh.

"You wanted the woman to be credible, Sarge. A witness who'd talk, testify. You wanted convictions. You got all that."

"And I could lose it all. If there was a conspiracy to withhold evidence from the trial, the world will lose it all and everything the girl went through—everything *you* went through—will be for naught. And the three sons of bitches who killed a kid by slicing off his fingers one by one in front of the girl, will be back in the cocaine racket, making millions. Tell me that's not going to happen."

Shrug met his eyes. "That's not going to happen."

Kindle hoped to God Shrug was right.

"Hey, Sarge!" Chad shouted as Kindle strode past.

He had something to show his boss, something Kindle wouldn't like.

"Look at this." He turned the monitor.

Kindle squinted at the grainy picture. "What the heck is it?"

"It's supposedly a photo of the Crown's mystery child witness sitting in the King's Ace before the cops shut down the drug den."

"I know that. But why is it on your computer?"

"I found it surfing the net. Someone's claiming, 'Key Eyewitness had Secret Nightlife.'"

"Surfing the what?"

"It's on the Internet." Chad sighed. "You really ought to take some of those computer courses the force is offering. The Web's not much more than a plaything right now, but predictions are it's going to quickly become a powerful tool of commerce—and thus, crime."

"The *web*?"

Chad shook his head. "You gotta take a course, Sarge."

"So on this web of yours, is Katrina a plaything, commerce or a crime?"

"Gossip. Another great potential of the Internet. Gossip that's accessible around the world."

Kindle straightened. "So much for keeping a lid on it." He headed for the break room.

"I take it that it's true and you already knew about it?" Chad called out.

Kindle froze. He swiveled on one heel and was back at Chad's desk before either of them could blink. "Chad," he said. "The girl knew the victim. He'd been a friend of hers."

Chad couldn't wrap his mind around the horrific idea. "Katrina knew Lukas?"

Kindle nodded.

"Lukas was Katrina's friend."

Another nod.

"She watched her friend get slaughtered?"

"Chad, shush!"

"And you're still going to defend Shrug?"

"Keep your voice down."

"Beyond anything this may mean to you and Shrug, or even the trials, have you considered what this means to Katrina? Have you thought about how immeasurably more brutal this makes the murder?"

"Perhaps why the defence didn't raise the subject."

"I'm not thinking about the defence," Chad snapped. "I'm thinking about Katrina."

"Chad!" Kindle gave a nervous look around the room. "Let's take this to my office."

Fuming, Chad followed his boss. None of this seemed fair to the girl. It was so wrong. Dead wrong.

"Sit," Kindle ordered, closing his office door. "This isn't something that's just happened and it doesn't change anything that has happened. It's the way things always were."

Chad rubbed his hands over his face. "This isn't right, Sarge."

"I know you were close to the girl, but don't let emotions run wild here. Keep rational about it."

"That son of a bitch," Chad said between his teeth. "I hate Shrug."

"I said, control your emotions. It wasn't Shrug who murdered Lukas. That brutality wasn't his. He did all he could to prevent that kill from coming down."

"My point is he didn't do all he could to keep the girl out of it."

"That's being dealt with. Don't judge so harshly. Please."

"Why would you even want to defend him in front of the review panel?"

"We've been there before. You know why."

Chad stared at him, wondering how he could be so blasé. How would Kindle feel if he'd been forced to watch his friend slaughtered? He stifled his resentment. "Did Shrug know Katrina and Lukas were buddies?"

Kindle closed his eyes and gave a quick nod.

"So why didn't anyone else know until now?"

"That's being dealt with."

"What's the rest of the story?"

"Gator chose Lukas as the victim because he was Katrina's friend."

"*That* was the lie!"

Kindle scrunched his face in confusion. "Pardon?"

"Katrina lied about it on the stand. I knew she did. I told Debra she did. When she was asked why Lukas was chosen, she lied. And that means that son of bitch Shrug lied on the stand too."

"Not necessarily. They both said Lukas was chosen because he was in Traz territory with his meth and had insulted the bikers. That's true. He'd still be alive if he hadn't done that. Shrug and Katrina didn't lie about that."

"They might not have lied, but they withheld information." Chad let out an angry huff. "We're going to lose it all, Sarge. They're going to overturn the convictions."

CHAPTER 25

Kindle leafed through the daily paper, waiting in trepidation for the phone to ring. He'd decided Chad was right. He'd have to enrol in a computer course or two. The Internet was obviously a powerful source of information.

It had taken only two days for the photo of Katrina to appear above in-depth reports on the front pages of major newspapers across the nation. Everything was there, from Katrina secret past life to accusations that the police had withheld evidence, insinuations of a police cover-up, and even reports on the internal review on Shrug.

Kindle sighed. How had his biker operation, so full of good intentions and excellent results, taken on such a nasty flavour so quickly? It seemed such a short time ago his department was receiving columns of glowing praise.

The telephone rang. Kindle answered and moments later lumbered up the steps to his boss's office, the newspaper tucked under his arm.

He cast a quick glance at the Crown prosecutor sitting in one of Staff Sergeant Peters' guest chairs, then addressed his boss. "I swear it wasn't like this, sir. I ran a tight ship. Above board the whole way. Not only well within the law, but with an eye to appearances too. There was nothing shady about that operation. It was good intentions all around."

"You're not being called to task over it," Peters said, "but these media reports have to be dealt with."

"The bikers' attorneys have already said they're going to launch an appeal to the Supreme Court of Canada," the Crown prosecutor said, moving his chair to make more room as Kindle sat. "It's likely they'll be successful."

Kindle groaned. "Successful?"

"I'm not counting on them being successful in getting the convictions overturned. However, it's likely they'll at least get their case heard. Things are starting to add up for them. This," the prosecutor said pointing to the paper, "will probably make it for them."

"How so?" Peters demanded. "The defendants obviously knew of the girl's relationship with the victim. He was her boyfriend, a drug dealer, a drug user. And the girl herself was running with a gang. If they'd wanted to attack her reputation, it was all there for them."

"We'll be arguing that. But what about Shrug's reputation? Throw in a tarnished officer as the other key witness, the judge's refusal to reveal the girl's true identity, a conspiracy theory regarding the missing information about the girl's past and it starts to look very much like justice wasn't served."

"A conspiracy theory?" Kindle said.

The prosecutor nodded. "Aside from Shrug, there are two other undercover officers in Calgary who knew the witness. Yet during the entire investigation *and* the trials, not one of them thinks to make it known the victim and the girl were friends? Nobody turns over the incriminating King's Ace photos? Nobody investigates the girl's past and questions her motives? Then the judge won't reveal her identity, denying the defence a chance to investigate the kid themselves? Has *conspiracy*," he made finger quotes in the air, "written all over it."

"The defence was given what they needed to know about Katrina," Kindle said.

"Concealing her identity was unprecedented," the prosecutor argued.

"So was their crime!"

"Of which they were innocent until proven guilty."

"But it wasn't like that. I won't go into the girl's reasons for not telling. They should be obvious to everyone. But the Calgary officers had valid reasons too. There was a stack of undercover photos they had to sift through. They weren't looking for ones to help our case. The pics with the girl in them weren't of interest to their investigation. And Shrug's reasons?" Kindle glanced from Peters to the prosecutor. "Do either of you realize how hard those four years were for that man? What was harder on him than anything he did while riding with The Traz was what he wasn't allowed to do."

"What do you mean?" the prosecutor asked.

"The things Shrug had to let slide, in order to get past the small guys to set up the big ones. Think about it. Every one of the murder investigators who went into that Quonset needed counselling afterward to deal with what they saw there. And Shrug? After the murder, he has to go back and eat and sleep and play with the buggers who did it."

"You're excusing his behaviour?" Peters asked.

"Maybe. But by not revealing Katrina knew Lukas, Shrug was simply trying to let the girl keep one little corner of her sanity. Was withholding information an illegal thing? Perhaps. Immoral? I'll let you decide. In any event, where's the police conspiracy? I don't care what the papers say. Neither Shrug nor the girl ever lied about Lukas."

"We'll argue all that," the Crown prosecutor said. "But we have to address the issue of why the judge didn't recess when the girl broke down on the stand."

"What? They're saying the judge was in on the *conspiracy* too?"

"It could look suspicious. The defence had to forfeit a key part of Katrina's testimony because the judge wouldn't recess."

"They forfeited nothing," Kindle said. "There was not a thing stopping them from asking Katrina about Shrug's gun and the shot she fired."

"And risk offending the jury? They'd have looked like malicious bullies, as evil as their clients, if they'd badgered the innocent little witness who was sobbing her tiny, virginal heart out."

Peters stepped in. "Enough!"

"This is more than enough." Kindle tossed the newspaper on Peters' desk. "Too much! Usually when I get after one of my guys, his fellow officers are on my tail about not supporting the ground crew. With Shrug, they're after me for supporting him. I need some understanding here. I need some support. I'm fighting not only my own men, but the internal review board—and now the damned media."

"Sergeant Kindle," Peters said evenly. "I've always supported you one hundred percent. I apologize if I haven't made that clear. Just tell me what you need and it's yours."

Kindle studied his boss, then lowered his voice. "Sorry, sir. I should be the one apologizing. I've misspoken. But let me make it clear. It wasn't just emotional reasons driving Shrug to withhold that information. He wanted Katrina to be the valuable witness he knew she could be. But he also knew how traumatized she was. If she'd been confronted about Lukas being her friend, she'd have shut down. We wouldn't have gotten any info from her, no testimony."

"Oh, bloody hell, don't be tellin' me stuff like that," the prosecutor growled. "I'm not the defence lawyer. It won't help my case any to argue the police kept secrets from the defence so the witness who nailed them to the cross would be sure to testify."

"You're a lawyer." Kindle grabbed the newspaper from the desk. "Twist it around so it looks good. After all, everyone's managing to easily do the opposite. About time someone got on my side."

He stormed out of the office and slammed the door. The harsh echo reverberated off the walls and tiles, easing some of his tension.

CHAPTER 26

Division Headquarters, Edmonton, February 1999

"We're reserving our decision on Shrug's involvement with the minor until we finish investigating the matter of him withholding evidence," the chairman of the review panel said.

Sceptical, Kindle narrowed his eyes. "What you really mean is that you're reserving your decision in case there's a retrial and Shrug's needed as a credible witness again. After all, we wouldn't want our star witness to have a serious reprimand on file."

"It has nothing to do with that."

"Yeah, it does. I read it in the paper this morning." He was pushing his luck and he knew it, but it had to be said.

"Don't believe everything you read."

Kindle shrugged. "The entire rest of the population does."

"I'll get you some help dealing with the media pressure," the chairman replied, making a note. "To reduce some of the other pressure, we've ruled on your involvement with Shrug. We've found no wrong doing on your part. You're cleared."

"Thank you." Kindle stood.

The chairman raised a hand. "Wait, please. We've taken to heart your recommendation to better train our undercover officers and those who supervise them."

Okay. Where's this leading?

"And," the chairman said, "we're asking you to head up that training session."

"I see." Kindle's shoulders sagged.

"Don't view this as underhanded retribution. We're very impressed with your cooperation with this review, and your honesty, insight, the integrity you've displayed. In fact, it's those characteristics that make you the best man for this job."

"Am I not the best man for the job I'm in now?"

"All those good at their jobs, sir, get to that place in their careers where it's time to move from *doing* to *teaching*. Preparing the younger set to take up the torch. We want a brand new type of cop out pounding the streets, Sergeant Kindle. Ones that have been bequeathed your wisdom."

"Thanks for the compliment." Kindle straightened. "But there's lots of *doing* left in this old soul."

"Your name's already in," the chairman said. "Approved."

"I see."

"We received recommendations for special training from several people aside from you during our investigation. One of them being the young witness."

"Katrina? You talked to the girl?"

The chairman gave a nod. "We did a thorough investigation. Of course we talked to her. In fact, part of the funding for the course will come from her."

Kindle's mouth hung open in disbelief. "You're actually taking her up on that?"

"She's adamant."

Kindle blinked, stunned. *Of course she is. She wants something.*

CHAPTER 27

Northern Alberta Police Detachment, Edmonton, September 1999

Debra dropped the file on Chad's desk and turned to leave.

"Are you free tonight?" he asked, hoping she'd say yes.

She flashed him a smile. "Yeah. Why?"

They'd been dating for over a year and a half now. At the beginning of last year, shortly after the verdicts were in, he'd taken her to see *Schrödinger's Cat*, a sci-fi chick flick. She'd loved it. They'd gone to several more movies, weekend dinners, walks in the park. He'd taken her to meet his parents, and she'd introduced him to hers. Last weekend, she'd spent the night with him.

He was in love with the woman.

"I want to take you out. Somewhere special."

"How special?"

"Very special."

"I see." Her eyes sparkled. "I'll make sure I dress for it."

Under the subdued lighting of Zario's Fine Dining, Debra's shimmering gown appeared liquid. Iridescence rippled and eddied around the curves of her breasts and hips. It seemed to Chad she was damned near flowing across the floor. He watched, entranced, as she slipped into the private booth he'd reserved. He let his breath out slowly and then slid in beside her.

"God, you're beautiful," he whispered.

"Thank you."

He always felt Debra put her entire being into that brilliant smile of hers. And her hazel eyes—mesmerizing, deep and inviting. He was falling into them.

"Are you going to kiss me?" she murmured.

His lips touched hers. Honest and warm. Giving and taking. Their bodies, their minds, their souls, their lives—entwined.

The waiter cleared his throat and Chad drew back. He saw everything he wanted in Debra's eyes, including her desire.

"Your champagne, sir," the waiter said.

Chad struggled to keep his eyes off Debra as the waiter uncorked the champagne and poured him a sample. He tried to focus on the clarity and aroma, but Debra's warmth and the sensual scent of her perfume overrode his senses. He quickly nodded his approval and the waiter poured their champagne and then disappeared.

She laughed, a soft tinkling sound that reminded him of innocence and light.

"I love your giggle," he said.

"Is that why you're always making me laugh?"

"I never thought of that. Perhaps, that's it." He chuckled and reached into his jacket pocket. "Debra Ann Carter..." He opened the ring case and she peered over the rim of her glass, her eyes widening with surprise. "I love you. Will you marry me?"

"Yes," she whispered, her lip trembling. She set down the champagne glass. "Yes."

He slipped the ring on her finger. Their eyes met and then their lips.

It was only when the waiter slid two menus onto the table that Debra pulled away. "I love you, Chad."

"I'm glad you said yes."

"Were you afraid I wouldn't?"

"I was so scared you were going to back away again, in case we have to retry the bikers."

"You should've known better. I'm not going to let Shrug's bad decisions control my life forever."

"I...I sometimes feel I'm just someone to fill the empty place in your life where Shrug once was."

Debra sighed. "You should know better than that. My relationship with Shrug never did get off the ground."

"But you wanted it to."

"At one time I did, but Shrug no longer has what I want. You're honest, kind, gentle. You make me laugh and you love me. Shrug—he isn't any of that anymore." She paused and stared down at the ring on her finger. "Do you miss her?"

"Her?"

"Katrina." She looked up. "Sometimes when her name is mentioned, you get a faraway look in your eyes."

"I guess I miss her at times. I think about her often."

"So do I. And then I think of Shrug and Kindle and the review panel decision that's due to come down any day now."

"Debra, I didn't want to think about that tonight." He was tired of thinking about it.

"I'm sorry."

"It's okay," he said. "We can talk about it if you want to."

She took a small breath. "How do you think it will turn out?"

"In my opinion, Kindle should be okay. Shrug might've been able to get away with involving Katrina. But the concealing evidence shit afterwards will kill him."

"Don't you find it ironic the thing he does to make amends to the girl is what's going to sink him?"

"I don't feel sorry for him. First, he said his dedication to the undercover operation caused him to make the mistake of recruiting Katrina. Now he's saying his concern for the girl made him screw up the operation. Where was that concern when he first met her? It doesn't wash."

"Shrug got really messed up out there, Chad. Before he went undercover, he'd have been mortified if anyone had even suggested he might do things like that."

"I didn't know him from before."

"I know, and that's why it upsets me when you demean him. He wasn't like this before. I swear! He was kind, down-to-earth, had a keen sense of reality."

"The fact is, he's not like that now. Not anywhere close."

"Perhaps he just hasn't come back yet. He's looking at the world through two different sets of eyes, a biker's and a cop's. And he doesn't know which image is right. Give him a chance, Chad."

He shrugged. "All I know is he's not a good cop right now. But I'll lay off him—because you asked me to." *Because I don't want to argue tonight.*

CHAPTER 28

Chad Leslie's Residence, Edmonton, March 2000

Six months after giving Debra the ring, Chad broke their truce. He simply couldn't listen to one more moment of her defending Shrug. Last week, the disciplinary review panel had set the date to finally announce their findings regarding Shrug. Ever since then, it seemed all she wanted to talk about was Shrug.

"Maybe you should toss me the ring back!" he exploded one evening during supper. "It seems like ever since I gave it to you, all I hear about is Shrug. 'Shrug this' and 'Shrug that' and 'poor Shrug.' What the hell, Debra? Do you have an obsession with the man?"

She tossed her fork on the table and gaped at him. "What—where are you coming from? Shrug's a friend, a co-worker. And the review panel's giving its decision on him next week. A decision, may I remind you, that could affect us all, affect the bikers' appeals, affect a retrial if ordered." She twisted the engagement ring. "I'm not sure I want to live with this jealousy. Maybe we ought to call it off."

"It's not jealousy." He toned down his voice. "I sometimes get the feeling you wish I was Shrug. If being with him is what's going to make you happy—"

"Shrug wouldn't make me happy. We've been through that. But he is an important part of both our lives and if he's going to be off limits even in our conversations, I can't live with that!"

"Maybe what's bothering me more is how you talk about Katrina. It seems you're always defending Shrug, but running down the girl."

"She's trouble," Debra muttered.

"You're just saying that because of what Shrug told you about her. His opinion of her is warped. More warped than the opinion he has of himself."

"You complain I'm always defending Shrug, yet you're always defending the girl. Should I be jealous of her?"

"You don't have to worry about that."

"You don't know Katrina like Shrug does. And you don't know Shrug. I swear if you got to know him, you'd learn to like the man. Plus, you'd start to believe what he says about the girl."

"I spent several months with Shrug and Katrina on the biker compound. I got to know the girl quite well, thank you. And I have no desire to get to know Shrug better."

"Until you do, Chad, you're always going to be jealous of him. He's always going to be a thorn in our relationship. Please. Do it for me, Chad. For us. Take the time to get to know the man."

He was trapped. "Fine. But I won't ever like him."

CHAPTER 29

Donald Hayes' residence, Edmonton

Chad waited in trepidation on Shrug's doorstep. Over his protests, Debra had phoned Shrug and then sent Chad off to meet him with a bottle of wine.

For the entire three months they had been together in the gang, Shrug had thought up ways to humiliate him. When Chad had finally had enough and mouthed back at the man, his jaw had felt the hard edge of Shrug's fist. Chad knew it wasn't likely they'd ever become best buddies.

Shrug finally opened the door. "Hey."

There was an awkward moment on the front step.

"If you'd rather me not be here," Chad said, "I'll leave."

Shrug opened the door wider. "Drink?"

"Sure." Chad kicked off his shoes and followed him into the living room. "Debra says you're feeling a little down over this review panel thing next week."

Shrug turned off the TV. "Sit."

"Things not looking too good for you?"

"Yeah."

As badly as Debra wanted him to get to know Shrug, Chad figured Shrug's one-word answers proved he wasn't of the same mind.

There's not much I can do if the man's not going to cooperate.

He glanced at his watch, wondering if Debra had a timeline in mind regarding this visit.

"Wine?" Shrug offered. "Or beer?"

"Wine's good."

Shrug disappeared into the kitchen. Chad heard him rummaging in a drawer, presumably looking for a cork screw.

"Congratulations on your engagement," Shrug called.

"Thank you," Chad yelled back. "Wow," he mumbled, "four whole words in a row—and two of them more than four letters long."

Shrug returned, set a six-pack of beer on the coffee table and handed Chad a glass of wine. "Be good to her." He flicked open a can of beer for himself and sat.

"Debra tells me you've known each other a long time."

"Yeah."

Great. Back to one-word sentences. "How long?"

"We were in depot together."

"She didn't tell me you took your training together. Was she good?"

"Good?" Shrug raised his brows and smirked.

Chad clenched the wineglass. "Good at the cop training, Shrug."

"Yeah, she did good." Shrug picked at the tab on his beer can. *Ting, ting.*

"You ever love her?"

"You come here to fight?" Shrug drawled.

With his eyes glued to his beer, he slowly raised the can to his lips, leaned back his head and drained it. A quick move of his right hand and the can became a tiny bundle of aluminum disappearing beneath his fingers.

"I'm a hell of a lot bigger man than you, Chad. It would be really smart on your part not to keep pissin' me off."

"I'll take that as a yes and shut up." He gulped his wine and again checked his watch. "Shit. That only took four minutes."

"What?"

"Debra sent me here to cheer you up."

"You ever cheer anyone up before? 'Cause you're really bad at it."

Chad chuckled. "Hey, big guy, could you get me some more of that wine? I figure I have to stay here at least forty-five minutes if I ever want to kiss Debra again."

Seconds later, Shrug set the bottle of wine in front of Chad and opened another beer. "It's gotta be worth it, I'd say. Forty-five minutes with me for a kiss from her."

Chad gave Shrug a wary look. There was a dreamy look on the man's face, as if he were contemplating the pleasure of a kiss from Debra.

You do want to fight, don't you? You'd love to take a round out of me and make yourself look good in Debra's eyes. I'll look like a snivelling, battered—I won't fall for it.

"She says you were a good cop before your stint with The Traz," he said. "Says you're different since those four years undercover with the gang."

"That surprise you, Chad? That I'd be different after four years with

The Traz? That a novel idea for you?"

"Yeah, it does surprise me. It surprises me that a good cop could recruit a thirteen-year-old girl into a biker gang. And it really surprises me a good cop could withhold evidence from a murder investigation. What has to happen in four years to change you that much? I can understand the cigarettes. I can see the cussing. Hell, even the lack of bathing, but withholding evidence? What happens to get you down that low?"

"I thought you knew the girl."

"Katrina? Yeah, I know her." *Where's he going with this?*

"Then you have your answer, don't you?"

Chad slammed the wineglass down on the table.

"What?" Shrug asked innocently.

"What I have to say might piss you off, but I gotta say it."

"Go ahead. I won't hit you, if that's what you're thinkin'."

"How the hell do you justify blaming the girl for what you did? Where are you coming from, for Christ's sake?"

"I'm not blaming her, like 'it's her fault.' I mean, she can't help the way she is, but she—" Shrug stopped short, shaking his head. "When you're with her long enough, you do things for her. She gets you to do things for her."

"Really."

"Kinda like how Debra got you to come here tonight."

"That's different. That's a man/woman thing. You've said it wasn't like that—"

"They say men are just little boys in grown-up bodies, but girls are grown women in child's bodies."

"She wasn't a woman."

"Nope. She was a girl. But girls always have it over us." Shrug stood up. "More wine?"

"I'll go for a beer."

Shrug held out the six-pack. "Go ahead."

Chad plucked a can from the box and rolled it between his palms. Then he popped the tab.

"You knew her in the gang," Shrug said. "Didn't you notice?"

"Notice? Like how she got others to do stuff for her? I noticed she was always trying to manipulate me. She hated that I caught her at it all the time."

"You're saying she wasn't able to manipulate you?"

"She tried, but I think I'm the one who did most of the manipulating."

"She let you think you manipulated her, did she?" Shrug chuckled. "You must've had a lot more of what she wanted than I had."

"I got what I wanted from her. She got what she wanted from me."

"What is it you think she wanted?"

"To get out of there alive. To be kept safe afterwards. Hell, I don't know. Maybe she wanted to suck up to me to avoid criminal charges. What does it matter?"

"Yeah, I guess it wouldn't matter to you."

Chad heard the challenge in his voice. "What don't I know, Shrug?"

"If she was wantin' out, she could've got out without you. I tried to get her out of there a half-dozen times. She wouldn't leave."

"Why not?"

"Obviously she liked what was on the inside better than what was outside."

"It wasn't the drugs inside that she liked, I hope."

"Never saw her use drugs. Only people." Shrug gave him a knowing smile. "She was exceptionally *good* at usin' people. That was somethin' I knew the moment I saw her. Figured I'd better ask her to ride with me, 'cause if I didn't and she started workin' for the other side, I'd lose the whole battle. I shouldn't have, though—shouldn't have asked her. Bin regrettin' that day ever since, and not for the reasons you're thinkin'. Not for any legal-type reasons or moral reasons, but for my own sanity reasons."

"What do you mean?"

"Let me tell you a story," Shrug began. "The Traz lost this huge shipment of coke to—well, not really—another gang. More like a group of businessmen with rather shady businesses. Hijacked the lot from us. Of course, we wanted it back. We knew who did it, but we didn't know where they stashed it. We wanted it back, and then we wanted revenge. So a bunch of us were out there hittin' the street, tryin' to find some tracks to follow." Shrug paused, lounged back and cast his eyes to the ceiling.

"I stop the Harley and tell Sarina, 'See that office tower? There's a guy in there who knows it all.' It was the head office of one of these businessmen. 'Who's the guy that knows?' she asks. I give her the guy's name—Robert Lawson. She gets me to go around the block and tells me to stop when we're in front of the building."

Shrug took a long pull on his beer and drained the can. Reaching for another he said, "So she says, 'Bob and I are gonna have a talk.' And she hops off the bike. This is a fancy building. I think they even have valet parkin'. At least there's some guy standin' outside the door in a hokey uniform. She's wearin' my Traz jacket."

"Why is she wearing your jacket?"

"Basically, because she wants to. I wouldn't buy Sarina her own jacket."

"Why not?"

"I wasn't gonna go into the cycle shop and ask for a size two biker jacket." Shrug paused. "I guess there were some things she couldn't make me do. Anyways, she did have my jacket on that day. It was down past her knees, just a little big."

"What happened," Chad asked.

"I holler to her, 'Take the jacket off!' Not because I thought it didn't look good on her. I'm no fashion expert that way. But Jesus, man, you don't walk into a fancy place like that with a biker jacket on. And she thinks she's gonna talk to 'Bob'? Like, right, she's gonna get past reception. Lucky if she gets past that valet guy. Lucky if she walks out alive."

"What did she do?"

"She stands and looks at me. 'Take the jacket off!' I repeat. 'No,' she says. Just like that. 'No.' I'm so mad at her I—" Shrug straightened and scowled at Chad.

"You wanted to strangle her?" Chad chuckled.

"She weighs what, ninety pounds? I get off the bike. I'm gonna rip that jacket off her back. Then she's off like a rabbit. Up these fancy brick stairs, past the little fountains. She runs right by the valet guy. Hell, he sees this little thing runnin' toward him with this huge biker dude after her, I think he even opened the door for her."

"What did you do?"

"I'm so fuckin' mad! I get on my bike and take off. I'm leavin' her there. I don't give a shit. I'm just leavin'." Shrug lifted the beer and guzzled. "I was probably lucky she hadn't started screamin' rape as she ran up them stairs."

"Yeah, you were lucky."

Shrug sighed. "Anyway, after about an hour, I cool down a bit and start to worry about her. I mean, like, she's thirteen years old, right? And she's wearin' a Traz jacket, and she's talkin' to 'Bob' about a missing $100,000 cocaine shipment. A guy starts to worry."

"So you went back?"

"Yeah. I go back, but she's nowhere in sight. I go down the street, and up and down the alley. Around and around, tryin' not to draw attention to myself, for a good fifteen minutes. Then all of a sudden she's there. Just like that, she hops on the bike. I swear she was hidin' somewhere and watchin' me hunt for her."

Chad set his empty on the coffee table.

Shrug frowned. "Need another beer?"

"Sure." He had the man talking. Debra would be happy.

Shrug motioned to the last can in the six-pack. "Help yourself. Anyway, I'm just fumin' again. I take off on the bike, and we ride. Ever put a Harley through its paces? Finally, I stop and I turn to her. 'Don't you ever do that to me again!' I say. She just looks at me, stupid-like. So I say, 'Do you understand, woman? Don't ever do that again!' She drops her eyes and sits quiet for about twenty seconds. Then she says in her little-girl voice, 'Are you finished yellin', now?'

Chad smiled. "I can see her doing that."

"How could I stay mad?"

"Did she get her chat with Bob?"

"She wouldn't tell me that day, but yeah. Later she told me. She finds Bob's name on the building directory and goes up to his office and walks in, up to the receptionist. She says, 'Tell Bob The Traz is here to see him.' Then she turns around and points to the letters on the back of the jacket."

Chad was captivated by the story. He had no trouble visualizing Katrina wrangling her way past the receptionist.

"Sarina has ears like a—what has good ears? Whatever it is, her ears are like that. She hears the woman say to her boss in the back office, 'There's a girl out there. Says to tell you Traz is here to see you.' The guy says, 'Traz?' I have to see this. Send her in.'"

"Then what?"

"God, I need a cigarette." Shrug patted his pockets. "Shit! You have a cigarette?"

"I don't smoke. Tell me what she said to him."

"She walks in and sits down quickly, before he even invites her to. She's an expert at stealing control of a situation. Before he says a thing, she pipes up, 'So Bob, where's the Melrose shipment?' The guy asks her what she's talking about. 'Maybe you know it as the $100,000 worth of cocaine you stole from The Traz biker gang last Thursday,' she says. 'They've sent me to find it.' The poor guy doesn't know what to say. He realizes she knows what she's talkin' about. She's told him enough. He just can't, for obvious reasons, believe the bikers have sent her to get it."

"So what did he tell her?" Chad asked.

"Nothin'. Neither of 'em says a thing. They start that starin' thing she does, sizin' each other up. Then Bob finally says, 'You think I'm gonna tell you?' Sarina's tellin' me this story and she turns to me and says, 'Of course I know he's not gonna tell me. But he doesn't know I'm lookin' around. I can see out the corners of my eyes. I read everythin' on the wall, his little sticky paper notes. I read the letter he has in front of him on his desk. I read all his appointments in his little day timer thing. When the receptionist left her desk to tell him I was there, I read the carbon copies in her telephone message book.'

Shrug looked past Chad and grinned. "She could do that you know. It's like she has a camera in her head. She could tell me word for word what every plaque in that office said. She kept it all up here." He tapped his temple. "Every name and phone number. I bet if you asked her today, she could recite them all back for you."

"I know. You told me before."

"You sure you don't have a cigarette?" Shrug scowled. "A cigar?"

"No."

Shrug inhaled and exhaled noisily. "So then—get this—she says, 'My father's a cop. He sure would be interested to know Ken called you three times last Thursday.' And she leaves."

"Who's Ken?"

"She has no idea. But those were the last three calls in the message book before the night the shipment went missin'."

"So later you're sitting on the bike and...?"

"Yeah. I don't know any of this Bob-stuff then, eh? She just says, 'Take me to the library and come get me in three hours. I'll have some addresses for you to check out.'"

"Did you?"

"Yeah. When we get there, Sarina climbs down from the bike, takes off my jacket and hands it to me. Then she says, 'And this time, be here to pick me up.' So I go back in three hours and she hands me a paper with three addresses on it. 'I'm pretty sure it's the first one,' she says. 'But we can check them all out.'"

Chad finished his beer and set the empty with the others. "Where'd she get the addresses?"

"She goes on the Internet, the phonebook, the reverse directory, the city map. Finds who's all involved as directors and stuff for Bob's company. Finds out what properties they own. Finds the names and address of all those phone numbers she has in her head. Looks at the map and decides if she were hidin' a shipment of coke, in which of these places would she put it?"

"Did she find out who Ken was?" Chad asked.

"Yeah, he was a partner in one of the other shady businesses that was probably involved in the drug heist. So anyways, we get to the first address and sure enough it's a warehouse. And she says, 'Ah, bonus!' She's pointin' to a high-rise goin' up next door. 'It's gotta be here,' she says. 'It's just too perfect. Who's gonna notice anything at the warehouse with all those construction people comin' and goin'? And that equipment, the noise.'"

Shrug crumpled his empty beer can and added it to the collection growing on the coffee table. "We see a couple of guys in the warehouse yard. So we go to Canadian Tire and buy a hard hat, steel-toed boots— whatever. Sarina says, 'I want you to walk over to the warehouse and scream at those idiots about parkin' in your guys' spots and gettin' in the way of your machines. Say stuff like, 'Didn't you get the message yesterday?' and see what you can find out.'"

"Seriously?" Chad squinted, trying hard to imagine Katrina and Shrug together on a shopping trip. "Did you do what she said?"

"Yeah. But she didn't let me wear the tool belt. She said it looked too new." Shrug reached for the last beer. "Too bad. I always wanted to wear one of those things. She kinda scuffed up the other stuff, but she said the belt was still too obvious."

"Find out anything?"

"Yeah. The guys were so nervous, kept flickin' their eyes behind them. The closer I marched toward the warehouse, the more vicious they became. They didn't like me suggestin' I might call to cops on them for trespassin' on my job site. When I maneuvered myself between them and the warehouse, I could tell I was seconds away from a meetin' with their fists. I figured I had what I needed so I left, all the while hollerin' back at them about what idiots they were."

"You just left?"

"That's the nice thing about biker work versus cop work. In The Traz, I didn't have to prove nothin'. A hunch was as good as DNA for establishin' guilt and meritin' punishment. I walk around the corner and climb back on the bike, ready to round up the gang and plan the takeover. But Sarina says, 'Shrug, could you do somethin' for me? Could we just call the cops and tell them where it is?' I couldn't believe her. 'Why would I do that?' I ask. 'There's $100,000 of mine in there.' She says, 'If the cops get the coke and Bob and Ken, that's kind of revenge isn't it? I don't want Biker revenge. I don't want that again.' She meant like what had happened with Lukas."

Chad shivered. "I get it. What did you do next?"

"Called the cops. Suited me. Got the shit off the street. Traz never found out what I'd done, though they knew the cops had gotten the stuff. That pissed them off. Bonus part was the thieves were safe from biker retaliation, behind bars. Bonus for the thieves and Homicide, anyhow."

"You're sure this story's true?"

"Well, for sure the parts of it I was there for are the truth. Honest. I don't know for sure what happened in Bob's office, but how else would she get addresses?"

"Wasn't she scared Bob would suspect she'd had a hand in the police action? She told him her father was a cop."

"What did she care? Bob was in jail. She's got the gang behind her. Then I tried to get her out. Because, like you are always remindin' me, she was a thirteen-year-old child."

"God, it's hard to remember that when you're hearing the story."

"It was a very long story, Chad. For me it lasted a year. How hard do you think it was for me to remember she was thirteen?"

They sat in silence for a while, savouring cold Pilsner and revisiting their favourite parts of the story. At some point Shrug went and got them more beer.

Finally, Chad said, "How did she keep herself safe? I mean, even before The Traz—at the King's Ace? Didn't she get bothered?"

"You look at her, she's a kid. Harmless. Looks seven, ten at max. Bikers and drug dealers are a lot of things, but most of them aren't paedophiles. Besides, she always made sure she had big friends, or in the case of the King's Ace, cop friends." Shrug chuckled. "And Syd and James thought they were usin' her. Hell, she got way more from those two than she ever gave back."

Shrug nodded to the beer on the table. "Drink up, buddy. You're falling way behind me." He popped open two beer and passed one to Chad. "Sarina was just a kid, until you saw her in action. Then you'd get confused. I didn't have any trouble between her and the guys in the compound for the first couple of months. The guys had seen her in action once too often. They began sensin' she was a she-devil. She was startin' to piss them off. They're used to punchin' out people who piss them off. What were they to do with her, though?"

"What'd she do to piss them off?"

"Everythin' from wearin' their jackets to antagonizin' their women. I'd give her shit. She'd rile things up like a hornet's nest. Like I said, I tried to get her out a half-dozen times, for my benefit more than hers."

"You couldn't control her? Come on. She was four-foot nothing and ninety pounds."

"Yeah, right. I couldn't even get a fricken jacket off her. How the hell am I going to get her out of there when she doesn't want to go?"

"But Gator got her, eh?"

"Yup." Shrug stared off into space, all amusement gone from his eyes. "Gator got her. That mean son of a bitch! Shit! He was every bit as smart as she was, but he was triple the evil. Sure, Sarina stirred things up and stuff, but mostly she was just doin' it to survive. You and me, if we piss each other off, we duke it out, but what's she gonna do when a three-hundred -pound ugly son of a bitch gets on her case?"

"I dunno. What'd she do?"

"She'd busy herself with gettin' a four-hundred-pound son of bitch angry enough at the other guy to take a round out of him on her behalf, though neither knew that's why they were dustin' their knuckles. Gator, though, wasn't mean in order to survive. Gator was evil because he just plain *wanted* to be evil."

"What did Gator have against Katrina?"

"Ah, Jesus, man," Shrug said, rubbing his head. "Let's not go there."

"You've gotta tell me this, Shrug. How much did she have to do with choosing Lukas as the victim?"

"Don't even think such shit! Lukas was her buddy. That bit about her bein' mad at the boy, or fightin' with him, or whatever—that's bullshit. She let him go because he got too heavy into meth and got mean. She still had a soft spot for him, no doubt. They had the same troubles at home. He chose his way to deal with it, she chose hers. It bothered her lots that he got so lost. Think about it, Chad. She was upset he's doin' meth, so she's sure as hell gonna be upset about him bein' tortured and murdered." He shook his head. "I should've let her shoot the bastards."

Shrug stood up and disappeared into the kitchen. He returned a minute later with another six-pack of beer.

"Well, I guess she sort of got even with Gator," Chad said. "She got him behind bars, right?"

"I hope the Court keeps him there. I thought I'd lost her after the murder." Shrug hiccupped. "She was out of it. Devastated. Did I ever tell you she didn't move for three days? She didn't talk. She didn't cry. She went into a...trance thing and stayed there. Hell, I don't think she even took a piss. What was I supposed to do, Chad?"

"I dunno."

"I couldn't handle the slaughter and I hadn't even been there when it happened. Even those cops that investigated the scene, they couldn't take what they saw. And, Chad, this was her friend...her *friend*. What was I supposed to do? I'm tryin' to, like, revive her or whatever. I tell her, 'Talk to me. Talk to me.' I say, 'Let's talk about the weather, or somethin', but she says nothin'.'"

Chad could swear Shrug was fighting back tears. "We don't have to—"

"Finally, she starts talkin'. She goes on about how it's her fault it was Lukas. If it wasn't for her, it wouldn't have been Lukas. If she hadn't told anyone about Lukas, Gator wouldn't have known. It was all her fault. So I'm listenin' and I don't remember how it all went, but she got me to promise not to ever talk about Lukas again. The only way she could get out of bed was if she never talked about it again. She was never gonna think about it. She wasn't his friend. Didn't know him—or somethin'." Shrug paused for another swig of beer. "What was it you asked?"

"I didn't ask anything."

"No, when you first came. You asked what could happen in four years to change me. Hell, I probably would've been fine if it hadn't been for the last year, after I met Sarina. Have another beer there, buddy. You know how pissed she is I'm actually a cop?"

"I didn't know she was pissed."

"She's pissed. She gets even when she's pissed. Kindle says, 'No, she's not gettin' even. She's a sweet little girl. She's thirteen. You're so screwed, Shrug.' She's not gettin' even? Yeah, right. What the hell is that 'Here's $100,000 to train your officers' thing, huh? What's that? Gettin' even. That's what it is. Shit, if I hadn't taken her to the compound, she'd have busted my neck. And next week, the concealin' evidence crap—does she care that I'll lose my job? Shit, no. She's hopin', probably prayin' to the devil, I do. She's not gonna say nothin' to stop it."

"You don't like her, so why'd you do it for her? Conceal the evidence?"

"I did it because I figured I owed her. I had to at least keep that promise. After all, wasn't she a little girl that I kidnapped? A little virgin girl? It was really *my* fault, wasn't it, that her friend..." He shrugged. "You know. Once she got out and knew how I felt, she decided to use my sense of obligation to get even with me for leavin' her in that Quonset. Next week, I'm out of here..."

By this point, Chad had noticed Shrug's slurred speech. Hell, he was feeling no pain either.

Shrug scratched his head. "What was your question?"

"Why'd you do it for her?"

"No, the question you asked when you first got here?"

"I can't remember that long ago. Do you miss her?"

"No, can't say I do," Shrug said. "I wish I had missed her a long time ago."

"You wanted her on your side, remember?"

Shrug stared at a hole in the bottom of his sock.

"Where do you think she's going to end up, Shrug. Which side?"

"Whichever side it is, it will be the winnin' one."

"Was she ever on your side?"

"Sarina's always on her own side. Whichever side suits her at the moment." Shrug sighed. "She's sure not on my side now."

"You can't really expect her to be. She was only thirteen,"

"Always boils down to that one fact."

"You think she should stick up for you at the panel hearing, take some of the heat for her part in the cover-up?"

"Dream on. That girl won't ever say anything good about me."

"Does she owe you something, Shrug? Does she owe you loyalty?"

"That's where I went wrong, Chad. Truth is, no one owes nobody anything. No one's beholden to nobody. She was with the gang because she wanted to be. I was there 'cause I wanted to be. She got me stuff I wanted. I gave her what she needed to survive. In the end, it was even."

Chad popped open another beer and waited. It was several minutes before Shrug continued.

"Nope. She doesn't owe me loyalty. But I don't owe it to her, either. And I don't owe her my career. I should've just told you guys right off the bat that she knew Lukas and they were friends. Lukas was chosen *because* he was Sarina's friend. I should've said that, because what did I owe her? I mean, after all, it was just one terrible night out of a whole year together, right? And, hey, the murder wasn't my fault, right? I figure her and I were even by the end of it all."

"No, you weren't even. You were the adult. You were the one responsible. You owed her big time for what you put her through."

Shrug banged his can on the table. "Exactly! I owed her. So don't ever again be askin' me why I concealed evidence!"

Confused and reeling from the alcohol, Chad blinked. The books on the shelf behind Shrug were blurry, dancing. The floor lamp in the corner appeared doubled. *Shit. I've obviously had way too much to drink.*

It was well after two in the morning when Debra showed up to rescue him. By then, Shrug's stories about life in The Traz were all sounding noble and heroic.

CHAPTER 30

Chad Leslie's residence, Edmonton

The next day was a very unpleasant one for Chad. Painful. Even lying absolutely still in bed didn't help.

"You weren't supposed to go there and get sloshed," Debra scolded from inside the bedroom door. "You were supposed to go there, have a few sips of wine and make Shrug feel better."

"If there's any justice in the world," he said with a groan, "Shrug will be feeling worse than I am."

"This is the first weekend we've both had off for months. I was looking forward to doing something together. Why did you have to get so drunk?"

"Debra, come here." He patted the bed. "Shrug and I hate each other. Drinking together was the only way we could be in the same room together without killing each other."

The motion of the bed as she curled beside him sent his stomach and head spinning. "This isn't working." He rushed to the bathroom.

"Chad!" he heard her call between heaves. "I'm going out for some fresh air."

It was late when Chad heard Debra return and saw the hall light flick on. He struggled out of bed and shuffled into the kitchen. Debra was on the phone, but she hung up just as he flopped down at the table.

"I'll take some coffee now," he said, his voice hoarse. "Who were you talking to?"

"No one." She poured him a mug and joined him. "I wanted to talk to Shrug to see if he's doing any better than you, but he's not answering his phone."

"Oh." He held the mug under his nose. It smelled like something that might stay down.

"He didn't seem as drunk as you last night."

"He's a better actor." He took a sip. It tasted good. "I'm going to find out if they'll let me visit Katrina."

"Why? Because of something Shrug said?"

"He told me stuff about the girl I didn't know before."

"I don't think it's a good idea to go visiting her. You shouldn't be stirring things up. She's trying to get her life back together. Let her go."

"Shrug's trying to get his life back too."

"And how is your visiting Katrina going to help Shrug?"

"She might be able to influence the review panel."

"Shrug's career isn't her problem. You've said that yourself. I don't know what he said to convince you otherwise, but he's got to take the heat alone on this one. Leave the girl out of it."

Chad stared into the mug. "I can almost see where he's coming from."

"Where he's coming from? It might have sounded great after thirty beers, but going after the girl just isn't right."

"She's a master manipulator."

"I know that, but what's your point?"

He looked at her. "Katrina's manipulations are screwing up the careers of four officers and she gets to walk away and start a new life." He snapped his fingers. "Just like that?"

"She was thirteen when she was manipulating. So yes, she gets to."

He swirled his coffee. Relieved that his head didn't spin with it, he took another tentative sip.

"Shrug's a master manipulator too, you know," Debra said. "He had to be, for what he was doing. Now, though, they both have to get real and quit blaming each other. They have to stop playing their silly games and move on."

Chad nodded, then said, "Katrina set Shrug up with the concealing evidence thing to get even with him for the way he treated her. She wasn't all that upset about the fact Lukas was her friend, but she knew Shrug's promise not to tell would eventually cause him major problems."

"How do you know that? How do you know how upset she was or wasn't? You weren't there, Chad—"

"I was there a few months after the murder, and she was so damned cool and collected it didn't even cross my mind she could possibly be the murder witness. If she—"

"I thought you said she woke up all the time screaming from nightmares?"

"Not *all* the time. And she didn't seem to have any issues during the day."

Debra shook her head. "Whether she set him up or not, doesn't matter. I think it's obvious she couldn't have set him up if he hadn't let her. Besides, look what Shrug set *her* up for."

"He'll pay for what he did. I just don't think he should also pay for what he did to protect her. He withheld evidence for her sake. She ought to—"

"In the biker world it was every man for himself. You know that, Chad. It's not like that now. Shrug will be judged on the standards of his profession, not any biker code of ethics. That's common sense." She studied him for a moment. "What the hell did Shrug tell you that's got you convinced the girl is the problem?"

"He told me lots of stuff."

"Chad, listen to me! As a woman, I know of what I speak. You don't want to tangle with the girl, for whatever reasons. Protect your sanity, Chad. Protect your career. Stay away from her."

"You're doing it again, Debra—carping on the girl."

She sighed. "At least promise me you'll sober up before you pursue your crazy idea of chasing down Katrina. Please, don't go messing with things because of something Shrug told you when you were both too drunk to walk."

"I walked."

"Stumbled, maybe. It wasn't really walking, believe me."

On Monday around noon, Chad closed his office door, making sure it clicked. *Time to track down Katrina. Cooper will know how to reach her.*

He picked up the receiver, knowing he probably shouldn't be using his office phone, but it *was* his lunch break.

When Cooper found out who was calling, Chad had to speak fast to keep him from hanging up. "Would you at least ask her if she would meet with me? Just ask her?"

Chad had no idea where Katrina had disappeared with her new identity, but despite Cooper's protests to the contrary, he was damned sure her ex-guardian knew.

"She wants to leave that all behind her," Cooper said. "Unless this is official police business, you're not talking to her."

"I'd like to hear *her* say that. After all she's an adult now, responsible for her own decisions."

Cooper gave a wry chuckle. "The papers can say whatever they want. She's no adult, believe me."

"She was adult enough to swing that witness protection deal. I think she's adult enough to decide if she'll talk to me. Just ask her. If she says no, I'll drop it. I promise."

Twenty minutes later, Cooper called back. "She'll meet you tomorrow at 1:00 in the Grande Hotel lobby. I want to reiterate, I'm not pleased with her decision. Are you sure this isn't about the Supreme Court appeal? If it is, I want her to have a lawyer present."

"I told you before, I'm not after an official meeting. This is strictly personal."

"She's only seventeen!" Cooper warned.

"Eighteen."

"Not for another couple of months."

"It's not that kind of personal. I'm an engaged man, for Christ's sake. I'm not looking to seduce the child."

"Her tender age hasn't seemed to matter much to the police in the past."

When Cooper slammed down the phone, Chad pulled the receiver away from his ear and winced. He didn't hang up until the dial tone kicked back in. It seemed to somehow soften the rejection.

Katrina was sprawled on the sofa in the hotel lobby, staring up at the ceiling, when Chad first spotted her. Although she didn't look like the twenty-two-year-old she was said to be, she no longer looked like a pre-teen, either.

"Hello, Katrina," he said.

She looked up as he approached. The youthful innocence that had captured his heart in The Traz was gone. Her blue eyes were cold and steely.

He stopped in front of her. "How are you doing?"

"I'm okay."

"Would you like to go out for a walk?"

"No," she replied, distant. "Sit.

"Thanks for meeting with me."

He took a seat on the high-backed, cushiony lobby chair across from her. His well-planned spiel designed to coerce a petulant teen, no longer seemed appropriate.

"We all miss you back at the station."

Katrina shrugged, as though she either didn't believe him or didn't care.

"You miss us?" he ventured.

"No, I'm too busy to miss anybody."

"What are you busy doing?"

"I'm going for my degree in computer sciences. We're into final exams right now."

"Good for you. Computers are one thing I don't know much about."

"I know everything about them."

He smiled. "I can believe that. I'm guessing you did okay on the high school diploma exams after the trials?"

"Nothing less than honours."

"How many years until you graduate?"

"A few more semesters. I was able to condense the program. They let me challenge some of the courses. If I pass the exams, I don't have to sit through their inane chatter." She cast him a quick grin. "I haven't flunked yet."

"What do you want to do once you've got your degree?"

She lowered her eyes and fingered the ribbon on her sleeve. "I don't know."

For reasons he couldn't pinpoint, Chad had the uneasy feeling she was lying. He cleared his throat and settled back in his chair. "Do you like computer sciences?"

"Yes. It's very fascinating."

Her cool responses were not what he'd been expecting and it was beginning to seem like a very bad idea to meet with her.

"So" she said, "do you like what you're doing?"

"Sure."

"Still going undercover?"

"No, I'm onto other things."

"Why? You were good at it."

"Not really." He tilted his head and grinned. "You spotted me right away. Remember? Not an encouraging sign, in my books."

Katrina shrugged. "Nobody else caught on."

"It only takes one person."

She looked past him. "I guess I wasn't too good either, considering you knew me right off the bat."

"You were a hell of a lot better than me, Katrina."

"Shrug was the best of us all. I think he even beat out Gator." She settled her gaze on the chandelier above them. "I hate what Shrug did, but one can't help but admire his ability to do it."

"He faces the panel next week, regarding recruiting you and withholding evidence."

"Good for him." Keeping her eyes on the ceiling, she leaned back and rested her sneakers on the coffee table.

"I don't think it's going to be good for him."

"Good."

What the hell does she mean, good? "I can't read your mind like I used to."

"I've been practising that."

"Can you still read *my* mind? Have you been practising that part too?"

"Let's see." She dropped her chin to her chest and closed her eyes. "You're here to ask me to do something to help Shrug." Her eyes sprang open.

Before he could reply, she dropped her feet to the floor and leaned toward him. Her blue eyes gleamed behind narrow slits. Her cheeks reddened. Every muscle in her face tensed. "What isn't coming to me, Chad, is why the hell you'd think I'd want to."

"Because I thought maybe...perhaps, you'd want to because you had a hand in getting him into this pickle. Maybe—"

"You think it's my fault he's in trouble? That's an interesting way to look at it."

"Katrina, he did it for you. He let you keep your secret—*and* your sanity."

"Really? That's what he told you?"

"Well? It's true, isn't it?"

"There are many reasons things happen, and they don't all come back to me. I'm not the master cause of the universe."

Chad took a deep breath. "The universe?"

"A few short months ago, you didn't have anything good to say about Shrug. What the hell did he say to change your mind?"

"Lots of stuff."

"Yeah, right. I can well imagine."

"You're saying he's been lying to me?"

"I don't know what the hell he told you, so how can I say he lied? I'm not *that* good at reading minds."

"He told me he tried to get you out of the gang several times and you wouldn't go."

She stared at him, stone-faced. "What else?"

"He told me stories about how you manipulated everyone, including him."

"You have one huge blind spot, Chad. Are you an idiot not to see?"

"See what?"

"You don't get it, do you?" She slid forward to the edge of the sofa.

"Get what?"

"Idiot! I'll explain it to you slowly. Listen. I-did-not-know-Shrug-was-a-cop."

"Oh."

"Do you know when it was Shrug first started pressuring me to leave the gang?"

Chad shook his head.

"*After* we'd chased down a missing coke shipment and I phoned the cops on the find, instead of letting The Traz take it back."

The fire in her eyes was dangerously close to being doused with tears and Chad felt his own eyes getting moist.

She blinked. "Do you know how scared that made me? I do something like that and whammo! Next thing I know, he wants me gone? He wants me far from the only people in the entire world who care about me. Out of the sight of anyone who might have an inkling to protect me. I'm thinking, chase me outta here, never to return, find my body under a sand dune. That's what I'm thinking."

She clenched her hands. "The more powerful he got, the more scared I got. He needed me less. Maybe not at all. I was just a kid. What gang leader wants to be babysitting a girl child? Him pressuring me to leave made no sense. Why would a biker want a murder witness to walk off into legal land? The only sense I could make of it was he wanted to get me away from the couple of bikers I had managed to befriend, so I'd be an easier target for a kill. Who the hell would've been there on the outside to protect me?"

She straightened and glared at him. The tears were gone, her eyes an icy blue. "But you knew all this, Chad. What the hell did that man say to you to get it to slip from your mind?"

"I'm sorry," he offered lamely.

"I thought Shrug was a biker. I thought I was manipulating a biker, to survive. So how the hell does that somehow make *me* evil? How does it make his problems mine?" She stood, wiped her palms down her pant legs and walked away.

He thought the conversation was over, but before reaching the elevator door, she whirled around. "The panel has talked to me. Shrug's going to do okay next week."

Chad opened his mouth to reply, but she had already stepped into the elevator. Then Katrina was gone.

CHAPTER 31

Northern Alberta Police Detachment, Edmonton, April 2000

Kindle didn't rise when Shrug walked into his office. He motioned for him to sit and kept on with his paperwork. He needed the time to compose his thoughts, figure out a plan of approach.

Shrug slid into the chair opposite the desk and stretched out his legs. He pulled a package of Nicorettes from his shirt pocket.

"Shrug, I'm giving you some advice for tomorrow when you face the review panel."

Shrug popped a chiclet in his mouth. "Go for it, Sarge."

Gritting his teeth, Kindle pushed back his chair. Standing, he leaned over, his hands on the desk, and stared at Shrug's feet. "Some humility on your part would be a good place to start. Topped with some respect."

Shrug pulled in his legs and straightened. "Gotcha."

"Unless, of course," Kindle said, sitting back down, "keeping your career is not important to you."

"Don't you be thinkin' I haven't considered resignin', Sarge."

"Perhaps law enforcement isn't the right place for you."

"Are you gettin' tired of defendin' me?"

"As I've already told you, I'll defend your actions in The Traz until I'm blue in the face, but I won't defend what came afterwards. At some point you have to take responsibility for your actions. I believe that's the point."

"I'm not askin' you to defend me."

"No, you're not. And I'm not asking you to stick with this career. You can go back to doing what you were before."

Shrug sighed. "I've considered that. But this police stuff, it's got in my blood. I'm hooked."

"I'm not speaking for the panel, but I know even if they let you keep your badge, you're not going to be allowed back on the street."

"No kiddin'."

"I have an inkling of what they're going to ask of you. If you want to remain a cop, I advise you to agree with it—without protest."

Shrug's eyes narrowed. "What are they gonna be askin' of me?"

"They're following through with our recommendation to institute additional training for our officers. I'm going to be setting up a few sessions and overseeing that. I'm thinking they might offer you the chance to come on board with me."

"That ain't what's in my blood."

"There was strong element of teaching and ethics in your previous career, right?"

"Yeah, but not like this."

"I have it on good authority the opportunity to assist in designing and implementing this course will be offered to all officers involved in this withholding of evidence. I believe Syd has already accepted."

"Those crazy buggers! Choose the people who need the trainin' to give the trainin'. The insanity of bureaucracy." Shrug tapped the underside of Kindle's desk with his boots.

Kindle ignored the tapping. "Who better to teach ethics than someone who's been there and done it, *and* faced the consequences? Isn't it better than having some pen-pushing book-learner do it?"

"The blind leadin' the blind."

"No, Shrug. The whole point of this is you're not going to be blind. You will learn to see things properly. You will come to such a deep understanding of ethical policing that it'll be something you can easily get across to others. You'll become the voice of experience—your *own* experience."

Shrug grunted. "It's an insane idea."

"Only because you don't yet see clearly. Believe me, I'll be damned sure you have perfect vision before you stand in front of one of my classes. I'll get you to that point if it kills me. You'll learn what you did was utterly and totally wrong, illegal and deceitful. You'll comprehend the irreparable harm you did to the girl, your peers, justice."

"I see. You're sayin' the review panel ain't gonna fire me?"

"I didn't say that."

"Yeah. You did." Shrug crossed his arms. "If I accept their teachin' offer, I keep my job—keep my reputation intact— just in case they need me as a credible witness in a retrial."

"That's not it at all!" Kindle argued, shaking his head. "It's giving a good officer a second chance to prove himself. A chance to learn something. A chance to undo some of the harm he's done."

Shrug clambered to his feet. "Sarge, you're getting almost as good as me at lyin'."

Kindle's face went hot and he could feel the veins in his neck pulsing. He strode around the desk. "Respect!" He wagged a finger in Shrug's face. "I demand *respect*."

"Sorry, sir. It wouldn't be like you to lie. I'll seriously consider your advice."

"I'm warning you, don't be a smart ass with the review panel tomorrow. Show them nothing but respect."

"Don't panic. Katrina says I'll do all right tomorrow, so I guess I'll do all right."

"Katrina?" Kindle dropped both hands to his sides. "You've been seeing the girl?"

Shrug ambled toward the door. "Oh, no. Not me."

"Then how do you know what she says?"

"Someone told me."

"Someone like who?"

"I think it was Chad." Shrug swung open the door and stepped into the hall.

"Chad's been seeing her?"

"I didn't say that."

Kindle leaned in the doorway. "I know you had a hand in this. Chad wouldn't have gone after the girl if you hadn't—"

Shrug looked back, an impish grin on his face. "Sir, it wouldn't be like me to do somethin' like that."

Kindle clenched his fists. "You stay away from the girl. And don't be sending anyone after her, either. Stay the hell away from her! You hear me, Shrug? Stay away!" *Or else.*

CHAPTER 32

Northern Alberta Police Detachment, Edmonton, July 2000

Chad entered Kindle's office and set a box of files down on the desk.

"This isn't exactly what I had in mind," Kindle muttered.

"What didn't you have in mind?"

Kindle flipped a letter he'd been reading face down and scowled.

Chad stepped back. "Sorry, sir." He pointed to the files. "I brought the—"

"I see that."

Chad nodded at the letter. "More Shrug stuff?"

Kindle shook his head. "More *Katrina* stuff. Steven Cooper phoned a while back asking if Katrina could use me as a job reference since her new identity pretty well wiped out all her past connections. I said I'd do what I could for the girl." His frown deepened and he handed the letter to Chad.

As Chad read it, his heart sank. "Oh, no. No! This mustn't be allowed to happen."

"I thought you liked the girl."

"My opinion of her has changed somewhat, since—" He closed his mouth.

"Since what?"

"Since…I ran into her a while back."

"You just happened to run into her?"

There was a rap on Kindle's door.

"Shrug," Chad greeted unenthusiastically. "You're the last person in the world I wanted to see. Thought you were on a 'well-deserved' paid vacation until the ethics sessions start."

"Worked four years straight, 24/7 with the bikers. Union says I'm owed some time off."

"Union? You started your own, or what?"

"Could you guys find another place to bicker?" Kindle asked.

"I'm here on a quick personal note," Shrug said.

Chad tossed the letter on Kindle's desk. "I'll leave."

"No need," Shrug said. "I'm just here to put in a good word for the girl. She asked me to and I guess I kinda owe her."

"You're admitting you owe her?" Kindle asked.

"Yeah. She put in a good word for me before the review panel, so I know she's expectin' somethin' back."

"How do you know what she said to the review panel?"

"I sent Chad to find out."

"You didn't *send* me," Chad protested.

"Yeah, I did. You just didn't know it."

Kindle cleared his throat. "Shrug, you told me you had nothing to do with Chad and Katrina meeting."

"I said that? No, I think I said it wasn't like me to do somethin' like that. Since you've been tellin' me everythin' I've been doin' lately isn't like me, I assumed I was tellin' the truth."

"Oh, for Christ's sake," Kindle muttered.

"Anyway, here's my good words for the girl. Ain't nobody who knows more about computers than Katrina, including Bill Gates himself. So I'm thinkin' we need the girl on our side of the law to keep up with the criminal use of the machines. Gotta stop the fraud artists dead, before they take over this new cyberspace thing. I'd like to see her accepted into police trainin'."

"When the hell are you going to quit lying?" Chad snapped.

"Didn't I sound at least a little bit sincere? I told her I'd give it a shot."

"Leave the girl alone," Chad said. "Quit insulting her. It's bordering on libellous to say she tooted you to the review panel simply to get a good word from you in—" He paused, remembering his uneasy feeling when Katrina had said she didn't know what she intended to do after graduating.

Had she been planning all along to join the force?

"The truth can't be libellous. I know that girl," Shrug said.

"So do I," Kindle said. "Which is why your glowing words about the girl aren't changing my mind."

"After what she did for us? She relived the horror of the murder for you. She testified against the bikers which has put her life forever in danger. She helped Chad disable perimeter sensors. What the hell, Sarge?"

"She's only, what, eighteen now? Something like that. Too young.

Too turbulent a history. Too..." Kindle shook his head. "I'm not having her on the police computers or anywhere else within the force.

"Shrug," Chad said. "Do you realize how often she's flipped sides? From being a cop's daughter to dealing drugs and running with a biker gang? Then flipped back over to the right side of the law when it suited her? What if she gets on our computers and flips again?"

Shrug grinned. "If it were to suit her, she damned well might."

Kindle pulled out the letter and re-read it. "We probably shouldn't be condemning her. She's never been found guilty of anything. And you're right. She did do a lot for us. It worries me, though, that I don't understand her motives."

"Ain't money that motivates her," Shrug said. "She's got a gazillion dollars of her own."

"Her memories of her father, sir," Chad said. "I successfully used her attachment to him to convince her to leave The Traz, to help with the sting, to talk about the murder, to testify."

"Ain't it kinda immoral to take advantage of a young person's grievin' like that?" Shrug asked.

"You probably used her grieving to get her on the back of your bike."

"I did not."

"She was an orphan. Looking for a father figure and zap! There you were, Shrug. Giving her some attention. Buttering her up."

"All I said was, 'Wanna' ride?' I swear. It was the Harley she liked. Yeah, Harleys. That's what motivates the girl, Sarge."

Chad turned to his boss. "We're supposedly an equal opportunity company here. Sergeant Kindle, if we let Shrug join the force, why the hell not the girl?"

"What motivates you, Shrug?" Kindle asked.

"My desire to make the world a better place for humankind."

"Oh, Lord help us." Chad walked out of the room.

Shrug watched Chad leave. When he was sure the guy was gone, he took a seat opposite Kindle. "Now that there's no witness, I'm gonna tell you this. Don't let the girl into the force, whatever you do. She's psychopathic, I swear."

"Is that a new word you learned from your counselling sessions?"

"Psychopathic—genius mind and no emotions. She makes up her emotions as she goes along, choosin' which ones will best serve her purpose. Drops 'em when they're no longer workin' for her. Psychopathic."

"Well, I'm not a psychiatrist like you're pretending to be, so I wouldn't know her diagnosis. Remember, she's undoubtedly scarred from her bereavement, followed so quickly by the murder."

"Oh, psychopathy ain't somethin' you acquire. It's somethin' you're born with."

"I see."

"You don't believe me?"

"Shrug, it's like this. You're painting the child evil to assuage your guilt over what happened. Don't do that. Accept responsibility and move on."

"Sarge, it's like this," Shrug said in a lazy drawl. "You have that girl in here on the computers for one month, and you'll be believin' every word I've said. In fact, you'll be sayin' them yourself."

CHAPTER 33

The Cooper Residence, Calgary, July 2000

Elizabeth Cooper turned off the kitchen tap and squeezed some dish soap into the sink. "What are you talking about, Katrina? What 'sucks'?"

"Everything sucks." Katrina pouted. *Life..this house...you.*

"Not everything," Cooper said. He turned to his wife. "She's complaining about the dean's note in her file, her lack of references for her job applications and the quarrel she had with Chad."

"Well, things do have a way of catching up with us," Elizabeth said.

Katrina glowered. "What does that mean?"

"You've been getting away with a lot of stuff for an awfully long time. Welcome to the real world. It's only going to get tougher from here on in."

"Tougher? Like it's been real smooth for me so far?" She stared at her guardians, then shook her head. *Yeah, right. My life's all sunshine and roses.*

"I'm not saying you've had it easy," Elizabeth said, "but you've certainly done a lot of things for which you've never paid your dues."

"What the fuck are you talking about?"

Elizabeth smacked the wash cloth on the counter. "Clean up your mouth! What I'm talking about is how most people who join biker gangs and deal in drugs do not end up safe and sound in a protection program. And that is just one example of how spoiled you are."

"I'm *what*?"

Elizabeth dropped the pot she was washing and strode over to the table. "You joined that gang on your own free will just like everyone else in there. Tell me, how many besides you are free to get on with their lives? How many are getting an education? A job? Answer me! How many?"

"None?"

"Do you think that's because you're special? That you're somehow better than everyone else? Let me tell you this..." Elizabeth lowered her voice. "It's because you're *lucky*."

Katrina let out a huff. *Lucky? Really? I watched my friend die.*

"Lucky to have had people around to pull you through," Elizabeth continued her tirade. "Or maybe not so lucky, since you've never learned to take responsibility for your actions. Here you are an adult in an adult world and everything 'sucks.'" She glanced at her husband, but he looked away.

Katrina pushed back her chair.

"You sit!" Elizabeth shouted. "Don't you dare run away from me when I'm talking to you. You're not a child anymore. You can't just run to your room and slam the door when things don't go as you want. I know you don't want to hear this, but you have to grow up, girl. You sit there complaining. Everything sucks because that's the way you've made it!"

"I made my life like this? I don't think so."

"Think about what you're saying."

"I understand what *I'm* saying, but I sure the hell don't understand what *you're* saying. I didn't tell the dean to put that note in my file about me sabotaging the university computer system. I'm not going to be able to get a high-level computer job with *that* staring me in the face. He has absolutely no proof it was me who crashed the system." She turned to Cooper. "That note can't be legal. I want you to sue him."

Elizabeth wiped her hands on her pant legs. "The trouble with that whole tirade is you don't deny it was you who sabotaged the computers. The crash *was* traced to your malicious software."

"BackTracker isn't malicious. I didn't design it to crash systems. It just happened, an unfortunate and unexpected side effect."

"Katrina!" Cooper chastised. "Even what you designed BackTracker for verges on the illegal."

"It simply erases the record of sites visited," she defended. "It is a protector of privacy."

"Even though I know nothing about computers or about software, I know you are lying," Elizabeth said. "Unless you start being honest with yourself, life's going to become even more hellish for you. Is *that* something you can understand?"

"No! And I don't understand why you're calling me a liar."

Elizabeth tossed her hands in the air. "I give up."

Cooper shook his head. "Give her time, Elizabeth. Although legally she's twenty-three, chronologically she's only eighteen. Socially and emotionally, she's much younger. Throw in an IQ of a hundred and sixty, then try to reconcile all that."

Katrina jumped to her feet. "If I hear how immature I am one more time, I'm going to scream."

"She's not going to make it out there in the world." Elizabeth headed back to the sink. "Katrina, you're smart enough, too smart maybe in some ways, and in other ways you're just not even on the map."

"Being called immature isn't the worst thing that can be said about a person," Cooper said.

Katrina scowled. "It sure as hell won't get me the job I want."

"Get real!" Elizabeth shouted. "The police aren't going to accept you into training. Not with your background. Or your...personality."

"Look for a different job," Cooper suggested. "Computers are probably a good place for you. You won't have to deal with people."

Elizabeth huffed. "She'll have to deal with people no matter what job she has. Bosses, customers, co-workers. She'll have to deal with criticism too. What are you going to when someone comes down on you, Katrina? Run to your room and cry?"

"Don't worry about it. With the dean's note on my file, the only computer job I'll find is with the mafia."

"Now *that* sounds like your kind of job," Elizabeth said.

Cooper stepped between them. "Give her a chance, dear. Katrina spent her teens, when she should've been growing up, down at the courthouse in the witness stand. Give her time. She'll learn."

Elizabeth gaze shot daggers at Katrina. "Four years and a degree later, and we still have a moping, self-centred, destructive...*child*. Half the problem, Steven, is you still treat her like an innocent kid who doesn't know any better."

"Can I go now?" Katrina asked.

"Yes," Elizabeth snapped. "Be sure to slam the bedroom door behind you and cry loud enough for me to hear."

Katrina spun on one heel, then strode down the hall to her room. Rather than do as Elizabeth had mockingly suggested, she closed the door quietly, flopped down on the bed and stared dry-eyed at a spot on the ceiling. She held her gaze until the daub of stipple seeped out of focus.

Closing her eyes, she listened to her breath and heartbeat. Thoughts tumbled in her mind. Not of computers, jobs, the Coopers or the dean. Mostly, she thought of Chad.

When Cooper had told her Chad had personal reasons for wanting to meet her, she'd thought he wanted to rekindle their friendship. Or since she was almost eighteen, maybe even wanted to start a romance. Instead, he'd been cool, distant and accusing. More interested in Shrug's wellbeing than in hers.

I didn't make Chad hate me.

She felt empty, alone and abandoned—familiar feelings that had haunted her ever since the night her mother had killed her dad. She'd felt this way when Lukas began using meth, when Syd and James had turned on her in the King's Ace.

She replayed her last conversation with Chad.

'You got Shrug into this pickle,' Chad had said. 'He did it for you, Katrina.'

When she'd left him in that hotel lobby, she'd felt just like she did when Shrug had left her in the warehouse.

She thought of her father.

"You're very much okay, Katrina," he had said the morning he'd died. "Don't let anyone ever tell you otherwise."

He'd said she'd do great things. At university, she'd begun to believe him. In the computer labs and with her peers after hours in the dorm, for the first time in her life, she fit in. But her classmates were now dispersed, she was living with people she couldn't stand and her dream of following in her father's footsteps with a law enforcement career was shattered.

Unless...

CHAPTER 34

The alarm buzzed and Katrina moaned, exhausted. Nightmares had ravaged her sleep—swirling darkness, splashes of crimson, incessant screams and Lukas...watching her always with his haunting blue eyes.

She slipped out of bed and headed down the hall to the bathroom. She paused when she heard Elizabeth and Cooper talking in the kitchen.

"You have to give her credit," Cooper said. "Most kids with her kind of money wouldn't bother getting a job, let alone take one beneath them."

"She didn't take that computer sales job out of the goodness of her heart," Elizabeth replied. "She's only doing it to get what she really wants."

"Are you worried about your chemotherapy tomorrow?"

"What does that have to do with it?"

"You're not making sense. There's very few of us who don't have our eyes on something better when we first enter the workforce."

"It's different with her. In some way, it's very different."

Katrina closed the bathroom door and started the shower. As she stepped under the steamy water, she began to cry. She watched her tough façade swirl down the drain.

She'd been reluctant to return to the Cooper's when her university dorm days were over. Still, she didn't want to wake up in the dark—sweating and terrified—and have no one but herself to hear her screams, make her tea and help her through to one more sunrise. As cold as the Coopers were, they at least did that for her.

She was always on edge. Eventually someone was going to recognize her as the witness at the biker trials. And the gang would hunt her down and terrible things would happen.

She didn't want to be alone if any of that were to happen.

Cooper had said she was too young to be on her own in the big city and he'd love to have her stay with them again. He said she would not be putting them in danger as no one outside of the police force knew he'd been her guardian in the first place.

She stepped out of the shower, wrapped a towel about her and stared at her misty reflection in the vanity mirror. *What do others see that I don't? I thought I was doing okay...considering.*

She grabbed a tissue and wiped at the glass until her eyes were revealed.

"You're brave, Katrina," she told her reflection. "No matter what anyone else says."

She'd considered herself brave for facing down the bikers at their trials. She thought she'd done well to leave the street life behind, get a university degree in under four years and programme a cutting-edge software package.

In the mirror, though, she spotted the haunting look in her eyes, just below the surface. That was the weakness others saw—loneliness and despair.

She gazed at her eyes until they became glassy and empty.

I've been on my own my entire life.

She could keep going it alone. In The Traz, with Shrug as her tutor, she'd mastered the art of hiding her pain.

"Is this a joke?" The receptionist grinned as she passed Katrina a phone message as she arrived at work. "Why would the Shasta Flash Show want to talk to you? The guy sounded so serious and the number he left does have a New York prefix."

"Don't be silly," Katrina said. "Of course it's just a joke. I don't think the top U.S. talk show would want me."

"He said something about biker trials and that you'd know what he meant."

Katrina froze.

The receptionist's mouth gaped. "*Do* you know what he meant?"

"He asked for me? Katrina Buckhold?"

"Yeah," the girl said slowly. " Are you all right?"

They found me! The Traz found me. They're going to kill me!

"No, I'm not. I'm going home. Give my ten o'clock appointment to the other salesman. He can have the commission."

"Are you ill?"

"Don't accept any more calls for me. If anyone asks, I don't work here."

CHAPTER 35

Cooper's office, Calgary

"Mr. Cooper!" Katrina jumped to her feet as Cooper emerged from his office. She grabbed his sleeve. "We have to talk. Privately."

"I'm due in court in twenty minutes. Now is not a good time." He brushed past her to the front desk. "Out until two," he said to his receptionist.

She hurried to his side. "Wait!"

Cooper plucked a file from the tray on the reception desk and opened it. "Is this something you can deal with on your own, Katrina?"

She forced back her tears. "This isn't one of my immature requests for a glass of warm milk. I wouldn't be bothering you if it—"

"Okay." Cooper slapped the file closed and motioned her into his office. "But make it quick."

As soon as he shut his office door behind them, Katrina passed him the phone message. "Somebody has revealed my identity and my whereabouts."

"Where'd you get this?"

"The receptionist at work said this guy phoned a few minutes before I got in this morning. He told her he wants to talk to me about the biker trials." She collapsed into a chair. "How would anyone know that I know about the biker trials?"

"Did you call him back?"

Katrina shook her head.

"Do you want *me* to?"

"I guess so."

She got up and paced around the room. "Nobody was ever supposed to know my real identity."

Not only was she under witness protection, her name had not been revealed in the courtroom. She'd only been referred to as 'Sarina,' and that's the only name anyone on the street or in The Traz had ever called her. No one but the Coopers and a handful of cops knew that it had been Katrina Buckhold on the witness stand. The gang would have had to wrest that information from one of them—and *that* wasn't likely.

She stopped pacing when she heard Cooper identify himself as her lawyer. He was already on the phone with the talk show guy.

She shivered and watched her guardian's face.

"John, you left Katrina a message saying you want her on your show," Cooper said. "For what reason?" He hit the speaker button so Katrina could hear.

"To discuss her side of the story, Mr. Cooper."

"Her side of what story?"

"Those biker trials that happened up there a while back."

"What makes you think she knows anything about the biker trials?"

"She was a witness for the prosecution."

"Who told you that?"

"I'm not revealing my sources."

"And who will be discussing the other side of this supposed story?"

"Well, we haven't confirmed that yet."

"I'll get back to you," Cooper said. He placed the phone in the cradle.

When he stood and faced her, the anxiety on his face increased Katrina's fear a hundred fold. She took a tentative step toward him. "Mr. Cooper?"

He hustled her toward the door. "Elizabeth is at home. Go there and don't let anyone in."

"I'm wondering what you've done about this," Elizabeth said. She poured herself a coffee and joined Katrina at the kitchenette table.

"What *I've* done about this?" Katrina stared at Elizabeth's cup, stung that she hadn't been offered one. *Why is it that even when I'm with people, I'm totally on my own?*

She headed to the counter and poured a mug of coffee. "I talked to Mr. Cooper—that's what I did."

"I know all about Steven calling this John guy and sending you here, but what I want to know is what *you* have done? This is *your* life in danger. Steven is supposed to be in court right now. Why have you handed it off to him?"

"Because I didn't know what else to do and I figured he would."

"The mature response to this would be for you to get on it right away. Talking to Steven was an okay place to start, but I suggest, as an adult, *you* ought to be the one pursuing the matter. You need to learn to fix your own mess."

Elizabeth picked up the cordless phone from the table and tossed it. The phone hit Katrina's arm and clattered to the floor. A slosh of coffee followed it.

"Are you saying I should call someone?"

"That would be a 'yes,'" Elizabeth said, walking away. "Use your genius to imagine who that *someone* ought to be."

CHAPTER 36

Northern Alberta Police Detachment, Edmonton

Katrina waited anxiously in Sergeant Kindle's office. It had been about four years since she'd sat in this very chair, huddled under an afghan, shivering. She felt as frightened and alone now as she had then.

As soon as she'd called Sergeant Kindle, he'd sent an officer to escort her all the way from Calgary to his Edmonton office. That response had made her all the more uneasy. She'd spent the entire tense three-hour ride from Calgary trying to figure out who had exposed her to the media—and why. She'd not been able to come up with any suspects. As far as she knew, no one on the wrong side of the law knew her name or where she'd been living.

She sighed, rested her elbows on her knees and her chin in her hands. It actually wasn't surprising someone had tracked her down. The Traz had unlimited power and could easily purchase information through bribery, blackmail, a lifetime's supply of cocaine, a free facelift...a thousand bucks. She knew from her time with Shrug that it was exceptionally easy to find people greedy enough, or vulnerable enough, to talk.

"Katrina?"

Katrina straightened and glanced at the door.

"Sergeant Kindle got tied up and asked me to drop in on you," Debra said, flashing Katrina a smile as she entered the office.

Katrina's eyes were drawn to the diamond on Debra's left ring finger. "You're engaged?"

Debra held out her hand. "Yes. Chad and I are getting married next month."

"Chad?" Katrina's voice caught in her throat.

Debra folded her hands behind her back. "Yes. Chad."

"Oh."

"I'm sorry..." Debra took a step toward her. "I know you had a crush on him...before...when you were a kid."

Katrina bowed her head and squeezed her eyes shut. "Chad and *you*."

"You were just a kid then, Katrina. He's past thirty now. I know you adored him, but he didn't think of you in that way."

"He told you that?"

"Yes."

Katrina clenched her hands and stared up at her. "Did Chad ever tell you that when he looked in my eyes it was as if we shared a soul?"

"No."

"Well, he told *me* that. So don't be telling me how it really was."

"He told me that you reminded him of the kid sister he lost. I think that's what he meant. Nothing romantic."

"You must be right." Katrina sprang to her feet, her blood boiling. "Because you're the one with the ring, aren't you?"

Debra took a small step back. "You're old enough to realize what was going on. Accept the facts. Chad wasn't sweet on you."

Katrina reached for her purse. "I'm leaving."

"Where are you going? So I can tell Sergeant Kindle."

"To The Traz biker compound. Seems to be the only place I ever fit in."

Debra widened her stance, blocking the doorway. "I can't allow you to leave."

The cold emptiness and fear that had been brewing in Katrina's core filled her chest and tightened her throat. She wiped at her eyes. "You can't *allow* me?"

"I'm sorry." Debra heaved a tired sigh. "I spoke too roughly. I wouldn't have said anything about the engagement if I'd known how you feel about Chad."

Katrina stifled a sob. "There's a lot you don't know about me."

Desperate to conceal her desolation, she walked to the window and stared down to the parking lot. "And a hell of a lot you don't know about Chad."

"Sometimes I think it's easier getting goods across the border than ideas," Kindle grumbled to Chad as they stepped off the elevator.

It was times like these that Kindle wished he had Shrug at his side— the Shrug that used to be. The one who could sweet-talk anybody into anything.

"Still no luck forcing the Americans to talk?" Chad asked.

"They're claiming under U.S. law, journalists aren't obligated to reveal their sources—as if they're journalists! In my books, the Shasta Flash Show is nothing but pure entertainment. All they're willing to concede is Katrina's identity will be well hidden should she agree to appear."

"It's not the TV appearance that's the issue here. Don't they understand it's the fact someone revealed her identity that's putting the girl in danger?"

"Apparently not. They keep insisting only John and his assistant know Katrina's name. But how can they be sure their source hasn't told others? And how can we find out for sure when they won't tell us who it is doing the talking?"

"Do we have any idea what this source's motive is? Is someone out to get the girl killed? Should we be investigating The Traz? Or is somebody just out to make some bucks from selling secrets?"

"Since the Show denies they pay their sources or their guests, we're left with the nasty feeling something more sinister than money is the motive."

Chad let out a frustrated groan. "How much are you going to tell Katrina?"

"I don't have much to tell, but Shrug says maybe *she* does. Said he wouldn't put it past her to have arranged this herself—for the publicity. She was in the limelight for so long, maybe she misses the media."

In better times, Kindle had valued Shrug's opinions and instincts more than his own. These days, though, he couldn't trust anything Shrug said.

"Shrug's full of bullshit!" Chad said. "I can't see that girl being anything but terrified at the prospect of the bikers tracking her down."

Kindle nodded. "Perhaps." He'd have to talk to Katrina, decide for himself. "As it sits, I don't know if I'm looking at something simple or more complicated. Staff Sergeant Peters is still working hard with the Shasta Flash Show, but they have the scoop on the mystery child witness who dismantled the biker gangs on both sides of the border. They're not motivated to cooperate. It was the story of the decade. A nubile beauty, barely able to peep over the witness stand, bringing down the tattooed giants of the drug and weapons trade. Katrina had the media mesmerized back then with her blue eyes and petite stature. What they wouldn't give to see her now."

"But she wouldn't be interested in the publicity," Chad argued. "She wants to disappear, never be found or identified."

Outside his office, Kindle paused and fixed his gaze on Chad. "There's some evidence she posted that photo of herself in the King's Ace to the Internet back when Shrug was facing the review panel. I have to agree with Shrug. This girl operates beyond the norm. Nothing's beyond the scope of possibility with her."

"Nothing's beyond Shrug, either. It's just as likely *he* released that photo. It proved quite useful in his defence against the child endangerment allegations."

"Are you suggesting Shrug revealed her identity to the show?"

"I don't know why he would, but it's not beyond him to do something like that."

Kindle pushed open the door to his office.

"Katrina," he greeted.

Curled up in his office chair, she looked small and vulnerable. She was not much taller than when he'd last seen her. She looked up at him, her eyes fiery and steady, like those of a defiant young teen protesting a curfew.

Kindle waved goodbye to Debra and Chad, then closed the door.

"I'm sorry I don't have much to tell you to put you at ease. I know how upset you must be."

Katrina rolled her eyes. "You have no idea how upset I am."

"Do you have any suspicions about who might have revealed your identity?"

She shook her head.

"*You* haven't told anyone?"

"Oh, for fuck's sake!" She shimmied forward on the chair until her feet reached the floor. "That's what this is going to boil down to? You have a leak in the police department and you're going to try nailing it on me? If that's the way it's going to be—" She started to stand.

"Sit!" he said. "Now!"

He was surprised when she obeyed.

"I'm not nailing anything on anybody, Katrina, so why are *you* nailing the leak on us? Is there something you know that I don't?"

She sighed, her eyes darting to the ceiling, the window and then back to Kindle's face. "Perhaps I'm nailing the link on you because nobody outside your damned police department knows my identity?"

"You refused to change your name after the trials," Kindle said evenly. "So perhaps one of your childhood friends made the connection?"

"Not likely. I never had friends and I've got no living relatives. I swear nobody from my previous life, except Cooper and Elizabeth, know I'm the one who testified. Besides, not only would this rat have to know my name, he would have had to know to look for a twenty-three-year-old woman and figure out where I was working. I don't think even you were privy to that info."

Kindle's phone rang. He picked it up and listened intently.

A minute later, he replaced the phone on the receiver. "Something's come up. Tell you what, I'll get someone to take you for lunch and we'll meet back here afterward."

"I don't eat when I'm upset."

"A coffee then?"

"Is Chad free?"

"He just might be," Kindle said, amused at the thought of handing the manipulative child off to Chad.

Chad caught Katrina's gaze from across the café table. He knew this wasn't going to be easy, but it had to be done.

"Debra told me how upset you were about our engagement," he said. "I'm sorry you feel that way. She and I thought you were old enough—that by now you'd realize how things really were back then."

Katrina arched a brow. "I see."

"I'm sorry if I've ever done anything, or said anything, to make you think otherwise."

"Would you like me to list those things for you?"

"List them?" He chuckled. "There's that many?"

She dropped a sugar cube into her coffee and slowly stirred it. She took a sip and reached for the sugar dish. Locking eyes with him, she picked up a handful of cubes and dropped them, one by one, into her cup. "Yeah. There's that many."

"How many things have I done to make you think otherwise? About as many as, say, the number of sugar cubes you're using?"

"You catch on fast." As she stirred, coffee sloshed over the brim of her cup and began seeping across the table toward Chad.

"Katrina, for Christ's sake!" He grabbed a napkin and sopped up the spill. "You were a kid back then. You've got it all wrong, I swear. Think about it! You were fourteen. I was almost thirty."

"I've got it all wrong? Yeah, maybe it would've been wrong back then. Wrong, like you back then promising me you'd be here for me when I left The Traz. Wrong, like you promising to find a family for me." Her mouth turned down in a sneer. "What the hell's wrong now? I'm not a kid anymore. I'm not fourteen. I'm a woman, Chad."

"You are. A beautiful woman. A beautiful, *young* woman."

Katrina shoved aside her cup, sending more coffee splashing to the table between them. "We kissed."

"*You* kissed *me*. I don't recall returning the favour."

"I believe you didn't protest too much."

Chad inhaled deeply and let it out bit by bit. "What would you rather I have done? Get angry and charge you with sexual harassment? I was gentle in refusing your advances because—*not* because I was interested in you, but because there was no one around to teach you—"

"Don't think I didn't notice the hesitation before you pulled away."

"I wasn't expecting you to grab my ears and kiss me. It took a second or two to sink in what you were up to."

Katrina picked up a spoon. Was she going to throw it at him?

"Elizabeth said I'm not honest with myself," she said. "Do you have a problem with honesty, too?" She put the spoon down, leaned back in her chair and stared out the window.

They sat in silence.

Chad watched her, curious. *Is she remembering the day we met? The azure autumn sky, the late summer grasses and the brush of fall colour?*

He didn't know what else he could do or say to make her understand he hadn't led her on. Not intentionally anyway.

"Chad?" She held his gaze for a moment. "Right after we kissed, you looked into my eyes and said we shared a soul. Without you, I have only a half a soul."

It was what he remembered most too—looking into her eyes. She'd said so much with them. He'd listened. He'd heard. He'd answered.

None of it, though, is the kind of love she's talking about.

"You made me promises you didn't keep," she said. "Thanks to you, there's no one here for me. No one! I don't fit in. Because of witness protection, I can't talk to anybody about what happened. Cooper's an idiot. Elizabeth is a bag and Shrug won't return my calls. I'm alone, Chad. You promised me that I wouldn't be."

"Shrug doesn't call because he's been warned to stay away from you—for obvious reasons."

"Yup. When it's convenient for him not to talk to me, he doesn't. Yet, whenever he needs me it's perfectly fine to dial me up. He can need me, but I can't need him. Very fair."

Chad grabbed another napkin, wiped off Katrina's cup and slid it to her. She tucked her hands under her thighs and stared into the half-empty cup as if reading the future.

"Shrug's the same as you," she said. "Same as Sergeant Kindle. Same as Debra. Trials are over and none of you gives a shit anymore. Cooper and Elizabeth hang around for the money. When I got that message at work, what does Cooper say? 'Make it quick. I have to be in court in twenty minutes.' And Elizabeth tells me to go fuck myself. No one gives a shit."

"It's not like that, Katrina. I care. I do. And I know the others do too."

"That's easy to say, Chad." She tipped her head, the light catching one side of her face. "I imagine anyone would say it. But will anyone do anything to show it? No. Not even a letter of reference. After the hell I went through for you. For Sergeant Kindle and Shrug. The hell I went through, and not one of you—not *one*—will put in a good word for me. Why? Because you guys don't need me anymore."

She smiled. "Except you guys *do* need me. You're just too short-sighted to realize that. Do you have any idea where cyberspace is heading? Where computer nerds are going to take it? Where criminals are going to inhabit? No one in law enforcement does because no one in law enforcement is under the age of thirty. You fucking old geezers need us nerds, us cyberspace geniuses. You have no idea how badly you need us. The criminals do, though. They know our value." Her eyes misted over. She blinked several times to clear them.

"You're planning to join the criminals?" he asked.

"So that's what you think of me." She grabbed her purse. "I'm out of here!"

"Katrina." Chad grabbed her arm. "I'm sorry. Sit, please. I know what you're saying, about computer technology. I understand how deeply you feel about law enforcement. I understand all that. I do."

"Easy to say, Chad. Easy to say."

"Listen," he said, struggling to find the right words. "I'll do something for you. I can't give you a letter of reference, but I'll give you a name. Leskiw."

He pulled a pen from his jacket pocket. On the back of a clean napkin, he jotted down a name and number. "Corporal Leskiw is reorganizing our computer department. I'll let him know to expect a call from you."

Sweat beaded on his forehead. *I hope to God I'm not making a mistake.*

CHAPTER 37

Chad peeked into his boss's office and saw a scowling Kindle flipping through a stack of papers on his desk. "Sarge, I hope you won't be needing Katrina for a bit. She's calling Leskiw down in Ottawa."

Kindle frowned. "Corporal Leskiw?"

"She convinced me with those blue eyes of hers to put her in touch with him."

Kindle's face turned a brilliant red. "What did you say?"

Chad took a step back. *I wonder if it's my mention of Katrina's blue eyes, or the fact I put her in touch with Leskiw that is upsetting him.*

"She says we're all betraying her by not giving her a reference," he said. "I figure if the computer boss himself turns her down, she'll have to admit it's not us keeping her from her dream career."

"Her career problems are not the worst of her troubles."

"Something new on the Shasta Show leak?"

"Have a seat." Kindle waited, then said, "Katrina's going to be wild."

"You found the leak?"

"We believe so."

"Who?"

"Take a guess."

"I always disagreed with the Witness Protection decision to let her keep her name. I'll bet it's an old acquaintance of hers. She said she had no friends. Maybe she had enemies."

"I guess you could say he's an old acquaintance of hers. Of Syd's too."

"Of Syd's?"

"Yeah, Syd's undercover partner in the King's Ace operation. Rusty James, the one who resigned rather than sign on with Syd and Shrug to run the ethics seminars."

"Oh no. Why? Why an ex-cop? Was he was pissed he had to resign? That wasn't the girl's fault. She had no role at all in that. Katrina didn't know those surveillance photos existed."

"Get this..." Kindle leaned back and began chewing on his pen. "James has apparently written a book on police incompetency surrounding the biker sting and trials. He figured a spot on the Shasta Flash Show would be great publicity for his work of fiction. Since he couldn't wrangle that on his own merits, he offered up Katrina's identity in exchange for a five-minute spot."

"Whoa! Wait a minute. He wrote a book on police incompetency?"

"We figure the book is revenge for losing his job. But we're not sure why the hell he's dragging the girl into it. We're after him. Big time."

"Oh, this is so not good."

"Tell me about it. We're attempting to prevent the book from being published, but that's a difficult concept for the Americans. As always, they're arguing free speech—the Fourth Amendment or whatever it is."

"First Amendment. Is Katrina's identity revealed in the book?"

Kindle shrugged. "No one's willing to give us a manuscript to review. Even if it's not in the book, we're worried. Has James been flogging her name to other media outlets in his bid to promote his book? Who all did he tell at the Shasta Flash Show and who all have they turned around and told? Did this John guy tell his wife?"

Chad could hear the frustration in his boss's voice.

"Katrina's going to have to change her name," Kindle said. "We've got to revamp her identity again. We don't have a choice now."

"You think she's going to agree to that?" *Good luck.*

Kindle wasn't looking forward to telling Katrina she had to change her name. She'd told him many times that her father had named her and it wasn't a name she'd let a criminal steal.

He tracked her down to one of the side rooms. She was sitting in a padded chair, her arms crossed and her feet swinging. She looked small and scared, although he could never be totally sure about what she was feeling. Katrina was a master at concealing her emotions.

She looked up when he walked in. He closed the door and stared down at her, wondering where to begin.

Katrina spoke first. "Debra says you wanted to talk to me about the leak. Have you found out who revealed my name?"

"We have good reason to believe it was Constable Rusty James."

"James?" Her eyes flared. Then she scowled. "That son of a bitch. Trying to get even."

"Get even?"

"I had a little quarrel with him behind the King's Ace."

"That's something I wasn't aware of."

"Oh, it was nothing. It was years ago. I doubt that's the reason he ratted me out."

"Tell me about it anyways."

"I didn't know he wanted me dead."

"It was a serious spat?"

"Oh, the spat wouldn't be why he wants me dead."

Kindle studied her face. Her smirk was a dead giveaway.

She's lying. Her life's in danger and she's not going to tell me a damn thing more about that quarrel. How can she be so stubborn?

"Any help you can give us in this matter," he said, "might mean the difference between you living or dying."

"Since the leak came from the police department, I'm counting on the police to protect me. Don't make it sound like it's my responsibility."

"Syd said you gave him and James the Coopers' address once, when they found you drunk out of your mind behind the King's Ace and sent you home in a taxi. Is that true?"

"I don't remember much about that night, but yeah. A taxi ended up dropping me off at the Coopers. I must've given someone my address."

"That's probably how James tracked you down."

"That was the one and only time I ever drank. And look at the trouble it got me in."

"Your connection to the Coopers is causing us concern for them too."

"I have no qualms about cutting that bond," Katrina said.

"I wasn't thinking of asking you to do that. They're your only link to stability. Your only 'family,' so to speak."

Katrina gave a dismissive laugh. "Family? Not likely. Besides, it's way too much to ask Cooper to change his identity. I don't imagine that would do wonders for his business. Leave the Coopers be, Sergeant Kindle. I've been on my own for as long as I can remember. I don't need them."

"Part of your original witness protection deal was you maintain contact with your guardians."

"The original deal's passé. Chronologically I'm eighteen, an adult under Alberta law. There's no longer a need for that guardian clause."

Her desire to rid herself of the only adult influence in her life and her only connection to her past sat uncomfortably with Kindle. The girl had been through way too much and was hurting way too deeply to be so alone in the world.

"It's something we'll discuss further," he said. "Right now we have to talk about you changing your name. We don't know who all is aware of your identity. There's no way to keep Katrina Buckhold hidden and safe. You must agree to change your name. First and last."

"That's fine," she agreed.

He blinked. "Your answer surprises me. You used to have such a strong emotional connection to your name."

"I have no choice but to cooperate. However, you must arrange to have my final marks and university degree transferred to the new name. I'd prefer you leave all other university records under Katrina Buckhold—to stymie anyone trying to backtrack through them to find me."

"Well, it won't be me doing that kind of stuff." Kindle withdrew a notepad and pen. "But I can note your wishes."

"Make sure all my assets get switched," she added. "Perhaps transfer the land I own to Cooper so my new identity won't show up as public information at Land Titles. He deserves something for his efforts in any event."

Kindle nodded. This was going far better than he'd expected.

CHAPTER 38

Northern Alberta Police Detachment, Edmonton, August 2000

Chad rapped on Kindle's office door. "The Supreme Court decision on the biker appeals is coming down tomorrow. I'm taking bets on which way they'll rule."

"I'm not a betting man," Kindle muttered, wondering why Chad had time to run around taking bets.

"Betting is legal, as long as the house doesn't take a cut."

"Did I say anything about legalities?"

"You don't have to put up any money," Chad said. "Just tell me your guess. What do you think the judges will say? Order a retrial? Overturn the convictions? Leave things as they are?"

"Whatever way they go, you can bet it'll be a split decision. A close split decision."

"I think the bikers will lose their appeal. They knew, even if their lawyers didn't, that Katrina and Lukas were buddies. It was *their* choice not to bring it up."

"If that was the only point they were considering, you'd probably be right. But it's not just that." Kindle motioned Chad to sit. "There are the photos of Katrina in the King's Ace. There will be judges hell-bent on sending a message to law enforcement that there's absolutely no justifiable reason to withhold evidence from a trial. They're going to cite precedence, saying if they let us get away with it this time, the floodgates will be opened for police in the future to conceal information from the defence."

"That's one side of the argument. It's been ruled before, though, that if the outcome of the trial wasn't affected, police errors are forgivable."

Kindle unfolded himself from the chair, walked to the cabinet and poured a glass of water. "The defence argued they were unaware of

Katrina's nightlife and could have used that information to tarnish her credibility. Of course, then there's Shrug's involvement in recruiting her and covering up her friendship with Lukas."

"They questioned his motive for doing that," Chad said.

"And, in turn, questioned his entire testimony, all the evidence obtained from his years undercover. It's not a slam dunk for us when both of the Crown's star witnesses are tainted. They argued those points tenaciously, almost had *me* believing. It'll be a close decision. They'd never simply overturn the bikers lose, but they may force a retrial."

"Maybe I ought to switch my bet."

Kindle took a sip of water. "They also brought up, again, the fact the judge wouldn't recess when Katrina broke down on the stand, and they never got her testimony about being in possession of Shrug's gun."

"But Shrug testified about giving it to her," Chad said. "The jury knew she was armed. Knew she pulled out the revolver after the murder, shot Lukas and then aimed it at the bikers."

"Like I said, it'll be a close decision."

"But you don't want to put any money down?"

Kindle raised a brow. "Do *you* want to put money down on whether or not Katrina gets accepted to police training?"

"Why do you ask?"

"I've fielded three calls already concerning her application." Kindle's mouth thinned. "Apparently, she impressed Leskiw."

Chad's eyes grew wide. "I didn't mean for her to. Didn't think she would."

"I tried to get permission to release some background info on her to the recruitment officers, but it was denied. All I could do was protest that's she too immature."

"What did they say?"

"They argued if they were to wait for a mature computer geek to apply, hell would be frozen over. She looks good to them, a computer pro who's willing to bypass the big bucks in private enterprise to follow in her father's footsteps. Twenty-three years old, a computer tech degree, exceptional IQ. I did insist they note in her file that I object to her joining the force."

"Is there anything I can do?" Chad asked in a sheepish tone.

"I think you've done quite enough."

"Syd? Shrug?" Kindle stepped into the meeting room, which had been converted to a session room for the ethics programme. He spotted the men at their desks in the back corner. "How's it going in here? Will you be ready in a month to start presenting this stuff?"

"Listen to this, Sarge." Syd picked up a magazine covered in sticky notes. "A quiz. I'm flipping a coin, heads or tails, and you walk in. The last six tosses have come up heads. You get to bet on the next toss. What will you place your money on, heads or tails?"

"I don't have time for this kind of—"

"No, this is important. I want to use it in our teaching. What would you bet on?"

"I don't know. I don't bet."

"Not even theoretically? Suppose I toss it twenty times and it's heads each time. Where would you want to put your money on the next toss?

"The fraud squad."

"It's not a trick coin or anything. Anomalies happen. Do you think you can take advantage of that anomaly? What do you think the chances are the next toss will be heads again?"

"It has to even out to fifty-fifty sooner or later so I'd say it's more likely to be tails."

Syd smirked.

"I take it that's not the right answer?" Kindle said with a sigh.

"It's the answer most people would give, but it's not the rational answer." He tossed the magazine to Kindle. "What you just said was past tosses will affect the outcome of the next one. That's not rational. Each and every toss has the same fifty-fifty chance of being heads, no matter what's happened before."

"Did *you* get it right?"

"No, but Shrug did."

It was Shrug's turn to grin.

Kindle raised a brow. "Are you saying Shrug's smarter than I am?"

"Not smarter, just more rational."

"You're going to use this in the ethics sessions?"

"I think we will. There's more to it than just coin tosses. The human mind has many blind spots. We often believe we're acting rationally when we're not. Scientists wondered how this trait evolved. You'd think it would be a dangerous one. Amazingly enough, they discovered our intuition usually gets us to correct answers despite the convoluted, irrational way we arrive at them. It's why we're always told not to change our answers on a multiple-choice exam. Chances are the first answer we choose is the right one—whether or not we arrived at it rationally."

"So I'd be correct to bet on tails in the coin toss?"

"You'd have a fifty-percent chance of bein' right," Shrug cut in. "On the other hand, you'd have a fifty-percent chance of bein' wrong."

Kindle slid the magazine back to Syd. "It would be comforting to know our intuition is usually correct. Out on the street, there sometimes isn't time for a lot of rational thought."

"Sarge," Shrug drawled. "I thought we were supposed to be promotin' rational thought and common sense."

"I don't want these seminars to be black and white issues. Life isn't. I want our officers to know that and think about it. Don't be giving them answers, boys. Be giving them questions."

"Speaking of questions," Syd said. "How far have you got writing the questions for the final exam?"

"I'm done."

"Done? How can you be done before we even have the course outline completed?"

"It's an essay-type final exam. One question. What's the number one rule, and why?"

"The number one rule?"

"If you can't tell your boss what you're going to do, don't do it because you'll be going over the line. It's the first thing I teach all of my officers and I get really pissed if they break that rule." Kindle raised a brow in Shrug's direction. "Right, Shrug?"

"It's not like you didn't know I had Katrina workin' for me."

"So that's where you at? You've given up blaming the girl and into blaming me?"

"You knew she was with me. That's the reason you sent Chad in."

"Ah, I see. You read minds now. Not only did you *not* tell me about Katrina, you lied to me about her. When you brought in that audiotape of the cocaine deal you set up, I asked what kid was wearing the wire and you denied a child was involved."

"But you knew I was lyin'. Your sound techs told you I was."

"It's called manipulation, Shrug. The only way I could challenge you on who was wearing the wire was to first call you a liar."

"Did you know," Syd interrupted, "that the human brain isn't physically finished developing until the age of twenty-five? The last part to come on stream is the one governing the ability to foresee the results of our actions."

"No, I didn't," Kindle answered, keeping stern eyes on Shrug. "Be sure to use that in the sessions."

CHAPTER 39

Gabe Kindle's residence, Edmonton

Kindle opened the door and smiled. His dinner guest had arrived.

"Have a seat," he offered, waving to the kitchen table. "I'll have supper ready in twenty minutes. Can I get you a beer?"

"Thanks. Sure." Shrug slid his giant frame into the nearest chair. "So did you win any money on the Supreme Court decision?"

"I'd have won if they'd let me place my dollars on a close split decision." Kindle set a beer before Shrug and poured himself a glass of wine. He took the chair opposite Shrug. "Did *you* win?"

"No. I thought for sure the media had it right. We were out to get roasted." He heaved a massive sigh. "It feels good to have that finally settled. You realize how close we were to having one hell of a mess? It would've gotten so dirty."

"Yeah, feels good."

"Think it would've been a different Supreme Court decision if it weren't bikers on the line? You think the pure evilness of the guilty gave us the one-vote edge?"

"Theoretically, it shouldn't have influenced their decision. They were ruling on the process of justice, not the crime or the criminals. But we'll never know. The Supreme Court, as usual, gave no reason for its decision."

"There are many reasons things happen," Shrug muttered.

"Like Syd pointed out to me, we think we're making rational decisions and can even present them as such, but inwardly there are other processes at work of which we're not even aware."

"Or perhaps we're aware of them, but don't care to admit it."

"Are you talking about the Supreme Court decision? About you not revealing Katrina's relationship with the victim? Or about me not following up on you having a kid in the gang?"

"All of it—everything. Unknown and hidden processes. If there'd been no threat of needin' me as a credible witness at a retrial for the bikers, you think the disciplinary review panel would've come down harder on me?"

Kindle cocked his head. "You're saying that in the end it all worked out in your favour?"

"These secret processes Syd mentioned—think they might be God at work?"

Kindle chuckled. "Could be. Sure hope it isn't the devil."

"You once asked if it was fair that I didn't tell you outright about the girl. It wasn't fair."

"When I asked you if it was fair, it's not like I already knew the answer."

"You know the answer now?"

"I know *your* answer now. Not sure about mine."

"You're talkin' in circles."

"I knew a kid was wearing the wire that recorded the drug deal. Since it was your tape, I was damned sure you knew that too. The fact you denied it was a kid told me you felt the undercover operation would be in danger if I pursued the matter. I could've called you a liar, Shrug."

"You could've."

"Wouldn't have broken my heart. I've done it before. I was the boss, and as you've said, it was my call. It seemed sending Chad in to keep watch on things was a rational decision, but maybe it was a decision based on Syd's unknown processes. Was it God or the devil at work that day? I wanted to get those bastard bikers so badly, Shrug. Wanted your efforts to really pay off. I was driven to succeed. Was that good? Or egotistically evil?"

"Damn it, Sarge. Don't screw me up more. I had myself convinced I'd fucked you around."

"You did. But I let you. Where does the blame lie? With me? I was your superior officer. And unlike you, I had all the information necessary to make the correct decision. But I didn't."

"It was hard on you too, wasn't it? The entire four years was hell for you."

Kindle shrugged. "We did okay. It was hard, but we did okay. We got the job done and came out alive on the other side. Nothing's black and white. The Supreme Court knows that. Review Panel knew that. *I* know that."

He sipped his wine, watching Shrug's expression soften with guilt and acceptance. "Did you come through it a better person? Or did you lose too much? Was it too tough?"

"Dunno."

"You went in thinking people were either good or evil. That it was God against the devil."

"Lost that innocence. Gone forever."

"Life's convoluted. Many themes, many streams. Many eyes, many hearts, many reasons."

The timer dinged, signalling their dinner was ready.

"I'll get the roast out of the oven," Kindle said.

With an eye on Shrug, he gathered potatoes and side dishes, and set them on the table.

"Sarge, I'm beginning to believe only God can comprehend the big picture. We shouldn't judge. We can only see through the glass darkly."

"You're quoting me scriptures?"

"Scriptures never hurt anyone."

"I could put in a good argument against that one. But I won't."

He carved the roast and rejoined Shrug at the table. They ate in comfortable silence. Not until he'd cleared away the dishes and wiped the table did either of them feel like talking.

"Speaking of many reasons..." Kindle slid an envelope across the table.

Shrug pulled out the letter and read it. "They want you to run the new computer crimes division? What the hell do you know about computers?"

"Nothing. Don't even know how to turn one on."

"What's this then?" Shrug waved the paper. "Punishment for your part in things?"

Kindle lifted a shoulder.

"I thought once the seminars were up and running, you were going to go back full time to bossin' around the undercover boys."

"That was my impression, too. When they assigned me the training sessions, they told me it was because I was the man for the job and it had nothing to do with you or the biker trials. They said they admired my cooperation and my honesty."

"So what are they saying about why they're giving you Computer Crimes?"

"When I asked, it was all flattery again. Should I believe them?"

"Flattery?"

"They're saying they're having problems getting the expansion organized. Leskiw's good with a computer, not bad with people, but sucks at organizing. Big dollars have come through to expand even more and they're scared Leskiw will be in way over his head."

"And you're good at organizing?"

"Not just that. They're saying the computer people are a

troublesome lot. Not fitting in well with the system. Wreaking havoc. The dream is to integrate Computers with Fraud and Gang and all they're getting is friction and contempt running both ways. They say since I handled the rough and rowdy undercovers, computer geeks should be a slam dunk for me."

"And you said...?"

"Told them I couldn't run a department I know nothing about. Told them their geeks could be using their keyboards to fire missiles at the Middle East and I wouldn't even know."

"I believe you actually can do that—fire missiles with a computer."

"Oh. I thought you were going to say I could actually head up a department I know nothing about."

"Ah, you can do it." Shrug gave the letter back to Kindle. "My advice? Do it and don't protest. The future's in those little silicone chips. Can't see it bein' anything but a great career move for you."

"So you'll be transferring down east to Ottawa?" Chad asked Kindle, unable to keep the disappointment from his voice.

His boss was staring at the new monitor on his desk, fingers poised over a keyboard. The look on his face was of a man about to touch a hot stove.

"You're not that lucky, Chad. The computer department is moving *here*. Renovations will start on the second floor within the next few weeks."

"So this isn't happening right away?"

"No, it'll be a few months before it's ready. In the meantime, you and I are going to be taking Computer Immersion."

"You and I?" Chad frowned. "*I*, as in *me*?"

Kindle nodded. He hit a key and squinted at the screen.

"Why me?"

"You're going to be my right-hand man."

"Is this still fallout from the biker trials?"

"Were you thinking you were going to walk off scotch-free from your role in things?"

"There was never much negative said about my involvement with the girl, and I definitely had nothing to do with the concealing of evidence."

Kindle pushed aside the keyboard. "You're wrong. I said a lot negative stuff about your involvement with Katrina. In fact, there was a lot of negative stuff said by a lot of people about everyone's involvement with her. That being said..." He picked up a stack of papers, rose and headed toward the door. "I've been assured transferring to Computer Crimes is not a step down but a fabulous career move. The reason I chose you was for your sense of humour."

Chad followed him to the exit. "Not my charm or my intelligence?"

"Definitely not."

"Not my people skills?"

"No."

"But I know next to nothing about computers. I don't think a sense of humour qualifies me."

"Our immersion will change that. Besides, they told me they had enough computer whizzes and what they need is someone to deal with the computer people. Leskiw will be maintaining direct control over the computer room. I'll be working hard at integrating and organizing, and you'll be translating computerese to English for me and vice versa. The go-between."

Kindle headed down the hall and Chad scurried to keep up. "Were you just kidding that I have no choice in this matter?"

"Even if you had a choice, I know you'd choose to do it for me. That's what I told them, 'No problem. Sign Chad up. He'll do anything for me.'"

"But computers?" Chad protested. "Computer people?"

CHAPTER 40

Northern Alberta Police Detachment, Edmonton, October 2000

A month later, Chad wandered into the detachment session room.

"I'm here," he said with reluctance to Syd and Shrug. "Kindle says you need some help adapting your ethics presentation to fit the needs of our upcoming special computer people."

"That man's out of touch with reality," Syd grumbled. "This course wasn't designed to deal with the temptations of cyberspace."

"But it will become so, right?" Chad said. "I mean, ethics are ethics. Conscience is conscience. If you do things on your keyboard you wouldn't tell your boss, you're over the line."

"You been around the Sarge way too much," Shrug drawled. "You're startin' to sound just like him."

"I'll take that as a compliment."

"You really enjoy being his little lackey, don't you? You bondin' with him? Is he your mentor? Is that why you were promoted to Corporal?"

Chad resisted the urge to punch him in the face. "I see he chose you for your sense of humour too."

"Is that why he chose *you*? I'm thinkin' the Sarge is the one with a sense of humour."

"I seem to make *you* laugh all the time."

"Laughin' *at* you, buddy."

"Shrug, you'd be a hell of a lot better off if you had someone besides yourself for an idol."

Shrug grinned like an idiot.

"Do you guys bicker all the time because you like each other, or hate each other?" Syd asked.

"I like him," Shrug answered. "I can see the Sarge's point. Chad was a source of great amusement for me in The Traz. Weren't you, Chad? Just the memory of watchin' him tryin' to mount a Harley brings a smile to my lips."

Chad strode toward Shrug. "The memory of you taking the girl into that Quonset brings *bile* to *my* lips. Have you learned anything from your ethics sessions—other than which words Kindle wants to hear you say?"

"Whoa!" Syd positioned himself between them. "Come on now. You're both over twenty-five and can foresee the results of your actions. Right?"

"Can you, Shrug?" Chad peered around Syd. "What was it you foresaw when you asked Katrina if she wanted a ride?"

"I saw a girl in trouble, no matter which way she answered."

Chad laid a hand on Syd's shoulder and nudged him out of the way. "And what do you think might've happened had she climbed on your bike and ridden with you to Children's Services?"

Shrug inched forward. "I foresee her runnin' away from a dozen foster homes—and no one around to care. A wild child with a million bucks and a genius mind. What would you have foreseen?"

"Stop it!" Syd ordered. "Both of you. This has nothing to do with computer ethics."

Chad clenched and then unclenched his fists. He took a small step back. His desire to lay Shrug out on the floor was overwhelming. But Syd had a point.

"Computer ethics is what you're here for," Syd reminded him. "Right?"

"Yeah," Chad said, keeping a wary eye on Shrug. "That's what I'm here for."

Syd waved a hand. "Come on then. See what I got. Some interesting pictures. Video cameras were part of the stepped-up security during the biker trials and I got my hands on the footage. I thought it might be a good training tool as Shrug has always said seeing Katrina on the stand was a turning point for him. That it made him realize just how tragic the results were after going over the line with her."

Ignoring Shrug, who was pouting in the corner, Chad said, "How could he not have realized that before the trial? He said himself that after the murder she curled up for three days, and woke up screaming from nightmares for months afterward. That, to him, wasn't tragic?"

The door slammed and he jumped.

"Don't worry," Syd said, not moving a muscle. "It's just Shrug leaving."

"He leaves like that all the time?"

"No. Sometimes he sneaks out like a shadow."

Chad let out a weary sigh. "Back to my question. How could he not know how tragic his actions were, and how they affected Katrina?"

Syd glanced up at him. "Perhaps it's because, when she was testifying, it was the first time he saw her distress away from the gang setting. Under the bright lights of the courtroom, back here in the real world, away from the everyday violence he'd become used to, her anguish suddenly looked much different. *Unacceptable.* I'm hoping the video will have a similar impact on our session-goers."

"Words aren't enough?"

Syd played with the controls. "We're having a hard time getting a resounding *yes* when we ask if Shrug recruiting the girl was a bad decision."

"You're kidding me, right?"

"Actually not. The question elicits more queries than answers. How many convictions did the operation net? How integral was the girl to its success? Did she want to be there? When we point out the answers to those questions weren't available to Shrug when he invited her to join The Traz, they start asking about her past."

"How are you wording the question?" Chad pulled up a chair and stared at the images Syd was fast-forwarding. "Are you actually asking if recruiting a thirteen-year-old into a biker gang is a good idea?"

Syd nodded.

"And you're not getting an immediate 'no'?"

"Not a unanimous, immediate 'no.'"

Chad sucked in a breath and pointed at the video. "Go back!"

"Back?"

"Rewind it up to where the girl lies about why Lukas was chosen."

"That's not the part we're interested in."

"Play it again. Slow it down." He leaned forward and stared intently at the screen. "What do you see, Syd?"

"What am I supposed to see?"

"Watch. Katrina casts her eyes down before answering. Play it again."

Syd rewound the tape and pressed the play button.

"She casts her eyes down," Chad muttered, "and to the right. Damn."

"I think she's just playing with the microphone stand."

"No. That's how I can tell when she's lying." He turned to Syd. "It's never a furtive glance. Always purposeful. She did it in The Traz compound too. She wipes at the table, fingers her sleeve, checks out her nails. But always down and to the right. Then she looks up and meets you straight in the eye—and lies. You got video of the drug trials?"

Syd tossed the remote control to Chad. "It's all there. I'll go find Shrug and try to calm him."

"Sure," Chad said absently.

Syd lowered his voice. "Shrug's hurting, you know."

"I know a kid who's hurting a lot more than that bastard."

"One person's misery doesn't negate another's. This isn't easy for him."

"So? It should be easy?"

"No, but I don't think you're doing anyone a favour by making it harder."

"I'll keep that in mind." Chad hit play and relaxed into his chair.

When Chad arrived home, he tossed his jacket on the sofa and walked into the kitchen. "Debra, you'll never guess what I saw today."

"What?"

"Video of the biker trials." Chad joined her at the table. "If my theory's right, Katrina did a whole lot more lying on the stand than just forgetting to mention Lukas was her buddy."

"You have a theory?" Debra cupped her chin in her hands and stared at him.

"Her body language telegraphs the fact she's about to lie. She not only lied to protect her secret about Lukas, she lied during the drug trials too. I can tell you which bikers she liked and which she didn't. The one's she liked, she lied to cover for. The ones she didn't, she lied to make worse trouble for them."

"You're grinning as if you admire her for doing that."

He shrugged.

"You're obsessed with that girl, Chad."

He scowled. "Why would you say that?"

"Because she's all you've talked about since you walked in."

He was about to deny this when she said, "Today's the day I went to the doctor to confirm if I'm pregnant. You haven't even asked."

Chad studied her eyes and a slow smile spread across his face. "I don't have to ask. I can tell by your eyes the answer is yes. You're pregnant? We're going to have a baby?"

He held out his arms and Debra nodded, walked around the table and nestled into his lap.

"When's the due date? Do you want a girl or boy? Have you phoned your mom yet?"

She passed him the handset. "Of course I haven't phoned my mom yet. You're the first to know. We'll make the calls together."

Chad set the phone on the table and cradled her in his arms. "I'm going to be a father, married to a mother." He caressed her cheek and then pressed his lips to hers. *Life is good. Very good.*

CHAPTER 41

Northern Alberta Police Detachment, Edmonton, March 2001

Kindle stepped into Chad's office, a harried look on his face. "The computer people are set to arrive at nine and something's come up. I'd like you to greet them and make them feel welcome."

"Can do. How many are there?"

"Seven or eight." Kindle checked his list, then passed it to Chad. "Eight."

"Where are their personnel files?"

"Lost in the move."

"The personnel files are lost? First it takes two months longer than scheduled for the equipment to get set up, and now this?"

"Chad, you're going to have to go with the flow. We'll get it all running smoothly once we've got them here. Besides, when I started complaining about the files, Leskiw told me if I knew anything at all about computers, I'd be able to find the information I needed on the net site. Or something to that effect."

Chad chuckled at Kindle's technical ineptness.

"Here are some notes for you," Kindle said. "Give them my apologies, tell them where the washrooms are, and no one touches the computers until they have my personal permission to do so."

"Gotcha!"

Chad stood in the doorway of the computer centre and sized up those in the room. Nobody was in uniform, everyone was talking too loud and the giggling was nerve-wracking. Totally inappropriate. He wondered if a school tour group had somehow ended up in the wrong spot.

He scanned the faces, looking for Corporal Leskiw.

Then he bit the proverbial bullet and strode into the room. "May I have your attention!"

He expected a swift silence to follow, but the chatter continued until a chorus of "shhh!" washed through the group.

"Where is Corporal Leskiw?" he asked.

Several people looked around. Some shrugged. Nobody said anything.

"You are the Computer Crimes people?"

A series of nods answered his question.

"Then you do know Corporal Leskiw?"

"We know who he is, sir, but we don't know where he is," a scrawny man in T-shirt with a beer ad called from the back of the room.

Chad took a deep breath. "Very well. Let's get to know each other. I'm Corporal Chad Leslie, assistant to Sergeant Gabe Kindle, who heads this department. He regrets he isn't here to greet you due to another commitment, but he'll be up to see you later today. When I call your name, please let me know you're here."

A soft murmur spread through the group.

"Constable Edwin Colins?" Chad's words were met with a roomful of blank stares. "Edwin Colins? I'm not mispronouncing it, am I?"

"He's there." A fellow who looked like he was at least five years from having to shave pointed at an empty desk.

"Edwin Colins is invisible?"

Chad cringed at the raucous laughter that followed.

"He's under the desk!" someone in the back shouted.

Chad walked over and stared at the feet protruding. "Constable Edwin Colins?"

"This is sure some funky wiring," a muffled voice answered.

"I'm addressing you, Colins," Chad said between his teeth. "I expect you to be on your feet listening to me."

"Oh, I can hear you fine from under here."

"If you can hear me fine, why didn't you answer?"

"I did, sir. Oh...maybe you can't hear me?"

Chad kept a fierce gaze on Colins until he had wiggled out from under the desk and stood before him with lowered eyes.

"Next on my list," Chad said, returning to the front of the room. "Felicity Randal."

Again, no answer.

"Does anyone know where Constable Randal is?" Exasperation crept into Chad's voice.

"She belongs here," the T-shirt guy confirmed. "I don't know where she is. Haven't seen her today."

"Very well." Chad rushed through the remaining names.

"I'm sorry I'm late," a familiar voice called from behind him.

Chad turned. *Katrina?*

She marched past him, threw an armful of books onto an empty desk and surveyed the equipment around her.

"What are you doing here?" he whispered, grabbing her arm. "You're not on my list."

"Felicity Randal." She ran her fingers over the nameplate on the monitor at her work station. "I'm on your list as Felicity Randal." She caressed the keyboard. "Did you forget that I was blessed with a new name after Rusty James told everyone my real name? However, everyone here knows me as Katrina, my *nickname*."

Chad cursed under his breath. "Why are you late?"

"I got lost." She straightened. "Honest, Chad."

Honest? That word wasn't in her dictionary.

His brow furrowed. "The entire second floor is Computers. How does one get lost?"

And there it was. A quick glance down and to her right.

Then she stared him in the eye. "Well, I was thinking about the tertiary system and how it's going to become the basis for artificial intelligence, and I got off on the third floor by accident."

"You're lying. You know this detachment inside and out."

She turned to the computer beside her, tilted her head and flicked at the floppy drive. "Fuck off, Chad."

A gasp erupted from the group. Chad couldn't be sure his own wasn't part of it.

"I find that offensive," a guy in size fifteen Reeboks chastised.

Chad scowled at him. "And you are?"

"Constable Josh Anderson, sir." He looked down at his feet. "Sorry, sir, but 'I find that offensive' is what Corporal Leskiw always says in such circumstances."

"From now on, no one in here says a word unless I specifically ask them to. Understand?"

His crew shifted uneasily.

"Understand?"

A series of nods moved through the group.

"The bathrooms are down the hall and to the right," he said. "We'll break for *recess*. Go out and get some fresh air. I'll ring the bell when I want you back. Except you!" He pointed at Katrina. "Constable Randal, you and I need to talk."

She heaved an exaggerated sigh, pulled a steno chair to the computer console and began typing.

Chad waited until the other officers were out of sight before hitting the power switch. Her monitor went black.

"No one is allowed on these computers," he said, "until Sergeant Kindle gives his approval."

Her hands remained poised over the keys. "You shouldn't have done that. Not exiting programmes properly can cause major problems."

"Constable!" He spun her chair so she faced him. "You will not be telling me what I should or should not do, and you will not be telling me to f-off, either. What you will do is apologize. Now!"

"Chad..." Her blue eyes peeked up at him through long lashes. "How about I apologize to you right after you apologize to me for all your broken promises? How does that sound?"

"Don't call me Chad. I'm Corporal Leslie to you."

"Don't call me Constable Randal. I'm Katrina to you. I'm only Felicity Randal on paper and in the phone book. Those who knew me as Katrina will still call me that. And so will my colleagues."

"Why?"

"It's legal. I can go by any name I want, as long as it's not for illicit purposes."

"There are reasons you were given a new name—life and death reasons. Why would you want to risk having someone from the gang track you down?"

She stood, sending the chair spinning toward the desk. She watched it until it came to a stop, then turned back to Chad. "You calling me Katrina won't tip them off. It's not like I'm the only Katrina in the world." A small smile lifted her lips. "It's nice of you, though, to care about my safety."

A dull pain throbbed behind Chad's eyes.

"Don't worry," she continued. "All the paperwork is in order. My SIN, employment records, birth certificate, Revenue Canada, my pay cheque, utilities—it's all under Felicity Randal. So you see, Corporal Leslie, there's no need for you to feel you have to protect me from anybody."

"I see." Was she remembering how he'd protected her in The Traz?

"Is it all right if I go for recess now?"

"Yes, please do. Don't get lost out there again."

He watched as Katrina turned on one heel and strode out of the room. Then he headed back to his office and waited for Kindle, who would want to know how the session had gone.

Fifteen minutes later, there was a knock on the door.

"Sarge." Chad motioned him inside. *Does he know about Felicity— Katrina?*

"You look ticked off."

"I am. Do you know Felicity Randal?"

Kindle scratched his chin. "Isn't she one of our new recruits?"

"Yes, but do you know *who* she is? Have you met her?"

"No, I've only met Leskiw."

"You're sure?" Chad studied Kindle's face. "Constable Randal wasn't the reason something pressing came up and you couldn't be there this morning?"

"I don't know what you're talking about."

"No, I guess you don't. You better take a seat while I tell you."

Kindle hovered over him, as if doubting the news was going to be difficult to take.

"Felicity Randal," Chad began, "is really...*Katrina Buckhold*."

Without a word, Kindle collapsed into the chair.

CHAPTER 42

A month went by before the personnel files were located, gathered and delivered to Kindle's office. He spent the morning browsing through them. He wasn't pleased with what he read. Contrary to the opinion of those who had trained and hired his crew, he wasn't at all certain that exceptional intelligence and high creativity scores compensated for the litany of behaviour deficits noted on every single performance review.

He picked up the phone and ordered Chad and Corporal Leskiw to his office. After hanging up, he surveyed his new, larger and more richly furnished office. It didn't seem to be enough of a reward for taking on this task. He dropped the personnel files onto the small meeting table in the corner and arranged three chairs around it.

Chad arrived first and then Leskiw. Kindle was pleased to be able to offer them fresh coffee from the small electric coffee maker he'd found room for on the bookcase.

"Corporal Leskiw," he said once they were all seated. He tapped the stack of files. "How many of these people know more about computers than you do?"

"I would imagine most of them know more than I do about one aspect or another."

"How many know a lot more?"

"A couple."

"Which two?"

"Well, one." Leskiw shuffled through the files and singled one out. "I know you have trouble with her, but this woman's brilliant."

Kindle eyed the folder labeled *Felicity Randal*. "How is it this girl, for whom I refused to give a reference—who, in fact, I verbally recommended on three different occasions *not* be accepted into training—ends up under my command?"

"I don't think anyone purposely planned it that way, sir," Leskiw replied. "Perhaps the universe has a reason. I don't know your history with her, but you really ought to give her a chance. I got to see her in action down in Ottawa. She's a whiz."

"Five seconds after we met, she told me to fuck off," Chad said.

"We're working on the language skills," Leskiw replied.

"That's what you call 'language skills'?"

"Look, the whole lot of them are lacking in the social competency department, but you," Leskiw nodded to Kindle, "knew that."

"More than just *lacking* in social skills," Chad said. "They're all social morons."

Leskiw frowned. "I find that offensive."

"I found it offensive she told me to fuck off!" Chad shouted.

"Chad," Kindle chastised. "Don't be getting offensive yourself. Respect, please. Katrina's language is just a small part of my objections." He pointed to her file. "She didn't do so well at depot, I see."

"I was hoping she'd do better," Leskiw said with a shrug. "I don't know what happened there. She scored high on the shooting range."

"I'm not sure that's a bonus," Chad muttered.

"How are you going to give Katrina the close supervision she needs, when you admit she knows way more about computers than you do?" Kindle asked.

"Why are you so concerned? Immaturity doesn't necessarily equate with irresponsibility. It's something we will watch for, yes, but it doesn't strike me as all that dangerous a trait. Her father was cop. She has a strong loyalty to the law. She could be making ten times the money in private enterprise, but she's chosen this. That has to say something good for the woman."

"Did you know the university had trouble with her?"

"No, what kind of trouble?"

"She crashed their whole computer system," Chad said. "They believe she crashed it while trying to cover up other illicit computer activity. What was she doing, where was she going, that she so desperately needed to cover up her tracks?"

"Did you ask her?" Leskiw said.

"She doesn't realize we know," Chad said. "She ingeniously obliterated it from her records."

"With a computer?" Leskiw eyes lit with interest.

Kindle shook his head. "No, with a new identity."

"Oh, the identity issue. I notice you call her Katrina, but I refuse to."

"I have the feeling that this name issue is not going to be our main problem. But I'll speak to her about it."

"You should speak to her about what happened at the university," Leskiw suggested. "I wouldn't assume what she did was sinister. Those kids all do it, as a challenge, not because of a criminal bent. I'm sure half the viruses out there originated in university computer labs. Then they write and market the software to block them."

"Those *kids*?" Chad let out a huff. "This happened little more than a year ago. She was hardly a kid. What challenges do you think would entice her now?"

"There sure would be a lot of them on our computers," Kindle said.

"I can see this is a big concern to you," Leskiw said, standing. "I understand that. I'll find out what I can from her."

Kindle motioned him to sit. "I wouldn't overestimate her loyalty. She's been known to flip sides." When Leskiw gave him a sharp look, he added, "I had more reasons than just her immaturity for not wanting her on the force. I've only now been given permission to tell you this and it must stay in this room. She testified for us at several biker gang trials a few years ago." He shivered at the memory.

Leskiw's eyes flared in shock. "She wasn't the...was she the Crown's child witness at The Traz trials?"

"She was."

"Oh." Leskiw slumped into his chair. "The vicious murder she witnessed. Are you saying she still has issues?"

"We don't know. We question her motives for being here. Perhaps she's here because of her father, as you say. Other than this latest fiasco at the university, she seems to have been behaving since getting out of The Traz five years ago. Back then, she was young, maybe foolish, grieving the loss of her parents. We hope she's grown up since then and chosen the right side of the law for good."

Leskiw scratched his head. "Back during the trials, there was also some impropriety involving her and an officer, wasn't there?"

Kindle avoided Chad's eyes. "Yes, there were issues with an officer—several officers. We'd hate to discover too late she's intending to use the privileges and power of her position to avenge what she perceives as unjust past treatment by the police."

"Have you asked her about any of this?" Leskiw asked.

"We haven't had the chance to say more than a few words to her since she arrived, but until we get answers that satisfy us, I suggest no computers for her. Teach her to make good coffee or something."

Leskiw scowled. "I can get her to work on programming."

"Like what?" Chad cut in.

"We're creating a system to enable us to track computer users. It's too easy for people to hide in cyberspace. We need to be able to chase down hackers, fraud artists, porn, all that stuff. It's an international project. It would keep her busy."

"Wouldn't she have to communicate with the others on the project, internationally?"

"Everything could be fed through my computer so I can monitor it."

"Considering her computer expertise, is it wise to assume she wouldn't bypass that safeguard?" Kindle asked.

Leskiw smiled and stood. "If she's going to screw around through the internet, she doesn't need our computers to do it. Yanking her access here isn't going to stop her from traversing cyberspace for nefarious reasons, if that's her intent."

"The point is," Kindle argued, "I don't want it happening on one of our computers." He passed the files back to Leskiw. "I want every one of these people to take my training course in ethics. I'm going to fit them in as we have room. Warn them if they don't pass my course after the second try, they're out."

"Okay. Consider it done." Leskiw moved to the door.

"One more thing," Kindle said. "Katrina's going to be the first to take it."

CHAPTER 43

Northern Alberta Police Detachment, Edmonton, May 2001

Kindle gathered Shrug, Syd and Chad in the computer session room. He knew they were all aware that teaching ethics to the socially illiterate computer people was going to be challenging, but he wasn't sure they realized that teaching Katrina ethics was going to be impossible.

"I'm fitting all eight of Leskiw's officers into our sessions as quickly as possible," he told them. "Katrina will be one of the first. I'm assuming you'll be able to integrate them?"

"Maybe we can do one special session for them all," Chad suggested. "I think Syd has pulled together enough course material to do that."

Syd nodded. "With video presentation from the trial footage that we've done up, we should have enough for a six-hour session."

"Excellent," Kindle said.

"You can't do that to her," Shrug said. "Her face is on that video."

"Why not? I made *you* face your monsters in public and you survived."

"I'm not doin' it."

"Sir?" Syd said. "If we're talking about Katrina sitting in on our ethics session when we show the video from the trials, maybe Shrug is right. It's intense. Once people view that video clip, there's no more waffling about whether or not it was a good idea for Shrug to invite her into The Traz."

"I won't show it when Katrina's in the room," Shrug said.

Kindle clenched his jaw. "I'm ordering you to."

"I'm not doin' it. If she's in, the video's out."

"There isn't anyone in that computer centre—hell, anyone in the whole force—who needs this training more than she does. And if there's anyone who needs intensity to get the message, it's her. Argue with me about that!"

"You can't show it. You're runnin' the risk of revealin' her identity."

"That isn't the reason you don't want to do it," Kindle said quietly.

"It's a good enough reason." Shrug leaned back and closed his eyes.

"I'll handpick the sessions-goers that day, people we can trust. Not necessarily her computer centre peers. There's more and more people all the time gaining access to our computers. I'll choose some mature, responsible people from administration, civilian members, some rural detachments. So now what's your excuse?"

"If the video's in," Shrug said, gritting his teeth, "I'm out." He chucked his pen across the table and stormed out of the room.

There was an uncomfortable silence.

"Sarge," Syd pleaded. "You've been busy with the Computer Department and haven't seen the final version of the video. Please, look at it first before you make your final decision."

Kindle heaved a sigh. "What have you got?"

"A good part of it is a split-screen image of Gator staring at her while she testifies. And it's not an absent stare. He's leering at her the whole while, running his sinister little pig-eyes up and down her. It's not something anyone seated behind the defence could see. Perhaps the judge and jury saw—she definitely saw. And once you see it, you'll no longer believe the accusation she feigned her meltdown on the stand to avoid testifying about shooting Lukas."

"Shooting Lukas. That's the last thing she ever did for Gator and she'd be damned if she'd give him the pleasure of reciting it in front of him."

"It wasn't that, I swear. Look."

Syd flicked on the video and upped the volume.

In silence, they watched as a young Katrina took down one of the most notorious gang's in Canada's history.

When the video ended, Kindle gave a nod of surrender.

"It's powerful," he conceded.

"Think about what it will do to the girl," Syd said.

Despite Kindle's promise that he wouldn't set Shrug in front of a class of students until he'd resolved his own issues, Shrug and Syd had been doing the sessions for some time now.

"What did it do to Shrug? He's not where he should be about all this, is he?"

Syd hesitated, then lifted a shoulder. "I wish I could say otherwise. He has so much going for him. He was doing okay until this." He nodded to the video.

"What do you mean?"

"Let's just say what he spouts in class isn't what he tells me afterwards."

Kindle frowned. Maybe Shrug would never recover. "Let me guess. Afterwards, he tells you Katrina wanted to be with The Traz. She isn't thirteen, but is the devil incarnate and has been around forever. If he hadn't taken her under his wing, she'd have been dead long ago. Sound vaguely familiar?"

Syd nodded. "Something like that."

"The time has come," Kindle said. "It's been damned near five years. He's had enough sympathetic understanding, enough counselling. We're upping the pressure, Syd. We're going to get him through it, once and for all."

"But what about Katrina? She isn't prepared, doesn't even know this video exists. In a room full of her peers, to throw that at her, with Shrug right there, doesn't seem fair."

Kindle felt a smidgen of remorse. Then it disappeared. "I need to find out for sure what's up with that kid. I need to know what's motivating her, where her loyalties lie and what's going on in her mind."

"That's what *you* need," Syd said. "What does the girl need? I know she needs maturity, to accept responsibility for her life, to quit blaming others. Needs to clean up her mouth. But none of that's going to happen in a six-hour ethics session. No matter how intense we make it."

"She's in way over her head with her top-security position in computer crimes, thanks to Leskiw and his computer gurus. She can't be there. She shouldn't even be in a uniform, packing a pistol. I'm not expecting her to pass the session, but at least I'll have something concrete to back up my objections to her."

"But, sir, what is it Katrina needs that we can give her?"

"You know what I'd like her to get out of this? Correct me if you think it's impossible. She's a far cry from twenty-five years old, with a brain developed for insight, but I'd love to see her leave this session with the insight she's not ready for this job." Kindle shot Syd a grim smile. "I want her to know determination, manipulation and blue eyes aren't what's required by an officer of the law. That it's her own self, not us, standing in the way of her career. I want her to know genius is nothing if it's not coupled with emotion and relationship skills. Can we do that for her?"

"I don't know, Sarge. Although we've designed the course to prompt insight, if she's not capable of that yet—"

"I'll help you. I'll get Chad in there. He has a much more realistic view of the girl than Shrug. Understands her pretty well. Knows how to push her buttons. And I'll get Bailey."

"Corporal Martin Bailey's going to an ethics session? Right, Sarge. I doubt he'll have time to attend with all the civil suits he's defending himself against. Not to mention the Force's disciplinary reviews."

"I'll get him here."

"You sound too confident."

"He's my most intelligent and outspoken undercover officer. No way will Katrina be able to manipulate him. I'll get him here and he'll keep her in line. Trust me. Now, to track down and deal with Shrug."

He found Shrug sneaking a cigarette out back.

"Come for a walk with me. We'll talk."

Saying nothing, Shrug lit a second cigarette from the glowing butt of the first.

"I thought you quit," Kindle said.

"Quittin' is easy. Done it lots of times."

"Well, Shrug, your smoking isn't my problem. But this thing with Katrina is. First of all, you *are* going to do the video. Now…tell my why you think you can't."

"You're always saying, 'Come on, people. Get real!' I say to you now, 'Get real!'" Shrug studied his cigarette and noisily inhaled.

"I think I am real. However, I have Katrina telling me she wants to get top-level security clearance on my computer system. I'm saying, 'Katrina, get real!'"

"Say it some other way."

"Why?"

"I was hopin' someday I'd be able to get the girl to like me again. I didn't agree to do these sessions to end up torturin' her."

"That my course might upset her doesn't scare me. What scares me is having her on my computers."

"Then just unplug the damn computer!" Shrug shouted. "This is the wrong way to do this."

"Why is the video so right for everyone else and not for her? Why is that, Shrug? Why do we want intensity for everyone but her? What makes her so damned special?"

"It's not 'everyone else' testifying on the video. It's *her*."

"She did a good job of testifying. We're not running her down, criticizing. The video is to give people a very real understanding of the consequences of our actions. It happened five years ago. It's not like it's a fresh and painful memory. Why should this be a problem for her?"

Shrug threw the cigarette to the ground and kicked at it.

"I can tell you why it's going to be a problem for her," Kindle said. "It shouldn't be, but we all know it will be because she hasn't dealt with it properly. She's not old enough to have dealt with it properly. Until that happens, she should not be where she is. I don't care if her IQ is two hundred and sixty. She's not functioning properly until she deals with this."

Shrug shoved his hands in his pockets and gazed up at the clouds.

"I'll tell you why it's going to be a problem for *you*," Kindle continued. "Because you haven't dealt with it properly, either. You talk about it lots, but you haven't settled it in your mind and heart. Until I hear you telling her face to face what you so willing share with everyone else, I'll know you haven't dealt with it. Until you can sit with her and watch that video together, I'll know *neither* of you have dealt with it. And I have a real problem with two of my officers having this big an issue simmering beneath the surface."

"Why?"

"It's not my issue you guys can't get your relationship straight. It's not even my issue you've both got resentments, guilt, whatever. But it becomes my concern when I ask myself why you two haven't resolved it. What is it about your characters, your outlooks, your thinking, your views of life, your attitudes? What's keeping you two from coming to grips with everything that happened? If there are problems in those areas, it will affect more than just how you and the girl get along. And then, it becomes *my* issue."

"Why do you say I haven't come to grips with it?"

"When I see the two of you watching that video together, when I see you telling her to her face what you yap all day to everyone else about, then I'll believe you've come to grips." Kindle sighed. "Shrug, when you think about that session, you're as scared for yourself as for her."

"She won't make it through, Sarge. She won't."

"I don't expect her to. I do expect you to, though."

"I don't know what you're wantin' from me."

"Yes, you do."

"You're wantin' me to apologize to her? Is that it?"

"If that's what it takes."

"In front of everyone? Like marriage vows made in front of witnesses to ensure their sanctity?"

Kindle chuckled. "Perhaps like marriage vows."

"What am I sayin' I'm sorry for? That moment in the café? 'I'm sorry, Katrina, that I asked you if you wanted a ride?'"

"That's not it."

"When Gator asked 'Ain't it time your woman got her hands dirty?' and I said, 'I got no problem with that'?"

"Think about it."

"Maybe it was the moment when I left her alone in the warehouse. The moment I said, 'Son of bitch! I'll be right back' and tucked the revolver under her jacket and left. Is that it? 'I'm sorry Katrina, I left you there alone.' Can I just say, 'Katrina, I'm sorry for everythin'?'"

"You'll figure it out."

At least, he hoped Shrug would. Otherwise, a class of computer nerds would be the least of Kindle's worries.

"I'm assuming the video is in?" Syd ventured when Shrug returned.
"Yeah." *Goddamn Kindle.*
He slid into the seat between Syd and Chad and tamped back the feelings of guilt. He didn't like where things were going.
"I still say it's wrong," he said. "She's gonna—she's *not* gonna get it. She won't understand. It's not right to do that to her."
"She won't get everything," Syd said. "But hopefully she'll get the message she's lacking something she needs."
"I think you and the Sarge have your hopes too high," Chad said. "She won't make it that far. Her insight is zero."
"Exactly!" Shrug said. "She's gonna interpret it all wrong. She's not gonna understand she's supposed to be learnin'. She's gonna feel we're shoutin' at her, antagonizin' her, displayin' her. She's gonna feel we've set her up to fail in front of her peers."
"Yup," Syd said. "What's your point?"
"My point is, who the hell is benefitin' from this pain we're gonna be puttin' her through? The girl's not benefitin' 'cause she's not gonna have a clue what's goin' on."
"Maybe she'll notice others seem to be getting something from it and wonder why she isn't," Syd suggested.
"She'll think she isn't gettin' anything 'cause we're purposely antagonizin' her above all the others. And basically we will be, 'cause we know it's not gonna sink in. Plus the fact, her face, her voice and her life are gonna be out there for all to see. The combination sucks."
"What are we supposed to do with her?" Chad snapped. "We have people pushing to give her computer clearance. We have her thinking she should have it. We have nothing but old stories to back up our negative point of view on the matter."
Shrug glared. "We have her depot evaluation. And the university thing."
"We don't have the 'university thing.' The paperwork isn't under her new name. All we have are general comments that she's immature," Chad argued. "Leskiw's already arguing immaturity doesn't equate to irresponsibility. We want to be able to go to him and say, 'Look. This is the way she thinks. This is the way she responds. These are the points she couldn't understand. Do you still think she should get her clearance?'"
"If nothing else," Syd said, "she'll benefit by not being in a career beyond her capabilities. That can be deadly. I guess I'm kind of an example."

"Good point," Chad said. "If she quits now, the door is always open for her to return to us when she's more stable. If she hangs around here until shit happens and she gets dismissed or whatever, it could ruin her chances to get a good career anywhere."

"By the way," Syd said. "Look at these charts I did up for the session. Is this what you had in mind?"

Chad squinted. "Looks good. Did you get the handout finished?"

"Working on it."

"Shrug, what do you...Shrug! What do you think about this?"

"Think about what?"

"The charts." Chad frowned. "What's up? You're not listening to us."

"Something Kindle said is botherin' me." It bothered him a whole lot.

"What?"

"He said the session was as much for me as for her. He wants me to say to her face what I say to everyone else, or something like that."

"He wants you to apologize to her?"

"I think so."

"And that's going to be hard for you to do? Still, after five years?" Chad shrugged. "I agree with Kindle. You have an issue there."

"I'd like to see *you* do it," Shrug said. "I bet you've never apologized to her."

"I apologized to her lots of times during the investigation."

"That doesn't count."

"I'd apologize if Kindle asked me to," Syd spoke up. "I wouldn't have a problem with it."

Shrug eyed him. "Just like that? It would be that easy?"

"Well, maybe not easy, apologizing is never easy. But I wouldn't lose any sleep over it."

Shrug wished he felt the same. He hadn't had a good night's sleep since the day he'd asked Katrina to take that ride. Maybe he *should* apologize. Maybe that's what it would take to make everything all better.

CHAPTER 44

Northern Alberta Police Detachment, Edmonton, June 2001

"Constable Randal, close the door and have a seat," Leskiw said.

Katrina obeyed. Although her boss's thin face was always stern, she'd learned how to release the gentleness resting just beneath his scowl. She tilted her head. *Hmm…if he were to put on a few pounds, he might actually be handsome.*

"You're booked for the ethics session tomorrow," he said.

"This whole thing is bizarre, sir. I know right from wrong. I don't need a six-hour session to learn that."

"It's about the grey areas between right and wrong, and how to morally and legally deal with them."

"I can't believe Shrug and Syd are going to be teaching me ethics." She gave an exaggerated sigh.

"It's not so much a teacher-student environment. Everyone's learning from each other."

"Sir, I'm not an idiot. I know I'm not wanted here. Sergeant Kindle's going to make sure I don't pass. I thought they'd at least give me a chance to prove myself."

"Be that as it may, I want you here, and I want you to make it through the session. The major complaints they have are your language and your immaturity. If you keep a handle on those two things, I'm sure you'll do fine."

"I can't be in the same room with Chad or Shrug and not tell them to fuck off."

"A big part of maturity is respect, which is having the self-confidence needed to not feel threatened by the space and power of others. Find ways to express that. Your work requires you to become part of the team, here."

"If I'd known I'd end up working for Chad, I wouldn't be here."

"Well, now that you are, how badly do you want to stay here? Enough to overlook your issues with that man?"

"I *want* to be here. I just don't want Chad to be. I went through hell and back to get this far, and I'll be damned if I'll let them fuckers kick me out now."

"A simple 'yes' would have been better. There's nothing wrong with your determination to succeed, but there's no need to insult others in the process."

She crossed her arms. "I'm going to do it, sir. I'm going to make it through their God damned session."

"Listen, it's those 'fuckers' who are going to decide whether or not you make it. Understand that. Accept that. Your entire career is resting in their hands. Respect that. If they tell you to dance, dance. Play the game with them."

"The game?" She was an expert at playing people games. It's how she'd survived as a child on the streets and in the gang.

"A high-stakes game," he said. "They win and you lose your career. Use the wits God granted you to come out the clear winner, young lady."

A slow smile spread across her face. "I hear you, Mr. Leskiw."

A knock sounded on the door.

"Come in," Leskiw called.

Kindle entered Leskiw's office, pausing when he spotted Katrina. He hadn't expected to see her there.

He gave her a brief nod, then turned to Leskiw. "Are you giving the girl some advice for tomorrow's session?"

He heard Katrina mumble something. She tossed her hair over her shoulder and brushed past him, heading out into the hall.

"Sorry," Kindle said. "Was I interrupting?"

"No. We were done," Leskiw said. "As for Katrina, she's going to surprise you and do fine."

"Must have been pretty good advice."

"I guess we'll find out tomorrow."

Kindle's mouth thinned. "She's not getting on my computers. No way."

"Is this spite because my reference overruled your objections to her?"

"Couldn't be. I didn't know you'd given her a reference."

"It better not be. I suggest you allow yourself to focus on the woman's good points."

"She has good points?"

"We all do. You seem to have no trouble looking past Shrug's rough exterior to find the man's heart. Why can't you do the same for Constable Randal?"

"There's a mighty big difference between that girl and Shrug."

"You're just saying that because you know Shrug better. To the rest of us, they're like two peas in a pod. No difference."

"Tell me what these two peas look like to you."

"Genius minds. Superb actors. Read people well. Master manipulators."

"You're right. They act very much alike. The difference lies in their motives."

"Shrug's are pure and Katrina's are evil?"

"I guess we'll find out tomorrow."

The following morning Katrina scanned the twenty or so people in the session room. She recognized a few of them. Last night she'd rehearsed in her mind the proper language, proper smile and appropriate attitude. She was going to give Sergeant Kindle nothing to hold against her.

"I'm Sergeant Gabe Kindle," his voice boomed out at exactly 0900 hours. "With me are Constable Donald Hayes—aka 'Shrug'—and Corporal Sydney Koots. And, of course, you all know Corporal Chad Leslie, our special guest who will help with the computer end of things. We've redesigned our undercover session to make it relevant to computer users. Our program will teach you about the dangers and pitfalls of going over the line. Isn't that right, Constable Randal?"

Katrina peeked at Sergeant Kindle, but he wasn't looking at her. "Yes, sir."

"By the end of the first hour," Sergeant Kindle said, running his eyes over the group, "I'll know all your names. Be ready to be called on. We're not going to be giving you answers here. We're going to be giving you the necessary skills and information to find your own answers. We'll have you reveal yourselves so you can gain insight into your behaviour. You must know both your weaknesses and your strengths in order to make better decisions."

"Is there a final exam?" Katrina asked.

"Yes. At the end. But don't worry, there's only one question on it. You're also going to be judged on your participation. Don't think by not contributing we can't judge you, because we judge silence as poor participation. Don't be scared to give the wrong answers. Be scared not to *give* answers. Don't be scared to disagree with me. I may be purposely telling you something you ought to be disagreeing with. Be honest with what you're saying. It will make things a lot easier for you." His eyes settled on Katrina.

Shit! He's getting ready to go after me.

"Ladies and gentlemen," he continued, "be prepared to give up control here. My team and I will run your lives for the next eight hours. You're going to talk about what we want you to talk about, respond the way we want you to. We'll ask you to go places you may not want to go, and make you admit to things you don't want to admit to." He paused and several coughs broke the silence.

"If you feel we're picking on you, it's because there's something you need to learn. If you feel we're prying, it's because so much of what you are today arises from what's in your past. You must understand where you're coming from. Right, *Felicity?*"

"Yes, sir. But do use my nickname. *Katrina.*"

She had the unsettling feeling he'd been speaking to her alone since the very start of his spiel. She snuck a quick glance at the dozen faces around her. It didn't seem possible everyone present was struggling with a troubled past.

"So how many here have at one time or another tried to hack into a site?" Sergeant Kindle asked. "Or launched a virus, or designed a Trojan?"

There was dead silence.

He shifted uneasily and glanced at Chad. "Did I use the wrong terms?"

Chad shook his head.

"What I want to know," Sergeant Kindle said, "is if anyone here has done anything remotely illegal on a computer?"

"Is it illegal if you try but don't succeed?"

Katrina peered over her shoulder to see who had been brave enough to ask that question. *Ah, Sarah Freeman.* She sat at the back of the room.

There was another moment of silence.

"Sarah asked a great question." Sergeant Kindle surveyed the group. "Come on, people. We a roomful of law enforcement officers in here. Someone must have the answer."

He didn't wait out the silence this time. "I saw a guy breaking into my neighbour's house yesterday," he said. "I ignored it. I mean, if you don't want someone to break in, get good locks, right? Right, Felicity?" He cleared his throat. "I mean, *Katrina.*"

"It's *not* right," she replied. "Just like it's not legal to hack into computers just because you can."

"You ever do that, Katrina?"

"Yes, I did. In university."

"And it was right to do that?"

"No. But we didn't think—"

"*We?*" he interrupted. "What's with the 'we'? You're the only one here from your class, I believe."

Katrina took a deep breath. "I never thought about it like that."

"Nobody ever told you it was wrong?" Chad cut in. "No one ever said, 'Don't do that, it's illegal?'"

"We—I was told that, but—"

"When you were told that, you stopped, right?" Sergeant Kindle's eyes drilled into her.

"No, sir." Her heart pounded in her ears.

"It wasn't a secret what you were doing, I'm assuming, because you weren't really doing anything wrong. It was just that the laws were stupid, right? It was just a game, a challenge. Your professors knew what you were doing. You told them, right?"

Her breath came in quick gasps and her face burned. "They knew, but I didn't tell them."

"The number one rule!" Katrina jumped as his voice reverberated through the room. "Remember it, because it will be on the final exam. *If you can't tell your boss what you're doing, you're over the line.* You shouldn't be doing what you're doing. Anyone have issues with that?"

She saw Josh Anderson raise a timid hand.

"Sometimes there are other reasons," he said.

"What's your name?" Sergeant Kindle asked.

"Constable Josh Anderson."

"Give me an example, Josh. You're doing something totally appropriate and legal, and yet there's no way you'd tell your boss what you're doing. Why not?"

"He wouldn't understand what I was saying?"

"You have a point there." Sergeant Kindle chuckled. "Chad, you have something to add here?"

Chad stepped forward. "Be aware of the dangers of not being able to communicate what you're doing. Watch out for the temptation to do things you wouldn't do if your boss *did* understand..."

As he continued listing all the things they should be wary of, Katrina picked up her pen and began to doodle. She felt like she was in school, trying to busy her mind with useful things, while the teacher prattled on.

She'd hated school.

Her father hadn't been happy when he discovered she'd wrangled her way out of most classes by promising to complete assignments on her own and show up to ace the exams. He'd told her there was more to learn at school than just academics. She'd successfully argued her case the day he'd died, eliciting from him the promise of a private tutor. But it was a promise Cooper had refused to honour.

Katrina eyed up Josh, who was talking again. He was a funny

looking character. Pale. A tiny nose, smooth skin and hair that looked uncombed.

"Like, if some software you're using to get a break on your investigation," Josh was saying, his lips dainty, his teeth, white and even, "also enables you to hack the Pentagon computers, you wouldn't want to do that."

"You would want to, or you *wouldn't* want to?" Shrug asked.

The room became a sea of laughter.

"I'm sorry," Shrug said. "I really didn't hear what you said."

"Well, I might want to," Josh conceded. "But I wouldn't do it."

"But that's obvious!" Sarah objected. "How could you not know you shouldn't do that?"

"Because if you did it, you wouldn't tell your boss, right?" Sergeant Kindle added.

Josh shook his head. "You should be able to figure it out, even without your number one rule. Other things, though, can be more tricky. Like if you're working credit card fraud and take advantage of your access to look up a friend's credit limit."

"Excuse me," Chad said, shaking his head. "That's not obvious?"

"Well, no one's ever going to know. It could be tempting."

"It's not obvious to you that using your access to acquire personal information not related to your job is over the line?" Chad asked. "You'd tell your boss you did this?"

"It's not like *I* would do it," Josh said, slumping into his chair.

Katrina smirked, happy someone else was under attack for a change.

"I would hope not," Chad said to Josh.

Sergeant Kindle strode to a whiteboard and wrote: *If you can't tell your boss what you're doing, you're over the line!*

Then he turned, his eyes drifting over each person until they rested on Katrina. "Maybe the serious issue here with you guys is that nobody's going to know. They're not going to know either because you don't tell them or because they don't understand what you're doing. Or maybe…they're not going to know because you know how to cover your tracks. Right, Katrina?"

"Learn someone else's name," she snapped.

"They're not going to know because *you* know how to cover your tracks. Right?" His gaze was unwavering.

She looked away and caught Syd and Chad staring at her. *Shit!*

A rustle swept through the room as people shifted in their chairs, shuffled papers, clicked their pens. A few nervous coughs punctuated the quiet.

The energy from Sergeant Kindle's silence enveloped her. It was hot, heavy, suffocating. She'd waited too long to answer. The quiet was now too dense for words to pierce. If she even had words.

"I'm letting it go," Kindle said. "This time. But from now on, when I ask a question, I expect an answer. Understand?"

She gave him a saccharine smile. "Yes, sir."

He stared at her through hooded, suspicious eyes. "If you know you can cover your tracks, does that line you don't want to cross move a bit farther away? Sure, you might not hack into the Pentagon, but maybe you'd visit porn sites in your spare—"

"No, sir," she interrupted. "I don't visit porn sites."

Someone snorted.

"That wasn't the question," Sergeant Kindle said. "Listen to the point I'm trying to make. If no one knows what you're doing and you can cover your tracks so no one will ever find out, is there a danger you'll start going over the line, even a little bit. And when no one finds out, maybe a bit more?"

"But your conscience should keep you from doing that," Josh argued, coming to Katrina's rescue.

She threw him a grateful smile.

"It's easy to fool yourself and start feeling justified," Sergeant Kindle said. "Perhaps you're saying you're going to try breaking into Suzy's computer to make sure this new software works before you try it on your bank fraud investigation."

"I can't see justifying something like that," Edwin Colins protested.

Sergeant Kindle shifted gears. "A thirteen-year-old girl is recruited into a motorcycle gang by an undercover cop."

Katrina gasped and looked at Shrug. He sat behind Sergeant Kindle and stared at the wall, his face stony and his grey eyes empty.

"Is he over the line?" Sergeant Kindle's voice boomed. "Come on, people. I'm not giving you the answer. Was he over the line?"

A chorus of yeses rose and faded.

"The girl had connections to the drug trade and contact with the gang before he recruited her," Sergeant Kindle added. "Is he over the line?"

"Did he know that?" Edwin asked.

"What difference does it make?" Katrina retorted. She kept her eyes on Shrug's face. *When the hell is he going to say something in my defence?* "She's a thirteen-year-old girl, for Christ's sake. He crossed the line."

Shrug arched his brows and a grin tickled his lips.

"Shrug," Sergeant Kindle called over his shoulder. "Did you know she was involved with drugs?"

Whispers erupted as the group realized Shrug was the officer in question.

"Yes, sir," Shrug replied.

Katrina jumped to her feet. "How does that matter?"

"It *doesn't* matter," Shrug answered calmly.

She cast her eyes wildly about the group. "See? It doesn't matter."

"The four-year undercover operation netted over two hundred drug, weapons and murder convictions," Sergeant Kindle continued. "The girl played an important part in the operation before the sting ended and during the trials that followed. Was he over the line?"

Josh raised his hand. "If she hadn't been there, would that have happened?"

"Did she know he was a cop?" Sarah asked.

Katrina glowered at Shrug. *Say something! Say something to defend me. Or are you still blaming me for everything?*

"Was he over the line, Katrina?" Sergeant Kindle asked.

She folded her arms and stared at her feet. "Yes."

"Were you over the line, Shrug?" Chad asked.

"Yes," he answered evenly.

She uncrossed her arms. *Thank you!*

"Josh," Sergeant Kindle said, "You said a moment ago that if you had any kind of conscience, it would prevent you from doing things which were obviously wrong." He threw his hands in the air. "How come your consciences aren't telling you this was wrong? Resoundingly wrong?"

No one had an answer.

"Shrug, did you feel justified in recruiting the girl?"

"Yes, sir. She wanted to come. I needed her contacts and skills to wrap up the operation. She was very clever. She seemed to be into the lifestyle."

"Did you tell your boss?"

"No, sir."

"Why not?"

"I knew he wouldn't let me do it and yet I knew I had to. I'd been undercover for three years and I needed that edge to get where I had to go. If he pulled the girl, it was over. Time and money wasted. And I was so close."

His words made Katrina flinch. *Just say it, Shrug. You used me.*

"Where was your conscience, Shrug?" Chad asked. "Was it saying anything to you?"

"It was sayin' she was too young. But I'd done lots of things in the three years before then that my conscience hadn't liked. It wasn't hard to ignore."

"But this was the first time you didn't tell your boss, right?" Sergeant Kindle probed.

"Yeah. Other things had been carefully scripted, justified and approved."

"You were thinking since you'd been allowed to do other things before that were pretty iffy, maybe this would be okay too?"

"It didn't seem a bad a thing to do, considerin' what was happenin' around me." Shrug looked everywhere but at Katrina.

She scowled. *Coward!*

"Watch out for that, people!" Sergeant Kindle said, raising his voice. "It can happen with your computers too. You're required to do magic with the keyboard during the course of an investigation and might start thinking it isn't all that bad to use your magic to change a zero on your bank account."

Edwin raised a hand. "Is this true, Shrug? You recruited a thirteen-year-old?"

"Yeah. I know how easy it is to cross the line and feel justified. Don't be so sure you'd never let it happen to you. Watch out for yourself. Watch out for your buddies. Stop it if you see it happenin'."

Katrina was mesmerized by Shrug. He was so calm, cool. She wasn't sure she believed his words, as detached as they were from emotion.

"What's the number one rule?" Sergeant Kindle bellowed.

The class responded in unison. "If you can't tell your boss what you're doing, you're over the line!"

"Remember that. It's on the final exam."

Katrina blew out a relieved breath. Things were winding down. She couldn't have been more wrong.

Sergeant Kindle strode toward her and stood in front of her desk. "Katrina, if the officer was over the line at the very start, was everything he did afterwards wrong too?"

"I don't know." She squinted at Shrug. He'd been a master at concealing himself in The Traz, and he'd had to in order to survive. But why hide his feelings now?

"I'll help you out. Pay attention." He tapped her forehead. "If you go over the line and illegally break into a computer system, and while in there you alter things so another breach can't happen and you tweak up a few other potential problems and then leave, were you over the line the whole time you were in there? Since you were there anyway, was it improper to fix things?"

She shrugged. "I don't know."

Sergeant Kindle moved away and addressed the class. "What if you get in there illegally and then find out by coincidence it's exactly where you needed to go to complete your investigation? Does that make it legitimate now? Does that mean you didn't really go over the line after all?"

"There's culpability there somewhere," Josh suggested.

"Shrug," Sergeant Kindle said. "You've been undercover multiple times. What do you say?"

"Just don't go over the line in the first place," Shrug growled. He caught Katrina's eye, then looked away. "It might jeopardize legitimate investigations. We were very close to losin' three murder convictions and untold drug and weapons convictions because I went over the line. Imagine all the time, money, effort and sacrifice made by so many people would have been for nothin'. I wasn't very popular around here. For a long time."

"But would it be wrong? Would your boss think you had crossed the line?" Sarah asked.

"He's given you a clue," Sergeant Kindle said. "Figure it out. Why do you want an answer? Planning on going over the line?"

"No, just curious."

"Curious about going over the line?" Chad asked.

Sarah shook her head. "No, curious about how the law views those kinds of situations."

"It has a very dim view of it," Shrug said. "Believe me. Your colleagues and bosses will have a very dim view of it too. They're out there bustin' their asses, maybe even puttin' their lives in danger to get their job done, and you're gonna jeopardize it all by doin' somethin' stupid?"

Katrina brows arched in surprise at his revelations. She looked from Chad to Sergeant Kindle and then to Syd. Which one of them had put the pressure to Shrug? *Probably all of them.*

"So Katrina," Sergeant Kindle came at her once more. "Besides your bosses and buddies and lawyers getting upset with you, what else can happen when you go over the line?"

"Innocent people can get hurt." She peeked at Shrug from beneath her lashes.

"Katrina," Sergeant Kindle said. "Let's say you're undercover, go over the line and piss someone off and they murder your friend to get—"

Katrina jumped to her feet. "I wasn't undercover. Don't go there!"

She realized too late by his triumphant smile she'd given him what he was after. She closed her eyes, clenched her jaw and willed herself to salvage the composure she'd practised. Gradually, the images of Lukas's accusing eyes retreated and she once more heard her breathing. When she opened her eyes, Chad was approaching.

"No, you weren't an undercover cop," Sergeant Kindle's voice began again to come through to her.

Chad put an arm on her shoulder. "Katrina," he whispered. "Breathe slow. Get some control here. Inhale...exhale."

"So only undercover cops can go over the line?" Sergeant Kindle faced the group. "Maybe computer cops, yeah, they can go over the line, right? Ordinary adults? Maybe they'll cheat on their income taxes, drive too fast, drive while drunk. Can kids go over the line? That ten-year-old selling coke, is he over the line?"

"Not when you're ten," Sarah objected. "He doesn't know any better."

"So he's not over the line? It's okay just to leave him there selling his drugs, because he's only ten."

"Katrina, breathe slow," Chad whispered again. Sergeant Kindle's questions and the answers wove in and out of Katrina's consciousness as she struggled to release images of the past.

"We were all kids once," Sergeant Kindle's voice boomed. "We shouldn't have gotten punished when we did wrong things? We resent that? Or it was necessary? Katrina, Katrina," he said moving back to her side of the room. "You ever get in trouble for things you did as a kid? Ever get away with something? Blame someone else for something you did?"

"Breathe deeply," Chad whispered. "Get control. Answer the question. It's an easy one." He patted her shoulder and stepped away.

"Josh," Sergeant Kindle said, finally breaking the silence. "If I were to ask you that question—did you ever get away with something as a kid by blaming by someone else—would it be a hard question for you to answer?"

"No. I'd say yes. I think everyone here would."

"You might even smile, remembering the incidence. A little bit of pride you'd managed to do that."

Josh grinned. "Yeah. A bit of guilt too. Most of the time it was an innocent friend or sibling who got shit for it."

"You wouldn't feel so guilty about something you'd done as a child that it would be hard to talk about it now?"

"No, it wouldn't be hard. I can tell you about one—"

"No, no. That's okay. We'll just all think of our own stories in our heads. They're all pretty well the same, I think. So, people, why won't Corporal Randal answer?"

"Maybe it was something real bad she did," Edwin suggested.

Katrina rolled her eyes at him. *Suck up!*

"But we just had this long discussion," Chad said, "about how kids weren't really able to take full responsibility for doing wrong. Don't you think we should all forgive that kid in us who did these wrong things on the way to growing up?"

"Sometimes it's hard to forgive yourself," Sarah said. "Especially if it had tragic results."

"Maybe," Sergeant Kindle said. "Or perhaps you've never forgiven yourself because you still haven't accepted blame." His gaze swept the room and landed on Katrina. "Katrina, are you still blaming someone else?"

"Blame?" Katrina rubbed her sweaty palms on her pants.

"That's what we're talking about. Getting away with something as a kid by blaming someone else."

"Oh."

"Or were you thinking about something you were unjustly blamed for as a child?" Chad asked.

"I don't know. Both, I guess."

"Well, was it your fault or not?" Josh asked impatiently.

"I've been told it wasn't."

"But you feel it was?" Sergeant Kindle asked.

"I didn't say that."

"I'm sorry. Tell me what you meant."

"I meant..." Katrina stopped speaking, lost in maze of violent memories.

It didn't matter whether or not she believed it was her fault. Or that Dr. Holeman, the jury and the whole damned world had absolved her of blame. Lukas had told her with his dying eyes that he believed she'd betrayed him. He was dead and there was nothing she could ever do or say to let him know otherwise.

And he wouldn't have even been there if I hadn't let Gator know we were friends. If I hadn't taken Shrug's side in the fight for leadership of The Traz. So who's fault is it now, Sergeant Kindle? Who's to blame?

"What the hell did you do, Katrina?" Edwin asked.

The others nodded, leaning forward in anticipation.

"They think you should tell us," Chad said.

She shook head. "No! It has nothing to do with anyone here."

"I can think of at least one other person here that it has a lot to do with," Sergeant Kindle said.

"That's his problem," she mumbled.

"What did you say?"

"She said, 'That's his problem,'" Chad repeated.

"So something we do affects another person badly, but hey, they can deal with it, right? Especially since you were just a child, right?" Sergeant Kindle turned to the group. "Katrina won't tell us. Do you think we should make her?"

While Sergeant Kindle took a vote, Katrina caught Chad's eye. "Chad, I can't do this." She stroked her arms, then covered her face and began to cry.

"You have to. You need to pass this course for your computer clearance."

She waited, head down, holding her breath.

"It was close, Katrina," Sergeant Kindle said a moment later. "Six to five that you tell us."

She lifted her head and her gaze drifted over the faces in the room, some she knew well, a few she didn't know at all. Keeping her tears at bay, she listened to her breathing and the thumping of her heart.

"A person wanting top-level security clearance," he said, his footsteps dissipating into the plush of the carpet as he walked to the front of the class, "has to admit their weaknesses and know their strengths. They don't have to tell me all the details of their deepest, most personal secrets, but they have to know why they aren't telling me. They have to understand their secrets. They have to have learned from past mistakes or errors in judgment and moved on."

She lifted her chin. She'd never felt so alone—or on display.

"Katrina," Chad said, "We need to know why you aren't telling us. Is it because you're avoiding responsibilities? Like when you tried blaming your classmates for going over the line on the university computer? Or have you acknowledged your mistakes and moved on, learning from them?"

Sergeant Kindle gave a nod. "You have a choice. Tell us what happened so we can explore it with you, or tell us why you shouldn't have to."

"What I've done or haven't done has nothing to do with computers or this course," she said. "My story doesn't affect anyone."

"But there *is* someone else here affected by your story."

She glanced at Shrug. "I'm not blaming Shrug. And I'm not blaming myself."

"Are you saying something bad went down, but no one was to blame?"

"The people to blame aren't here."

She reached for her water bottle and fingered the droplets of condensation. She slumped over the bottle, afraid to look up, afraid to see the accusation in everyone's eyes.

"Katrina!" Syd said. "Sit up. We're not going to attack you for what you did. We're going to help you through it. Look at me. If you don't want to look at everyone else, just look at me." He took a spot a few feet from her.

With tear-filled eyes, she raised her head.

"Good," he said. "We know you have questions about what's going on here. You share your story and we'll help you answer them. We can't go much farther if we don't hear your story."

Her story? *Lukas's story.*

"We aren't going to tell it for you," Syd said. "It's your story."

She blinked and a single tear rolled down one cheek. *My story. Lukas's dead eyes. The expression in them. Hurt. Betrayal.*

"Keep looking at me," he said. "Keep looking at me. What happened?"

She recalled the gun in her hand, the bullet piercing the skin and—

"I can't!"

She jumped to her feet, the chair crashing to the floor behind her. The water bottle went flying into the aisle, rolling toward Syd's feet.

Without a backward glance, Katrina rushed to the exit.

CHAPTER 45

Katrina grabbed her sweater from her desk and headed outside. She found a sheltered corner, sat in the grass in the shadows and sobbed. When the emotion and her tears had exhausted her, she closed her eyes and leaned against the building.

"Listen!"

She opened her eyes and searched for the owner of the voice, but there was no one in sight. She heard distant traffic and leaves rustling in the breeze. She sighed and drew her knees to her chin. An ant was at her feet, trying to get through the thick grass.

"You'll make it, little guy," she said. "I know you will. You'll get where you're going. It's what nature designed you to do."

Even though it was the city, it was nice out here in the sun. Her grandpa had been an outdoorsman and she'd spent hours with him in the forest. And her Grandma had liked gardening. It was Grandma who had taught her yoga and how to control her breathing and slow her heart.

Katrina's eyelids slid closed.

"Listen!"

This time she recognized the voice. *Grandma Buckhold?* She'd know her grandma's quiet but intense voice anywhere.

"Listen!"

Grandma Buckhold's voice took her back to that first day when she'd hopped on Shrug's Harley. She'd wrapped her arms as far around his middle as she could and laid her head against his back. With her eyes closed and the growl of the Harley, with the whisper of the wind and the roar of the road, for the first time since her dad had died, she'd found peace.

She'd not meditated since Lukas had been killed. She'd not wanted to listen to the universe. She'd met Lukas way back. He'd seemed a man to her, but he'd been only seventeen. Like her, he'd been alone in the world, with a drunk mother at home demanding he find money for the rent. So he'd started selling drugs.

"Listen."

She awoke to the screams of sirens leaving the detachment parking lot. As the cop cars wove off into the distance, a robin chirped. She gazed at the colours of the world and searched for the bird in the weeping willow. She could not spot him, but noticed the stark difference between the yellow-gold of the leaves catching the sunshine and the deep green of the shaded boughs. Illusions. In reality, every healthy leaf on that tree was the same colour.

Sometimes things are different than they seem and sometimes they're not, but you wish they were.

She thought of her life and how she wished it were different.

I wish Lukas and my Dad were alive. I wish I was strong and mature like Corporal Leskiw wants me to be. Like Dad anticipated I'd be.

She stood and dusted the grass from her pants. *And I wish Gator were dead.*

She headed inside and went to her desk. Sitting down, she picked up the framed photo of her father in uniform. He had such a proud smile.

"Maybe someday, Dad," she whispered. "But not now. I'm not ready yet."

"Aren't you supposed to be in Sergeant Kindle's session?"

She looked up and saw a young officer with chubby, dimpled cheeks. She'd seen him around but didn't know his name.

"Well?"

His eyes twinkled and she couldn't help but smile back.

"I didn't make it."

"Maybe next time. Not many of us get through the first go-around."

"I don't think there will be a next time. I walked out."

"You walked out on the Sarge? Uh-oh. Now you're in trouble."

"What's your name?"

"Stanley, from the Gang Unit."

"Ah, that's where I've seen you. Do you have a minute, Stanley?" She motioned to the empty chair.

"Sure." He sat down.

"A long time ago I saw my friend murdered," she said, testing each word. "Sergeant Kindle wants me talk about it. He said I couldn't move on until I dealt with it. But I couldn't talk. Just couldn't."

"Tough."

"They were talking about blame, accepting blame and blaming others. I do blame myself sometimes. I blame Shrug. Mostly it's just too difficult to put into words. The memories...are awful."

"Did you tell Kindle?"

She shook her head. "I couldn't."

"Why not? The session is mostly about being honest with yourself. If you'd just told him it wasn't about guilt or blame, but that it was too difficult to talk about, you'd have probably made the Sarge happy."

"No, he wants proof I'm dealing with it."

Stanley shrugged. "Maybe just proof you're aware of your problems. You *are* dealing with it, right?"

"I'm not," she whispered.

"You just talked to *me* about it. That's called 'dealing with it.' You're dealing with the past and are ready to move on. If the Sarge corners you again, just let him know you're aware of the issue and prefer dealing with it outside the session room. Tell the Sarge you talked to me about it. I'll back you up. I want you to make it." He put a hand her shoulder and then walked off.

"Stanley!"

He stopped, turned slowly and faced her.

She frowned. "Why do you want me to make it?"

"Because you're…beautiful."

"I am?"

"You must know that."

"My father used to always tell me I was beautiful. But it's been a long time since anyone else has. The last one was Zed, one of The Traz bikers. He told me he could tell I wasn't dead inside because I was beautiful, and dead people aren't beautiful. That was before the murder." She sighed. "I thought I died in that Quonset. Didn't think I was beautiful anymore."

"Well, you are."

Katrina watched as he sauntered off down the hall. Then she looked back at the picture of her father and traced the outline of his smile.

"Katrina?" Sergeant Kindle said with calm patience. "Don't ever walk out on me when I'm instructing you." He sounded like her father.

"I'm sorry."

"You obviously failed your first chance at this," he added. "Your *last* chance is starting right now. Go eat with your colleagues down in the cafeteria and be back in that session room at one o'clock."

In the blink of an eye, he was gone.

She let out a moan. *Crap!*

CHAPTER 46

The detachment cafeteria glistened and smelled of Mr. Clean. The clatter of dishes sounded from the kitchen. In the far corner, the others from her class had gathered at four tables.

Katrina took a seat at an empty table.

"May I join you?" an older gentleman asked.

She recognized him from the ethics session, but couldn't recall his name.

"Sure. Have a seat."

He set down a lunch tray and slid in across from her. "George McMullen."

"Nice to meet you, George. Guess you know who I am."

He nodded. "You okay, Katrina?"

"Yeah. Fine."

George settled into his chair and unwrapped a tuna sandwich. "You sure had us all worried."

"Worried?"

"Kindle was damned near frantic. Had us all out looking for you."

"Are you serious?" She squinted at him. "Didn't strike me anyone would care if I left."

"He cared," George said with a nod. "Screamed at us for an hour about how if anyone else felt the need to leave the room, they must take someone with them."

"Why the hell would he be worried about me?"

"He said people breaking down was just the first half of the process, and until the group had a chance to build you up again, you were living in a dangerous space." He gave a faint smile. "I'm glad you're fine."

"Definitely looked more like rage than worry on his face when he found me."

"The Sarge rages when he's worried."

"Sarina, Sarina..." someone whispered in her ear.

She jumped as a giant, hairy arm slipped over her shoulder. Dirty nails capped calloused fingers. Spinning around, she glared up into a burly, bearded face she'd never seen before.

"Get off me," she demanded, pushing his arm away.

"Sweetie," the stranger hissed in her ear, "all you would've had to say was 'no.' Shrug asks, 'Wanna ride?' You say, 'No.' If you'd have said that, everything after that sunny September afternoon woulda collapsed like a house of cards in a late summer's breeze. None of it woulda happened. But you said 'yes.' Yet somehow Shrug takes all the heat?"

"Step back, Bailey," George said, getting to his feet.

With a scowl, the man drew his arm from Katrina's shoulder and stalked off.

"Who the hell is he?" she asked, clasping her hands to stop them from shaking.

George's eyes widened. "You don't know him? Thought everyone knew Martin Bailey. He's one of Kindle's undercovers. Has more complaints against him in his file than the rest of the detachment put together. Keeps our lawyers busy fending off the lawsuits."

She scanned the crowded cafeteria. "What does he want with me?"

"Ignore him. He'll eventually go away."

But she wasn't that lucky.

She was back in the session room at one o'clock. She hadn't intended on participating in the afternoon session, hadn't thought she'd be allowed there, but Sergeant Kindle had given her no choice.

"A thirteen-year-old girl is recruited into a motorcycle gang by an undercover cop." Sergeant Kindle once again asked the class. "Is he over the line?"

"Hell no!" someone shouted.

Katrina flicked a look over her shoulder and saw Bailey standing in the doorway. She froze. *What the hell is he doing here?*

"Ladies and gentlemen," Sergeant Kindle said, "this is Corporal Martin Bailey. Thanks for coming."

"Glad to help out." Bailey strolled into the room and squeezed his oversized frame into a chair.

"Why is he here?" Katrina managed to spit out between clenched teeth.

Sergeant Kindle smiled. "Bailey works undercover. Mostly."

Bailey snorted. "Hell, you wouldn't want to tell 'em what I really do."

"You heard my question when you walked in?"

"Yeah. If that's the kind of questions we have to answer in here, I'm going to do real good on this course."

"So you're saying the undercover cop didn't cross the line?" Sergeant Kindle crossed his arms. "Anyone care to disagree? Come on, don't be scared. Bailey only looks mean. Besides, what did we learn this morning?"

Katrina bit back a nasty reply. Bailey's arrogance riled her, as did the silence of the group.

"She's only thirteen, so of course he's over the line," she blurted.

Bailey swiveled in his chair, his mouth pinched. "Holy Christ! Aren't you too tiny to be takin' me on?"

She narrowed her eyes at him, refusing to look away. "She's thirteen. He's a cop."

Bailey grinned. "Where have you been all my life? You're sure a sweet little thing. You a farm girl or something? Spent your summers playing with the kitties in the hayloft? Hey, I bet when you were thirteen, your daddy was taking the training wheels off your bicycle."

She leapt to her feet and started toward him. "You don't know anything about me."

Chad stepped in front of her and lowered his voice. "Think about the results of your actions, Katrina. He's a hell of a lot bigger than you."

When Chad stepped aside, Bailey winked at her. She had a clear path to his taunting face. She took another step.

"Think about the results of your actions, Katrina."

Chad's words sank in and she stopped.

"Don't let these two hog the conversation," Sergeant Kindle said to the others. "Remember, you get marks for participating."

"You're an idiot," Katrina said to Bailey before walking back to her seat.

"An undercover shouldn't be looking at girls that young when he's out in the field," Josh piped up. "If he were one of my guys, you can bet I'd take him to task over it."

"Is that so?" Bailey sneered. "What planet are you from? You been on the streets since the '80s? They don't make kids like they used to." His seedy gaze shifted to Katrina "You got some hot biker bitch groupie who wants to set her crotch on your Harley—hey, what's the problem?"

She had her path in sight and a plan in mind as she vaulted over chairs and tables toward Bailey.

"Holy shit," Chad muttered as she flew past him.

Counting on the element of surprise and her speed, she approached, unafraid, within inches of Bailey's massive frame. "Where the hell do you get off saying things like that about someone you don't even know?"

She lined up her knee with his crotch and when his head jerked down, she threw her fist at his face. Before she connected, Sergeant

Kindle's arms were about her, and Shrug was yanking Bailey backward, out of reach.

"Let go of me!" she demanded.

Bailey escaped Shrug's grasp and took a step toward her. "You're all thinkin' she was an angel back then. Just an innocent little girl. She got on the back of a Harley with a giant-of-a-dude wearing Traz colours." He spat on the floor by her feet. "She weren't no fucking angel."

Shrug grabbed Bailey by the neck and whispered something in his ear. Bailey's kept his eyes on Katrina the entire time. When Shrug's thick fingers tightened around Bailey's neck, his face turned a brilliant red. It was almost purple before he finally dropped his gaze and began clawing at Shrug's hands.

Shrug released his hold and shoved Bailey into the nearest chair. "Stay!"

"Katrina, sit down," Sergeant Kindle said, nudging her.

Oh crap. What have I done now?

She sat down, ignoring the curious stares of her classmates.

Sergeant Kindle strode to the front of the room. "I've never done this before, but today Katrina and Bailey will each get full marks for sitting and saying absolutely nothing for the next twenty minutes. Understand?"

"Yes, sir," Katrina said.

"Yo, my man," Bailey said. "Gettin' paid to do nothin'. Life's back to normal."

Sergeant Kindle ignored him. "Now back to our discussion. The girl who got on the back of the Harley." He turned to Shrug. "Did you know she was only thirteen?"

"Hey, it *was* you!" Bailey shouted, giving Shrug the thumbs up.

Katrina opened her mouth, but Chad touched her arm. "Don't get mad, Katrina, get even. I know you can do it. You've done it before."

"I don't have a gun this time."

"Actually, I was thinking of the other time you got even." He squatted beside her. "Use the group. They don't like Bailey. Get them to like you. Make some friends here, girl. You can't do it alone." He returned to Sergeant Kindle's side.

Katrina scoured the room for a friendly face. Half the people were looking at her and half at Bailey.

I have no idea how to get people to like me.

"We have a video for you," Sergeant Kindle said. "Before we view it, I'd like to warn you, we went through many hoops to get permission to use this footage for training. What you see here *doesn't* leave this room. This video does not exist once you walk out of here."

"Something we'll do and not tell our bosses?" Sarah asked.

Sergeant Kindle chuckled. "Just don't be using this exception to justify other behaviour. Shrug, introduce the piece, please."

"This video of courtroom procedure was part of the stepped-up security during the biker gang trials," Shrug began.

Katrina's heart sank. *Please tell me you're joking.*

Shrug's baritone voice filled the room. "You'll see the testimony of that thirteen-year-old girl. I never fully accepted I'd gone too far until I saw her on the stand at the murder trial. Until I saw her and heard her. It just hit me. How many charges? Two hundred and fifty-six charges? At that moment, I just knew it hadn't been worth it. None of it was worth it. That one night just erased anything good that ever came afterwards."

His words hit Katrina hard, like a sucker-punch to the gut. Did he really mean it? Was he sorry?

Syd hit the play button.

"Holy Christ, Shrug!" Baileys voice rang out. "That's her? Let me guess. You didn't think she was thirteen. You thought she was nine, right?"

Katrina was amazed at how young she looked in the video. Her hair was in braids and she was wearing a pastel-pink frilly top. Her voice was so soft.

She studied the others in the room. No one was connecting the child to her.

Shrug pulled up a chair beside her and rested his giant arm on the table.

She knew there was a tapestry of tattoos under his sleeve. She remembered her childhood fascination with the lines and colours that covered his bulging muscles.

She studied his face. His grey, stony eyes were veiled in a mist.

If he blinks, a tear's going to form in the corner of his eye and roll down his cheek.

Curious about what it was that made him realize what he'd done to her, she turned her eyes to the video. It didn't seem like it was her on the screen. How tiny she'd looked. And vulnerable. No one had guessed it was all an act. Though it was vulnerability she'd projected, she'd actually felt strong, triumphant. She'd stared right at the bikers when she testified.

But this...this *child* on the video is what the jury had seen. What Shrug had seen. This is what the prosecution had asked for—innocence. It looked like she'd spent her summers playing with kittens in the hayloft.

But I was playing with much more dangerous things in The Traz compound and in the King's Ace Bar.

She sobbed on the video as she testified about the moments before Lukas's murder. Every word, every memory, was a dagger to her heart.

She looked up at Shrug. He nodded, closed his eyes as if he were in pain, then opened them. He gently folded one hand over hers. When he locked eyes with her again, she saw past her reflection in his granite eyes. He was hurting. Badly. She saw remorse in his eyes.

What does he see in mine?

Her gaze returned to the air of innocence being played out on screen. It didn't bother her that she'd come across to the defendants and jury as naive. But it was discomforting to realize Shrug and Syd had jeopardized their careers, and James had lost his, so she could protect that false image so no one would know she knew Lukas, played around after midnight in drug-invested bars and ran cocaine for the big boys.

The sobs on the video grew louder, more anguished. Young Katrina was shaking, traumatized. The defence lawyer's frustration was obvious as he tried to get the judge to call a recess.

She recalled the Supreme Court ruling, which had struck down the bikers' appeals. The Crown had argued that, since she'd been in tears for most of her testimony and yet had still answered questions, there was no reason to conclude she wouldn't have answered at this point. The judge made no error, the prosecutor had said. If the defence had wanted to question her about Shrug's gun, they could have. The Supreme Court judges must have agreed.

Katrina watched her young self being led, weeping, past the jury, through the Plexiglas tunnel to the secured entrance. She'd been so small she could hardly be seen through the uniforms surrounding her. Then the video clicked off.

"Great ending!" Bailey cheered, breaking the silence. "The jury buys it, the judge buys it and the defence lawyer's left wondering what hit him."

Shrug stood up and pushed his chair against the wall. As he walked to the front, he flicked his eyes to the ceiling, to the floor, to the wall.

Katrina could tell he was not doing well.

"You're such a prick, Bailey," George muttered. "I'd like to have seen you do any better."

"Oh, I know I couldn't match that performance. She even got to you, eh, Shrug?"

Katrina stood. "It wasn't a performance, Bailey. I know for a fact it wasn't, because that child was me."

Josh gasped. "You?"

"It *was* her!" Sarah said.

Edwin nodded. "That was Katrina."

"So sweet and *innocent*," Bailey jeered.

Shrug clenched his jaw. "Leave her alone, Bailey."

Katrina watched as tension sucked all the air out of the room.

"Stop it!" she cried. "All of you just stop!"

A hushed expectancy enveloped the room and she felt stares stabbing her from all angles.

"Bailey's right," she said. "I didn't play with kittens. It just...comes off that way."

"What *were* you playing with, sweetie?" Bailey asked.

She zeroed in on him. "Drugs, bikers and undercover cops."

He matched her stare. "Funny that never made it into your testimony."

"Nobody asked."

"Funny thing about that." He stared at her for moment and then turned away.

"Are you saying you weren't as innocent as it looks on the video?" Edwin asked.

Katrina took her seat. "I was prepped. The Crown attorneys wanted a credible witness with an emotional testimony."

"You were acting?"

"No. I didn't know I looked like that. I was testifying at a biker gang murder trial. I was looking the killers in their smug little faces. I didn't know I looked so...like *that*."

"You were prepped, eh?" Bailey said. "Were you prepped to answer the defence's questions about the gun found at the scene?"

"I was told they would probably ask. They didn't."

"What did you think their next question was going to be? If you'd stopped crying, what would they have asked?"

"I don't know."

"You know damned well they'd have asked about the gun."

She shook her head. "I didn't know that at the time."

"You knew. You knew if you kept sobbing your heart out, the defence would look like bullies if they kept haranguing you about the gun."

"Why would I care if they asked me about the gun?"

"Oh, you didn't want the jury knowing you were an armed bitch. That it was *you* who put the bullet through the vic's head."

A collective gasp swept over the room.

"You wanted to be the naive, credible, vulnerable—"

"If you're saying I planned my tears, you can go to hell, Bailey. I don't care what you think of me, I was just a fifteen-year-old kid on that stand. I wasn't some devious siren with an Academy Award under my belt."

"It's okay, Katrina," Shrug said. "Leave it, Bailey. Just leave it alone."

Bailey motioned to the video screen. "That really move you, Shrug? You think that's who she really was? Innocent? Is that what she was like undercover with you?"

"That's what she was really like—underneath her constant struggle to survive. Beneath her guilt, behind her grief. That's who she should have been that year. With a little help, that's who she would have been."

When Shrug met her eyes, an unexpected rush of sobs racked Katrina. She sank deeper into the chair and covered her face.

"I'm sorry, Katrina," Shrug said.

She glanced up and found remorse, acceptance and forgiveness in his eyes.

"People," Chad said, "let's help Katrina and Shrug reconcile this. Anyone have something to say to them?"

"They're both okay," George said. "I'd be proud to have either of them as my friend or partner."

Sarah cleared her throat. "Katrina, I admire you for what you're doing. It must've taken a lot to deal with the stuff that happened. And you still chose to join the force." She wiped at her eyes. "I think you're going to do real good for us."

"Thank you," Katrina whispered.

"Anyone else?" When no one answered, Sergeant Kindle added, "Katrina, did you learn something about yourself today?"

She wondered if she'd ever been sweet or innocent. Maybe before her mom took to drinking. Before her dad died. Maybe it *had* been there, in that inner calmness her grandma had coaxed from her during their meditation and yoga sessions. Was it her innocence that had lit up Grandpa's eyes when he strolled beside her through the autumn leaves to the hunting blind?

Was I like that? Ever?

She took a deep breath and looked up at Sergeant Kindle. "I feel I did the best I knew how at the time. I was a kid who made a bad choice. I was hurting."

"And now?" Chad asked.

"Now? I don't know what I'm like now. I don't know what kind of a person I am. I don't know if I'm okay."

"You're okay," Sarah said.

The others nodded.

"Yes." Katrina sat straighter and wiped her eyes again. "I'm okay."

A long pause followed.

"We'll wrap things up early today," Sergeant Kindle said. "It's a small group. I think you all got your money's worth. Before we pass out the exam, Chad wants to say something."

Chad nodded. "Our buddy, Shrug," he began, "has been taking the brunt of this for way too long. Syd and I knew Katrina back then as well. Both of us had a part in keeping Katrina from being the person she should've been—as Shrug so eloquently put it. Syd?"

"I knew Katrina before she hooked up with Shrug," Syd said. "When she spoke of playing with drugs and undercover cops, I was one of those cops. Bailey told Katrina if she'd just said 'no' to the bike ride that day, the rest of the story would've collapsed like a house of cards. However, before she even had that chance to say 'no', I could've told her father she was on the street, instead of pestering her to find me the latest designer drug, or news on the latest cocaine shipment."

His eyes flicked about the room, resting briefly on Katrina. "If I'd done that, or something as simple as not referring her to Shrug, she wouldn't have had to say 'no.' Katrina, there are many reasons things happen. Take away any one of those reasons and the story collapses. I regret my part in all of this."

Syd walked through the group and stopped beside her. "I'm so sorry," he whispered, so only she could hear. "About *all* of it, Katrina."

She understood. He was apologizing for everything. The King's Ace, Daiga's Lounge, Suzy Q's, stolen computers—that whole spring of hurt and betrayal while she'd played on the streets with Syd and James.

Syd patted her shoulder and returned to the front.

"This is the first time Shrug and Syd have spoken to Katrina about their roles," Chad told the class. "Katrina and I have had many conversations over the course of our relationship. Lots of fights, lots of accusations, broken promises, pressures to talk, to testify. Katrina, I have to honestly say, my life has been better for knowing you. I wish you luck in finding your way back to being that special person the universe meant for you to be."

"Oh for Christ's sake!" Bailey muttered, stomping out of the room.

"It's exam time," Sergeant Kindle said.

The six-page exam landed in front of her. She flipped through it. It was blank except for Sergeant Kindle's single question at the top of the first page. *"What's the number one rule, and why?"*

She riffled the papers, enjoying the soft whisper and the movement of cool air across her face and her fingers. In the surrounding quiet, her classmates were intently bent over their tables, scribbling away.

"Listen!" Grandma Buckhold's voice said.

She squeezed her eyes shut and listened. And remembered…

There she was, young Katrina, so bold, daring, hurting, angry at the world. She had crossed the line far too many times. One fatal error in judgment—getting on that bike with Shrug—had cost Lukas his life and had almost claimed her own. Men had lost their careers, the police force its reputation. Taxpayers had lost thousands.

Yet somehow it feels different now. It feels like I've walked through all that and right on past it. It feels like…I'm going to be okay.

She stared at the exam and clarity washed over her. There was no need to answer Kindle's exam question. She'd listened and now knew she wasn't ready for a job in Computer Crimes. She also knew that this session hadn't been about her keeping her job. Kindle could have just fired her, transferred her to Traffic, assigned her to revamping manuals, or something. But he hadn't.

He made the effort to get me through this. Syd, Chad, Shrug...Bailey. They were all here for me.

She remembered Elizabeth Cooper's words about how lucky she was to have had people to pull her through. Suddenly, the woman didn't seem so wicked anymore.

Minutes later, Katrina walked to the front, her eyes on Shrug, who was busy at a table near the window. She slid the exam onto Sergeant Kindle's desk, then headed for Shrug. With a small breath, she tapped his shoulder.

"Katrina." He stood, wrapped enormous arms around her and squeezed.

Her heart soared. *This is the Shrug I knew. The one who made me tea and wiped my tears.*

When she pulled back, she swore Sergeant Kindle and Chad were both looking at her approvingly. She cast Chad a teary smile and left the room.

Kindle strolled to the desk and flipped over Katrina's exam. "'Special thanks to Shrug,'" he read. "That's all she wrote."

Chad grinned. "She just can't follow rules, that girl."

"Actually, it's not a bad response. Katrina Buckhold is finally growing up."

Message from the Author

I hope you enjoyed travelling with the BackTracker characters through their struggles and pain. I hope you rejoiced when they attained small victories as they chased big dreams.

Despite the fact that, in fiction, traumas and rewards are amplified for dramatic effect, we can't help but see ourselves and our lives in the pages of a book. I hope the courage, persistence and spiritual strength of Katrina, Shrug, Syd and Kindle inspire you to forgive yourself and those who hurt you, admit your errors, face down your demons and pursue the greatness that was meant to be yours.

Oh, and along the way, please be inspired to lend a helping hand to fellow travellers on this rough and rugged road called life.

Courage to you all,
Eileen Schuh

About the Author

Eileen Schuh is the author of *THE TRAZ* and *FATAL ERROR* (the first two books in the young adult BackTracker series), and *SCHRÖDINGER'S CAT*—a sci-fi novella.

Eileen lives with her husband in the remote northern boreal forests of Alberta, Canada. Drawing inspiration from the wilderness, she creates entire universes populated with fascinating characters doing intriguing things.

Eileen recently retired from a life of careers that varied from nurse to journalist to editor to business woman. She remains active in her adopted community of St. Paul and basks in the love and loyalty of an entire flotilla of family, friends and fans—virtual, imaginary and real ones.

She invites you to visit her online:

Blog: http://eileenschuh.blogspot.com

Website: http://www.eileenschuh.com

Facebook: http://www.facebook.com/#!/profile.php?id=609330070

Twitter: http://twitter.com/#!/eileenschuh

IMAJIN BOOKS

Quality fiction beyond your wildest dreams

For your next ebook or paperback purchase, please visit:

www.imajinbooks.com

www.facebook.com/imajinbooks

www.twitter.com/imajinbooks

Made in the USA
Charleston, SC
05 September 2013